This Charming Angel
By
Sharon Gartner

Illustration and cover design - Libby Reed. ©
www.libbyreed.com
Editing Janine Ogden

ISBN-13:
978-0-9873750-3-2

www.sharongartner.com

For all my angels here on earth.

Acknowledgements

To the beautiful Libby and Janine for their hard work.
My awesome family and friends
Thank you for being you.

Also available by Sharon Gartner

This Charming Shack

Facebook Profile.

Lisa Collins.

In a relationship with Rick Crankshaw.

President of the Country Women's Association.

About me. I'm over 5 foot tall, blond, and after brief time in property investment which didn't work out due to discovering a squatter in my ceiling and having my heart ripped out by Jake, who ran off with a woman old enough to be his mother, I have discovered my true calling as a wedding planner. I have fantastic friends (Millie) and I'm so in love with Rick (used to live in my ceiling, but not a pervert or anything. Also Jake's twin brother, but nothing like Jake, is sweet and sensitive). I live with my best friends Millie and Sid in my rural property which can be hired as a venue for weddings (complete with own petting zoo).

Member of 'The Impulse Behaviour Management Support Group'. (As an adviser, not actual member).

1

9am

God I wish Mum and Dad would leave.

They've been here for three weeks now and have worn me down with all their questions and tuttering. It's so annoying and I feel like I have to justify everything to them, like 'why did I buy a condemned house without a building inspection' and 'why did I quit a perfectly good job to become a wedding planner'.

I still haven't told them about the plans for the petting zoo but I'm a big girl and feel that's none of their business. Not that I'm scared of them or anything but Mum's disapproving looks followed by 'tch' is wearing thin. So best they know little. Millie and Sid are due to return from their honeymoon and I am so excited.

Millie and Sid's wedding was the first event I have planned after I discovered my true calling as a wedding planner.

They also moved in with me so they can finish off the renovations. Millie and I went into partnership after I brought the property. Me, the owner, and Millie, the project manager. But after deciding not to sell the house for profit I proposed that Millie and Sid live here for free and Sid do the renovations. Millie's not exactly a country girl so she is going to stay in the city during the week and come home weekends. It works out perfectly for Sid as he's gotten quite attached to the country and can spend his time doing renovations and building a guest house and pens for the petting zoo. Well, I haven't exactly told Sid about the petting zoo or guest house yet but I'm sure he'll be fine with it. I'm also hoping Mum and Dad will realise that newlyweds need their space and leave.

Rick is dropping by later to help me move furniture to my new office space in the village. I'm so excited. Rick is gorgeous (nothing like his brother Jake who dumped me for an old woman). Things between us are going great, apart from the fact he hasn't even hinted at wanting to get married. And since Mum and Dad have been here,

Rick hasn't wanted to stay a single night with me, saying that he feels a bit weird with Mum and Dad around even though they are camped out in their Winnebago. And when I stay over at his place he seems to just want to cuddle and talk and not have *sex*. I mean cuddling and talking is nice but I need to tell Rick that I'm a warm blooded woman with needs and not a daytime talk show host.

I have also built a website for my wedding planning business and after Dad's annoying lecture about how many small business fail in the first five years and overheads, blah, blah, I went back and begged Debbie, my old boss at the retirement home, to take me back to do a couple of shifts a week to make ends meet. Debbie is the best boss ever as she gave me three afternoon shifts a week and didn't even say I told you so.

I'm also been looking on e-bay for animals for the petting zoo. I'm convinced that adding a petting zoo to the property would attract even more events.

It used to be an old abattoir back in the mid century and the remnants of the old slaughter yards are situated at the rear of the house. I was very disturbed by this so decided that having cute and cuddly animals who will be loved by many (those who are prepared to pay for the experience), will bring a good omen to the old slaughter yards. Bonnie and Clyde, my two Boer goats, will make a great start and I'm thinking about getting alpacas, small horses and maybe even an emu.

Arrival of Matt

I heard a car pull up and got very turned on at the thought of Rick arriving, but it's not Rick, it's only Matt.

"Hey," he grunted through his mop of youthful hair as he sauntered in all moody and hormonal.

Matt and I met after a wee incident involving high alcohol consumption, and then ended up having sex. Matt is only nineteen so I'm very ashamed about the whole experience.

He is also the son of Pamela, the woman who ended up having an affair with Jake. But when Jake left town after selling the family farm to mindless developers,

Pamela had a small mental breakdown and is recovering at some hospital in town.

"I thought you're meant to be working?" I asked as he planted his dirty, greasy backside down on the nice clean sofa.
"Yeah, lunch break, thought I come and say hey."
"Why haven't you gone home to Neroli for lunch?"
"I thought she was here." He said puzzled.

Neroli is an old friend of mine who came to stay with her demon child Tom and surprised us all by having another baby without telling anybody she was pregnant. Matt (who was also staying with me at the time after being kicked out of home by his snotty mother) was smitten with Neroli and Tom, and they now live together with the demon child and baby Bailey.
Matt tucked in to his greasy pie in equally greasy jeans.
"So when do Sid and Millie get back?" asked the spotty youth through a mouthful of meat pie.

I had a sudden panic attack as I totally forgot about the time. Millie and Sid should be here any minute and I haven't even put together plans for the guest house or petting zoo. You see, the plan is that if I present all plans to Sid then that should lesson the risk of his new wife pulling me back to impulse behaviour meetings and insisting I take prescription drugs. I also promised that as part of my wedding planning service I would set up the marital bedroom and make it nice; so when they return from their honeymoon and Sid carries Millie across the threshold they can start their marriage off in perfect ambiance.

"Matt you need to help me put this bed together, Millie and Sid will be here any minute and they have nowhere to sleep." I said pulling him from the sofa.
"Yeah whatever, as long as it doesn't take long. Why are you worried about it now? They're probably all shagged out anyway."
I dragged the spotty youth to the marital bedroom with tools in hand. Matt put the bed up in no time flat while I busied myself throwing furniture around the room to make it look more presentable.

I almost got the thrown together effect of the bedroom down to a presentable finish when Matt asked me whose bed it was that he just assembled.

"It's Millie and Sid's," I answered him a bit puzzled. "It's my wedding present to them."

"Yeah but where did you get it from?"

"Pff, old garage sale," I said, waving his silly question away.

"This used to be my bed," Matt said with a hint of concern in his voice. "Where did you get it from?"

I didn't want to tell him but it was a clearance sale that Matt's father held at the family's estate. So I didn't answer him, hoping he'll move off the subject.

"This is my bed!" Matt exclaimed. "Look you can see my initials in the headboard."

"Okay, okay. Yes Matt, I got it from the clearance sale your dad had but I didn't realise it was your bed."

"How much did you pay for it?"

"I'm sorry?"

"Lisa!"

"Fifty dollars."

"Fifty dollars! Do you know how sentimental that bed is? That's where I had my first shag."

Matt is so overreacting. I told him that it's not my fault that his bed was sold. Matt offered to buy it back but I declined on account of the fact that I just got throw pillows with love hearts on them to match the tones of the headboard and more to the point, Millie and Sid would have nowhere to sleep. Now Matt's gone all moody again and left without saying goodbye.

God what *is* his problem?

Arrival of Rick

He's so sexy.

Mum and Dad are out shopping and Millie and Sid have not yet arrived home, so I hinted to Rick that we make the most of our time alone.

Arrival of Mum and Dad

Phew, that was a close one! Five minutes sooner and they would have been scarred, not quite for life though, because not much happened anyway on account of Rick being terrified of getting caught shagging by parents.

Arrival of Neroli and baby Bailey

God what is this, Grand Central Station?

Arrival of Millie and Sid

So excited.

I ran out to greet them and cannot wait to show them their new room. Millie is barely out of the car when I pull her into a big embrace. This is the longest that Millie and I have ever been apart since we met and I'm getting all choked up because I have missed her. Millie's pleased to see me too and surprised that my parents are still here. I don't know why she would be surprised; she knows my parents cannot resist annoying their only child.

We are now all seated around the table on the patio and Millie's passing around her camera so we can all look at their honeymoon shots. It's a lovely peaceful scene taking place and it makes me realise how blessed I am. Neroli's staring into space twirling her long dark hair around her finger, and Rick's bouncing baby Bailey on his knee.
Rick's so adorable and sexy; he would make a great father.
I so want a baby.

"So what's been happening here?" Millie asked when all the photos had been seen.

"Well Lisa was about to move her furniture into her new office." Dad informed her.

"Office?" Millie exclaimed shooting me a look.

Oh god, I haven't told Millie that I rented office space for my new wedding planning business.

"Yes, I thought I would need an office, you know, for um, office stuff."

"Lisa, you don't need an office, it's not viable. What about the overheads?"

"Yes I agree," said Dad.

I need to change the subject as I feel a lecture coming on.

"Lisa you didn't sign a lease did you?"

"Um, just a tiny one?"

"Oh Lisa!" Millie groaned.

"Actually Lisa while we're all here, it's about time we talked about this," Mum said in her annoying tuttering way.

What is this? Intervention?

Dad starts, "this wedding planning business, I'm not disapproving but don't you think this sort of profession would be better off if you had some clients first, before you start opening an office?"

I look to Rick for support, he'll tell them.

Shit, Rick's also looking at me in a tuttering way.

"I do have clients," I said in a hoity tone.

Truth is I don't, but Mum and Dad had announced they're leaving at the end of the week so I'll just have to pretend I have clients until they leave.

Millie opened her mouth to speak when she was interrupted by Matt throwing a wad of bank notes at me.

What the..? I thought he had left.

"Give you a hundred bucks for the bed."

"What bed?" Millie asks.

"Ah..."

"Lisa who are these clients of yours?" Dad asks.

"Ah..."

"Alright two hundred..."

"What bed?" Millie asks again.

"Lisa what are you charging these clients?" Mum asks.

Now everyone's looking at me for answers and it's so unfair. I feel like I have been railroaded by the wedding planning police. I fake a coughing fit and run to the kitchen where it is quiet and no one is asking questions.

Rick came in to see if I was okay in his sexy way.
"Do you still want me to take the stuff down to the new office?" he asks as he wraps his arms around my waist.
"I don't know, you have to ask the office police." I said in a sarcastic tone.

Rick laughs and turns me to face him, "I see your cough has improved. Listen how about we do that later, I have to go and do some work anyway. Will see you after?"
He gave me a kiss and told me to be nice to my parents, I went to go back out to tell Mum and Dad that how many clients I have is not their business, when I turned around to see them all standing in the doorway.
Shit!
"So these clients?" Mum asks again.

"All right," I said defeated, "well um ... didn't want to tell you as it's a big secret but it's um ... Matt and Neroli."

Mum's hand flies to her mouth in a pleasant gasp before pulling a stunned looking Neroli into a big embrace. Matt's looking at me in total shock, Millie's looking at me suspicious like and Neroli's stunned look as been replaced with a very confused expression.
But Neroli always looks confused.

I grabbed Matt by the arm while the distraction of congratulations being said was going on, and pulled him in to the storeroom.

"When am I getting married?" he asks totally bewildered.
"You're not!" I hissed, "but I will make a deal with you, you pretend to be getting married just till my parents leave and I'll give you your bed back."
Matt's thinking about the proposed offer and a big dreamy smile comes over his face.
"Yeah okay, whatever," he agrees, "now give me back my bed."
"Not right now," I hissed. "Let me find another bed for Sid and Millie first, but don't tell them it's your bed alright?"

Matt nodded.

"Great. Now get back in there and tell Neroli she's not really getting married before she opens her mouth."

Back in the little gathering full of joy and confusion. Matt now has his arm around Neroli telling Mum and Dad how he knew the first time he met Neroli, she was the one and all that mushy stuff. Neroli must still be in total shock as she still looks very confused and hasn't said anything yet.

Millie cocked one suspicious eye at me and I diverted her attention by asking if she and Sid wanted to see their new bedroom. I don't give her time to answer as I grab their belongings and lead them to the marital bedroom.

In marital bedroom
Millie and Sid seem pleased about the room and they look so happy together with their little affectionate banter. Sid declares he is going to have a lie down as he is tired.

I went to leave the room but Millie grabs my arm.
Great, here comes another lecture.

"Tell me that Neroli and Matt aren't really getting married and you have done this to shut your parents up."

What? How does she..?

"Lisa?"

"Yes," I said in a defeated tone. "Matt agreed to go along with it just until Friday."

Millie shook her head, I know she really wants to say that telling my parents about a fake wedding is a dumb idea and the office is an equally dumb idea, but she simply sighs.

Back in kitchen

Mum and Neroli are now sitting around the kitchen table looking through bridal magazines.

Matt must have gone back to work as his ute's gone.

Later

Neroli is now gone and I have to say, thank god she's gone, as it looked like she was enjoying looking at wedding stuff and I'm not sure if Matt's told her she's not really getting married.

Mum and Dad haven't mentioned it again and now all that is left to do is just get through the next three days until they leave.

Rick rung to tell me that if I was still getting a hard time from the office police then he may know someone that will take over the six month lease I signed and he'll let me know. Rick also thinks that it may be a good idea if I start the business off from home first and build it from there.
He's so brilliant and sexy.
So that's what I've decided to do.
I had just got off the phone with Rick when Millie sauntered out onto the porch stretching and looking very restful.
"Lisa that bed is so comfortable, where did you get it from?"
"Oh… you know, pff."
"And the room looks great. Thank you, I know you must have put in a big effort."
Millie's glowing, married life must agree with her. She suggested we open a bottle of wine to toast the new bedroom.

Two bottles later

Ha, ha, so funny, Millie was just telling me about their honeymoon and that Sid forgot his board shorts and had to wear budgie smugglers to the beach.

Mum joined us for a short time but she cannot see why we think wearing budgie smugglers was that funny, as the whole point of tight bathing costumes was to keep the sand from getting into awkward places and in fact, my father wears them all the time at the beach. Millie and I are now roaring with laughter and Mum's in a huff and has gone away to cook something.

Millie is putting on her serious lecture face and I know she's going to start on the whole office thing again so I told her not to worry. I assured her that I had had a think about it and decided to set up office from home and that Rick's found someone to take over the lease and everything is working out well.

Sid's joined us; he also said the bed was comfortable.

Three bottles later

I now have enough courage to tell Sid about the petting zoo and guest house.

I was prepared to state my case like lawyers do in court, when shock comes upon me as Millie and Sid think it's a great idea.

Now I'm worried because they do think it's a great idea and Millie's not dragging me off to an impulse behaviour meeting.

Sid suggests that he could get some plans done. I tell him not to worry because I already have plans and have already ordered timber for the petting zoo yards. I suddenly remembered that I had bid for some geese on e-bay and the bids will be closed. Millie's shocked at the thought of bidding for animals online and I point out it's not like selling a teapot, animals online come from breeders and it's very much an acceptable practice. I race through to my laptop and discovered that I am now the proud owner of a flock of geese.

Millie's now even more shocked and Dad's lecturing me about buying livestock over the internet.

Next morning

I cannot believe I brought a flock of geese. I don't really want geese but can't get out of it now.

Rick came around last night and announced he has a surprise for me and he needs to go to the city, he also offered to pick the flock of geese up for me on his return.

I'm so excited about my surprise and have spent a sleepless night wondering what it could be. Cannot help but think it could be a ring.

I woke Millie up in the small hours of the morning to ask her if she thinks my surprise could be a wedding ring and she said that if it was a ring then Rick would be a first prize dickhead on account of telling someone as neurotic as myself about a surprise in the first place.

Mum and Dad are cleaning the Winnebago in preparation for their next trip. Millie's heading back to the city tomorrow to start work so she's offered to give me a hand to set up my home office.

I'm so excited about my wedding planning business and petting zoo and I had a tiny thought last night that a Bed and Breakfast would also be a great business. But when I mentioned this to Millie, she gave me her usual warning look and said, "one step at a time."

"Nothing wrong with setting goals," I shot back in defense.

The office didn't take long to set up, just a desk and my laptop, a few bridal magazines, oh and a chair.

Now I just need clients; real ones.

I'm not due to start work at the retirement home until next week but I have to say I'm not really looking forward to it, it feels like I'm going backwards not forwards. But for now I shall sit in my new office and wait for clients. I advertised in the local paper so am confident the phone will be ringing off the hook soon.

Hour later

No calls yet but I am surfing the net for some sexy lingerie. With Mum and Dad leaving on Friday and Rick with his policy of no shagging around parents, I have decided to make Friday night extra special and spice things up so he will not be able to resist me. I'm trying to decide between a white lace chemise with white stockings or a leather suit with crotchless knickers. I have also booked myself in for a bikini wax and because Sid will be here on Friday night I have decided to also give him some space.

Also, cannot have noisy sex with people in the house, so I have it all planned out. I will put on the sexy lingerie and a big trench coat and drive down to Rick's with a bottle of wine and surprise him.

Then if Rick pops the question the night will be even more perfect.

Phone ringing

Oh my god this is it, my first customer. I clear my throat in preparation for a professional manner.

"Good err morning, Lisa Collins event planning."

"Hey."

Bugger, it's just Matt.

"Matt," I hissed, "how many times have I told you not to call me on the land line. This phone is for business purposes only."

"I want to set a date," Matt informs me.

"For what?"

"For our wedding."

"Matt you're not getting married."

"Yes I am, on May 20th."

I rubbed my brow in frustration; Neroli's dim-witted ways seem to be rubbing off on Matt.

"Matt you can't set a date if you're not getting married, if my parents ask I'll just..."

"Nah man, I really am getting married. I've thought about it and talked to Neroli and we have decided we do want to get married."

"Matt don't be ridiculous you can't get married, you're only nineteen."

"Really?"

"Yes really, now get off this line."

"Can I still have my bed back?"

"Yes, yes! Now get off this line in case clients are trying to call."

I hung up from Matt and checked the phone to make sure I hadn't missed a call from Rick. I'm so excited about my surprise and I have decided on the white lace chemise to go with the whole proposal slash wedding theme.

I was just processing payment when I heard a tiny knock on the door.

Ooh could be a client?

No they'd phone first.

"Lisa dear?" came the faint shrill from behind the door.

Mrs Crankshaw. Rick's aunt and the most meddlesome person on earth. She is also my neighbour.

"Lisa dear, there you are. Where is everybody? I've been knocking for ages. Busy with the new interest I see."

She cranes her neck to see what I'm doing on my laptop and I move my screen around just a tiny bit so she can't see pictures of leather bondage gear on the screen. Not that Mrs Crankshaw is an old prune or anything, a few months back she was the mastermind behind a fundraiser the Country Woman's Association held for a member who had breast cancer. We put on a *Kinky'n'nice* party and sold heaps of adult products to raise money for breast cancer research.

Oh did I mention that I'm now the President of the local Country Woman's Association.

Mind you, no one else wanted the job.

"Now Lisa, Rick has just rung and asked Max to drop off your geese, he's been held up but he'll give you a call later. He's going to stay in the city for a couple of days."

My heart sank. Rick's staying in the city for a couple of days, is he having trouble finding me a ring?

I quizzed Mrs Crankshaw about the reason why Rick would stay on in the city for a few days but the old lady is giving away nothing other than his message that he'll call me later.

Day turning to crap.

Mrs Crankshaw has gone to make a cup of tea and check out the newlywed suite like a nosey person.

I can't wait that long for my surprise and am horrified to think that Rick would make me wait. If he really loved me he would just tell me, ooh phone ringing.

Oh my god it's Rick! I will answer the phone in an unsuspecting manner.

I answered the phone and on came Rick shouting over the top of what sounds to be a crowded bar. I checked the time on my laptop and realised it's only eleven in the morning. I was about to change my unsuspecting tone into a frosty one when Rick informs me he's at the airport.

Oh!

"I'm not going to tell you what I'm doing at the airport it's a surprise," he teased after I panicked and asked him if he's leaving the country.

"Sorry sweetheart," Rick went on, "didn't plan it like this, it just happened. I'll be home on Friday."

He hung up and I'm still a bit stunned as to why Rick would be at an airport, strange place to buy an engagement ring unless it's on mail order and is so rare that customs have intercepted it and he's gone down to sort it out. But jeez how long does it take?

Mrs Crankshaw returns with a steaming hot cup of tea.

"Lisa dear your parents inform me that Matt and Neroli are getting married."

Oh shit

"I have to say I'm a bit shocked," Mrs Crankshaw said as she planted her chubby backside on the chair.

"Oh you know," I said waving my hand at her, "it's probably just a phase I don't think it will happen."

"Your parents tell me that you're going to be coordinating the wedding."

"Well nothing has been discussed yet."

God I wish my parents would leave before this white lie snowballs out of control.

"Still," Mrs Crankshaw comments, taking a sip of her tea and leaving the comment hanging in the air.

I need to change the subject so I asked her if she knows of any garage sales in the area as I still need to find Millie and Sid a new bed. Okay a second-hand bed is not nice but I just need the frame.

I've decided to buy Millie and Sid a new mattress; finances are not good so I can't afford to buy them a whole bed. And I still haven't worked out what to tell them when the time comes to take their current bed away.

But I'm confident that will work itself out.

Mrs Crankshaw is now going over the list of items that the CWA needs to cater the up and coming garden clubs' afternoon tea. I'm a bit bored but it's a good distraction from the fact no clients have rung. Mum has now joined us and Mrs Crankshaw and her are discussing Hibiscus cuttings. In looking at the time, I realise we've been sitting here for one hour and forty minutes.

But to show Mum that I'm not clock watching and the wedding business is going well, I'm pretending to be busy, but really I'm looking at baby names online to see what goes well with Crankshaw.

Dad gingerly knocks at the door and tells me a man has arrived with some geese. Mrs Crankshaw informs Dad that it's her husband and insists that Dad meets him.

I'm not that excited about geese but it's a great start to my petting zoo. Max Crankshaw was unloading the cage that housed the three geese from the back of his ute. I directed him to the chicken coop in a nonchalant manner. Geese are unexciting creatures and I have to say, a bit noisy and quite big for baby geese. I watched them for a while as Dad and Mr Crankshaw chatted like old friends. Now we are all having a tour of the Winnebago and I feel like I'm in an old peoples' village.

Back in office
No calls and so bored.

Hour later
Still no calls.

I went to see what Millie's up to. I tapped at the bedroom door and realised Sid must be in there as well because it sounds like hanky panky. I tiptoe away with my face burning red, so embarrassed, but am going to mention to Rick that Millie and Sid don't have a policy of no shagging around parents.

I need to get over this boredom and I figure if Millie can kill her boredom with something physical then so can I.

I have a vision of what this place would look like with a petting zoo and guest house but the garden lets it down, so I've signed up for a garden tour with the garden club for inspiration. But now I need to weed, not with weed killer this time, but actual bare hands weeding. Mum's not a gardener so no good asking her for help.

Hours later

Gardening is very therapeutic and I cannot believe I haven't discovered the benefits of being with the earth before. Now I'm thinking of starting my own garden business as well as wedding planning so after I finish this patch I'm going inside to do some flyers to pass round the garden club members at the garden tour.
I also have discovered that I'm not even thinking about Rick and my surprise engagement at all.

Millie came out to see what I was doing. I wasn't going to ask her what she's been doing as her and Sid seemed to be at it all afternoon. I told Millie about my idea for a garden business to fill in the time between wedding clients and she swore under her breath, mumbled something, then in a loud voice said, 'one thing at a time', and if I'm still keen on gardening tomorrow then I should think about it then.

Millie's so negative.

Mum also came out to see what I'm doing but I didn't mention to her about starting a garden business. She'd only tut at me.

I heard the phone ringing and ran to it like Forrest Gump hoping it will be Rick.

Alas it's not Rick, just bloody Matt.

"You're wrong!" he said when I picked up the receiver.

"Wrong about what?" I panted down the phone.

"I can get married, I looked it up on the internet and the legal age is eighteen. Google it if you don't believe me."

"Matt," I sigh, "I know that. When I said you can't get married you're only nineteen, I meant you're too young to be tied down."

"Well I'm gonna."

"Yes one day…"

"Nah man, I'm gonna get married on May the 20th."

"Matt don't be ridiculous, that's only a few months away."

"Yeah we decided not to wait. So can you do it? You know, organise it and stuff?"

Panic is now rising in my throat. I have gone and planted a silly idea in the spotty youth's head that he should get married to a single mother fifteen years his senior and unaware of what planet she's on.

I need to stop this.

"Matt," I pleaded, "you're making a huge mistake, don't do anything, I'm coming round."

"Nah man, I'm not arguing, made up my mind, told Mum and everything."

My heart stopped.

"You told your mum? Oh god what did she say?"

"Yeah, she's sweet with it."

"Matt is your mum still on the medication?"

"Yeah but she's doing okay, I told her not to worry, that you're sorting out the wedding arrangements."

Oh my god! I cannot believe Matt has told Pamela. And worse still, told her that *I'm* arranging it all. Pamela, Matt's mum, my mortal enemy. Not only did she have an affair behind my back with Jake, she's also a snotty woman who went out of her way to be mean to me and is a total control freak I might add.

Now I feel she'll be sitting in her hospital ward in the metal health unit plotting revenge on me for ruining her teenage son's life and taking over her position as President of the CWA.

I pleaded with Matt once again but he's absolutely sure he wants to marry Neroli and they're coming around tomorrow to discuss wedding plans. I told Matt that I don't want anything to do with it and he can make his own arrangements but he said that he will tell Sid and Millie about the bed so I said I may be able to help a tiny bit.

"Oh and Lisa," he said, as I was about to hang up and cry.

"Yeah?"

"I still want my bed back."

Facebook Status Update.

Lisa Collins.

Lisa changed from 'in a relationship' to 'almost engaged' to Rick Crankshaw.

Lisa added 'soon to be petting zoo owner' to her work info.

2

I cannot believe Matt and Neroli are getting married; I feel so responsible for this and need to stop the wedding. Matt's too young to take on a ready-made family and he's still doing his apprenticeship as a mechanic. He doesn't earn enough to support a young family. And what is up with Neroli for letting Matt marry her, I mean how responsible is that?

And oh my god they want to get married in three months! Why so soon?

I just had a sudden thought that it's obvious, Neroli is pregnant again! Does that woman know how to do anything else but have babies? Yes that must be it; Matt's going to marry Neroli because she's pregnant. Phew, that's a relief, I mean I can't be held responsible for that!

Better tell Millie."They're what!" Millie exclaimed, almost choking on her orange juice.

"Yes, I think Neroli's pregnant again, they're getting married in May."

"They're what?"

Millie's repeating herself but it's understandable as it's a bit shocking. I told Millie about Matt telling Pamela so it must be serious. I also told Millie that I need to visit a witch doctor or something and get a counter spell because I feel Pamela has a voodoo doll of me and is going to spend her days sticking pins in it for putting the idea into Matt's head in the first place.

Millie's not lecturing me this time, she said if Neroli is pregnant then Matt's doing the right thing and we should be supportive.

I told Millie that Matt is not doing the right thing and I will not support a child wedding.

Millie disagrees again and she ends up getting snotty with me because she thinks that I'm making this all about me and I said.......

Never mind, point is I need to stop this wedding.

Sid's hammering away down in the proposed petting zoo area, finally things are moving forward.

The boring geese are settling in well and Sid thinks it's time I let them out of the pen so they can be free-range geese, so now they're resting on the bonnet of my car.

I'm so not impressed with Sid and when he comes back from the petting zoo yards I'm going to make him clean the geese excrement off my car.

Back in office

Still no calls from clients so I googled witchcraft. And because I do not have chicken's feet or badger's hair in stock I'm going down to the crystal shop later to get tiger's eye to ward off any voodoo attacks from Pamela.

Also (even though I have no clients) I have had a very productive afternoon. I brought a bed for Millie and Sid, a mattress online which will be delivered tomorrow (love internet shopping) and have hatched a plan as to how I'm going to switch beds. You see with Millie going back to the city for work and Sid's preoccupation with the petting zoo yards, switching will be easy.

I texted Matt and told him to bring his work ute as his bed will be available for pick up when him and Neroli come round to discuss so-called wedding plans.

I've also done an estimated budget sheet for Matt and Neroli which I will present them with tomorrow in the hope that they will be shocked with wedding cost (not to mention my fee) and then decide that living together is much cheaper and there's no need for a wedding after all.

I'm very tempted to call Rick but do not want to seem like I so want to know what my surprise is, so sent him a wee text with kisses and hugs and he sent the same back.
So cute.

I need to sort out a license for the petting zoo. I mention this to Millie and she said that's a very grown-up thing to do and it's nice to see me taking the right avenues and looking before you leap and all that crap. Millie seems a bit drained and tired today but I'm not surprised as Sid and her have been non-stop shagging since they got back from their honeymoon.
There seems to be a lot involved in obtaining a license for a petting zoo so I printed information out and set it aside for another day and in the mean time, made a list of animals needed. I've already got goats and geese but I'm thinking of furry, fluffy things that you can hold, so rabbits and guinea pigs are a must, also a pony, alpaca and cow.
And they all have to be white in colour.

I started looking on the internet for white animals when I heard Sid come inside and Millie call out to him from the bedroom. Surely they can't be about to shag again?

I mean Millie doesn't like sex all that much and Sid normally just does what he's told so I'm certain that Sid's not the instigator of this shag fest. Millie is a very private person but I feel I need to ask her what's going on.

But I think I'll wait until they're finished first.

Arrival of rural postman

I heard Rob's van pull up and sprinted out there before Dad starts talking to him again. Rob and Dad seemed to have hit it off and Dad insists he stays for a cuppa before continuing on his rounds.

But I have a slight problem because Rob's not your average postman. Rob's like Mrs Crankshaw, a very nosey person who likes to gossip. So far he hasn't mention to Dad about Rick squatting in my ceiling or the fact I had slept with Matt.

Okay Neroli's the same age as me and she's sleeping with the spotty youth but I'm convinced Dad still thinks that I'm saving myself for marriage because he mentioned to me about Rick being a decent young man who has good intentions by giving me time and not giving into temptation by sleeping over (poor Dad, if only he knew). So I don't want to burst his bubble.

Also if they found out that Rick was squatting in my ceiling without my knowledge then Dad's opinion of Rick will turn sour quicker then a ripe lemon, not to mention my parents marching me back to the city and locking me away till I'm old enough to retire.

"Hey there lassie," Rob greeted in his Scottish accent as I sprinted to his van.

"Oh you seem keen today, waiting on this are you?" he said as he handed me my parcel.

Ooh my mail order massage oils have arrived.

"Something for our young Rick is it?" Rob chortled.

Great. Rob's obviously seen the company name on the package.

"No!" I shot back, my cheeks burning. "Anyway Rob, Dad's not here today so… you know, I'll tell him you said hi and all."

"Whatcha talking 'bout lass, he's right there."

Dad's standing in the door of the Winnebago waving the kettle in the air and Rob shuts the van door to join him. I have to remind myself that it's only two days until my parents leave.

It's so bloody exhausting; all this running around trying to keep my parents from acquiring top secret knowledge about myself. I planted myself down on the small fold-out table of the Winnebago waiting for Dad to make the tea. Dad's Australian but his parents were Scottish so Dad thinks he's an expert on all things Scottish, which is fine, as that's about the extent of the conversations between him and Rob. But just to be sure that their subjects don't run off course and move onto things like cougars and squatters, it's best I sit in on their little chit chat.

Even though Rob thinks it's his company I crave.

Conversation so far seems to be about the weather and the shocking story on the news about some RSL club banning boiled sweets from bingo games. I haven't contributed to the conversation as I have no interest in weather or bingo. Trying so hard not to let thoughts drift off to things like engagement rings and Rick because the conversation subject could turn so quickly, but already I'm bored and Dad hasn't even poured the tea yet.

Conversation switched to current affairs.

Tea served.

Oh god, now they talking about home invasions.

Oh no, now conversation is swinging towards citizens rights against intruders.

Rob is now opening his mouth and looking at me with a devilish glint in his eye. Any moment now he's going to tell Dad. *Shit, shit,* got to stop this.

Oh my god, here it comes, his lips are moving, quick, need a distraction.

I grabbed my mug of steaming hot contents and threw it at Rob, I didn't mean to hit Rob with the steaming contents, it was only meant as a distraction but now Rob is on his feet clutching his groin.

Oh my god I have scolded Rob's manhood!

Dad's gasping and grabbing at his heart upon witnessing my unprovoked attack on the postman. I snatch a tea towel from the table and begin rubbing Rob's groin area in a desperate attempt to show how sorry I am. Dad's yelling at me but I'm unsure what he's saying.

I realise that Dad may be even more shocked at the sight of me rubbing postman Rob's groin with Mum's good tea towel that she brought to commemorate Charles and Diana's 1980's visit to Australia.

I'm so embarrassed but in too deep to rectify the situation so I asked Rob to take his pants off so I can wash them, telling him how sorry I was.

I didn't hear Mum come in, I only knew she was there when she started smacking my hands away from Rob's groin. Rob has now found his voice and told me 'not to worry lass, accidents happen and have done a superb job in stain prevention'.

I'm now walking back to the house after being banished from the Winnebago but not before Mum gave me her 'we'll talk later' glare as she reached for an icepack. Great, now I'll never get to know if Rob's going to tell them about Rick's previous life as a squatter.

Back in office

Cannot concentrate. Rob is still here and after trying to sneak around the side of the motor home to eavesdrop and being caught by Mum, I knew the mother of all lectures not to mention 'damn good explanation' is going to be forced upon me anytime soon.

Now I'm wondering how I'm going to get through the next one and a half days before they leave.

Crystal shop

I've decided avoidance is the best defense against my parents. Rob was just leaving as I got into my car. It can't be all bad as he gave me a friendly wave as he left; I didn't look at Mum and Dad but could feel the wrath of their stares as I drove away.

At crystal shop

The crystal shop has lovely ambiance, I could feel the peaceful serenity the moment I stepped inside.

 I need to buy a tiger's eye to ward off attacks from Pamela, also thinking maybe a crystal to cope with parents.

"Hi Lisa."

"Oh hi Tim. Buying crystals as well?"

Tim is the local baker and believe it or not, Millie's ex.

Well not an *ex* exactly. Tim and Millie had a brief relationship a few months back when her and Sid split up before getting back together. And when I say brief relationship, I mean that it lasted only a week. Tim was smitten by Millie and a wee bit heartbroken and bitter about Millie going back to Sid.

"Oh you know?" he shrugged glumly under the black cloud that seemed to hover over him.

"Well that's err, great Tim."I quickly moved away from him before he involved me in a conversation. I didn't want to ask how he was 'cos then I'd get the whole sob story about how his life is not worth living since Millie decided to go back to Sid etc, etc. Poor Tim, lovely guy, but wish he would get a life.

I made my way over to the displays of crystals. There were so many and each listed their healing functions and spiritual benefits. I found my tiger's eye and quickly skimmed through the meaning on the information card. *'Builds confidence, releases stuck states, good for digestion...'* Ha! Found it, also *'protects against evil eye demons and witchcraft'*. Can't believe my luck, I not only found a stone that will protect me against Pamela but against the wrath of my parents as well. I made my way over to the counter to pay for the magic stone when I saw the little sign *Tarot Readings Here Today.*

I stood staring at the sign like a complete dummy. Not sure what to do as how easy would it be to march in there and find out in ten minutes whether or not Rick is going to ask me to marry him. But if I do that then I'm going to have to act all surprised when he does propose.

No, I'm not going to get sucked in to it.

No future is one hundred percent certain and if Rick does ask me to marry him then I'd rather not know. I marched myself over to counter, snubbing the sign and telling myself that I'm better off not knowing the future as it's not my business to know. I paid for the magic crystal and left the shop feeling very proud and in control.

Back in crystal shop

I'm waiting on my appointment with the tarot reader, I decided that a little glimpse into the future is harmless.
It's also good to be prepared.
I can't see Tim anywhere so presume he left the store, however I didn't see him leave.
 I'm feeling very excited about the reading, wonder how many children Rick and I will have?
A door opened snapping me out of my thoughts. Tim appeared looking very pleased with himself.
"Oh, hi Lisa."
"Tim! Did you just get a reading done?"
He looked embarrassed but pleased at the same time. He said that the tarot card woman was amazing.
 She must be good 'cos this is the happiest I've seen Tim in a long time.

"Who's next?" came the voice from inside the door. I gingerly entered the room and was a bit startled as the woman looked more like my mum then a gypsy.

I sat down but am not quite sure what to say, I don't want to give away too much about myself.

She looked at me and smiled.

"Hi, I'm Angela," she said.

"I'm Lisa." I smiled back, *shit I shouldn't have told her my name.*

"Have you had a reading before my dear?"

"Err, no."

"Okay, well the first thing I want you to do is close your eyes and focus on the question you want answered today."

I close my eyes. I feel her take both my hands, I feel silly sitting here with my eyes closed in front of a complete stranger who is holding my hands, she has lovely soft hands I must admit, wonder what type of skin care she uses?

"Clear your mind," she said softly.

Oh right I forgot.

There was only one question I wanted to ask.

"Um err, excuse me," I asked, raising one eye open to see she also had her eyes closed and was rocking back and forth, "um do I ask out loud?"

"No, just focus in your mind."

"Oh alright, got ya." Closing my eyes once again, I begin to think that I could ask all sorts of things, not just about Rick and I, but about my petting zoo and wedding planning business and how many kids I will have and if Pamela is going to come after me with a carving knife.

I felt her hands slide away from mine. "Okay, let's begin," she said taking a deep breath and handing me the deck of cards. "Shuffle the cards my dear and cut the deck into three piles."

I'm so excited. I cut the deck into three piles and watch as she gathers them up and lays the first cards on the table.

"Hmmm," she said, her brow crinkles up in a disapproving manner.

I bend forward to see what could be so horrible but can't understand the pictures, looks like a sword.

Oh my god, Pamela *is* going to come after me with a large sharp object.

"You have some issues with making decisions, you seem to lack focus with your life," Angela said, tapping her finger on the card.

Oh phew is that all, so that doesn't mean Pamela coming after me.

"You don't seem to look before you leap..."

Yes, yes, get to the point.

"You seem to burden yourself with projects..."

Just turn over another card.

"Absorb other people's energy's..."

God I wish she would just move on, I'm not paying her $50 to tell me stuff I don't want to hear.

She turns over another card and her expression changes.

"There's news of a pregnancy soon."

Ha! So Neroli *is* pregnant.

"I also feel there is conflict around an event," she looks puzzled and kinda moves her head to one side as if she's listening to someone beside her. Bit freaky.

"There are some past issues that need to be addressed. Is this making sense to you dear?"

I wanted to say that I have no idea what she's talking about, but didn't want to spend all day talking about anything other than Rick and so I said "oh yes," and nodded in a knowing way.

"That's good," she smiled and patted me on the hand. "Just remember your guides are there to protect you and guide you, don't be afraid to ask for help."

"Err right, okay."

She turns over two cards and I craned my neck to see. Looks like a tower and some rider on a horse.

"An unexpected visitor may arrive, could be some issues there."

Well that's nothing new, I get visitors all the time and they all have issues.

"You're in a relationship at the moment."

Finally! I lean forward in anticipation.

"He's a good man," Angela continued, "I feel he has your best interests at heart, however you're not absolutely sure if he is the one for you."

What? I cannot believe she just said that. I know Rick *is* the one for me, for a start we get on really well and he is nothing like Jake was, he respects me and I love the way he thinks I'm funny. He is really supportive with my wedding planning business and Millie likes him so that's got to count for something.

The old lady doesn't know what she's talking about, can't believe I paid $50 to a crazy lady.

Angela smiles and puts down the deck of cards. "You're not very open about this are you?"

What. How does she...

"My dear, let me elaborate," she said taking my hands again. "You're not sure if this man is the right one for you because you're not sure what it is you want for yourself."

I thought about this and have to admit she's a tiny bit right.

"You know the universe only responds to what you put out there," Angela continues, "and your spirit guides are there to guide and protect you and right now I feel they are telling me to tell you that you haven't figured out what your true path in life is. You can't move forward if you are not sure where you want to go."

I could feel tears bubble up in my eyes and I don't know why. I don't feel upset but a flood of emotions are running through me.

"Sorry," I sniffed.

"That's okay dear, just let the emotions flow freely."

"Do I really have spirit guides?" I sniffed, taking the tissue she handed me.

"Oh yes, they are here with you right now."

"Really? That's so cool." I looked around the room wondering where they could be.

"But my dear you must listen to yourself, trust your gut feeling, open yourself up to the angels."

"What about Rick, err I mean, my boyfriend?"

Angela smiles and pats me on the hand, she picks up the cards and turns them all over.

"You will be fine but remember what I said, in order for things to move forward you must decide what you really want, it's only then that the universe will grant you your wishes."

I feel so much better, it's like a veil has been lifted. I mean Sid is always going on about this stuff, with his meditation and all and I could never see the point up till now. And how cool is it that I have some higher being following me everywhere, it's like I know something that others don't. Ask and you shall receive, why hadn't I realised that before.

I grabbed my bag from beside the chair and leaned over to hug Angela. I thanked her and told her that I must be off as I have to make a list of all the things I need to ask the universe for.

She said something but I didn't hear her.

I stopped at the counter to pay the well spent $50 when I saw a flyer on the counter for a meditation group that is held every Tuesday. I think it's a sign from the universe so I grab a flyer and one for Sid as well, as he could be my meditation buddy. I paid and left the shop.

I stepped out into the glare of the sun holding the door to the shop open so my guardian angel doesn't have to walk through it and felt the gentle breeze across my face. For the first time I saw my surroundings in a different light, the universe is now my friend and I'm going to love and give to the universe from now on.

"Hi Lisa."

I looked around to see Tim waiting outside the shop.

"Oh hi Tim."

"Did you have a reading with Angela as well?" he asks.

"Oh yes and it was wonderful, I didn't know you were into this stuff Tim."

Tim went all coy and scuffed his boot on the pavement.

"Yeah well, you know, Mum was and I guess it just rubbed off on me. Do you know about the meditation group?"

"Oh yes, just picked up the flyer. How was your reading Tim?"

A grin spreads across his face the size of Africa. "Fantastic, she said that I will cross paths with my true love and seems to think I have already met her."

"Oh that's great Tim."

Tim catches my eye and there is a flash of emotion in his gaze. Bit weird.

"Okay then, bye Tim."

"Bye. Um see you at meditation on Tuesday?"

"Err, yes, bye."

"Bye."

Facebook Status Update.

Lisa Collins.

Lisa updated her Relentionship status to "Almost engaged to Rick Crankshaw".

Lisa added 'meditation and anything spiritual' to her interests.

3

Friday

Thank god it's Friday.

It's a very important day because not only will Rick be home later but my parents are leaving.

And thank goodness they're leaving because after I got home from the crystal shop yesterday, they were waiting for me with their arms folded across their chest's demanding an explanation as to why I would throw hot tea at the postman. When I told them it was an accident, I then had to endure Mum's lecture me about how I could have scarred him, third degree burns blah, blah, and then to top it off they insisted on spending some time with me, so all afternoon I was forced into a game of scrabble in the cramped surroundings of the Winnebago leaving me no time to make my wish list to the universe.

But I'm sure the universe wouldn't mind waiting.

Mum's in the kitchen making pancakes for breakfast and it smells so good, I have to admit as much as Mum and Dad are a pain, I'm going to miss Mum's cooked breakfasts.

Millie must have smelt the pancakes as well, as she's sitting at the kitchen table sipping her coffee. Millie's also going back to the city today to work her very last weekend shift at the Irish Bar before being rostered onto week days only.

I sat down next to her as Mum brought over my stack of pancakes lavished with maple syrup.

Gotta love mums.

"So I hear you have Matt and Neroli coming over later to discuss wedding plans." Millie said quietly. "So I guess you have finally agreed to make the arrangements."

"How did you know?" I asked.

"Because Matt phoned, he said to tell you that all systems are go, whatever that means."

I think that was Matt's tactful way of telling me without Millie finding out, that he's going to bring the ute with him and take home Millie and Sid's bed.

"So do you still think Neroli's pregnant?" Millie asked, not so quietly this time.

"Pregnant?" Mum interrupted, "whatever makes you think she's pregnant?"

"Because Matt's too young to get married so there must be a reasonable explanation as to why and so suddenly."

"Nonsense dear," Mum tutted, "your dad and I were only twenty when we married and we didn't have you till later on."

"Yes Mum but this is different," I mumbled.

"It's not. Clearly that boy is smitten by her, it's written all over his face. I think it's lovely."

Millie nodded in agreement.

Up against two people who think they know what's best for everyone. It's true, Mum and Millie are always talking about people they meet or celebrities and spouting off about how much better off they would be if they just got a job or changed their hair colour. So best I don't say any more on the subject.

"Oh and Matt called," Mum said as she joined us at the table, "he said to tell you he's bringing the work ute to collect the bed."

"Lisa what bed is this?" Millie asks.

Bloody Matt, he's as discreet as a herd of elephants. Better come clean, after all it's just a bed and Millie seems in a good mood.

"Okay Millie, don't get mad but I brought your bed from Matt's father. But I didn't know it was Matt's bed and then when he found out, he wanted it back, so I've ordered you and Sid a new bed which should be arriving today."

Millie looked at me a bit puzzled.

"So why didn't you just tell us that in the first place?"

"'Cos I wanted it to be a, err, surprise."

Millie rolled her eyes at me. "Well as long as this new bed is as comfortable as the old one, then fine."

Phew, that was easy.

Millie stood up and gathered her mug, "better go and wake Sid so I can get going I suppose."

"Yes," agreed Mum moving from the table as well, "we better get organised ourselves."

Small leap of joy in my stomach, not only because parents are leaving, but it's Friday and I'm going to see Rick tonight.

In office

There's a parcel sitting on my desk and I'm guessing it's my sexy lingerie. Dad must have put it there, which means Rob must have been and gone this morning. Thank god. After yesterday I don't think I'm able to face him again.

I opened the box and pulled out the contents. Very impressive and I'm dying to try it on, but it's not the appropriate time. Although, I have to say with confidence, Rick is going to love it. I must remind myself to ask Millie for her big trench coat before she leaves.

I checked the phone for any missed calls relating to the wedding business but alas, none so far. I'm thinking I may need to hold a wedding expo in the village to get unwed couples in the wedding mood.

Millie's hollering at me from her room so I make my way to find out why Millie feels she needs to summon me like I'm her personal slave.

"Lisa, Sid doesn't want to give up the bed," she said sounding frustrated, as she throws clothes into a bag.

"Yeah," agreed Sid still under the covers, "this bed is too comfortable, it's taken a long time to find a mattress that moulds to my body, I'm not giving it up."

"Well what am I supposed to do about Matt?" I pleaded.

"Just give Matt the new bed," Millie suggested.

"The reason he wanted his bed back in the first place is because of sentimental reasons, that's where he had his first shag! Doesn't that even bother you in the slightest?"

Millie shrugged and Sid mumbled something but didn't sound too concerned.

"Okay fine, have it on your conscience."

"Lisa stop being a drama queen," Millie sighed, "why don't we swap headboards around, we will keep this mattress and give Matt the new mattress that way he still gets to keep part of his stupid teenage years."

"Fine, whatever!" God so much drama over a bed.

Now Mum is hollering at me. What is this? Holler at Lisa day?

I left Sid to sort out the bed and went to find out what Mum's yelling about. Not that she needs much to yell about.

A blemish on her polished prize silver tea set is enough to set her off.

"What!" I shouted back.

Mum appears, "Lisa, Dad and I are leaving now."

Oh. I'd been waiting for this moment to come but now it's here I'm not entirely sure I want them to go, I feel so sad.

"Give's a hug poppet," Dad says pulling me into an embrace, I'm trying so hard not to cry but I can't help it. God what's happening to me?

"Now come on darling," Mum says pulling me from Dad's embrace and folding me in hers. "We're only going up to Queensland for a few of weeks, then we'll be back for the wedding."

"Err, what wedding?"

"*Tch*, Matt and Neroli's silly, Matt's invited us."

"Now don't let that Rick take advantage of you," Dad warns.

"Err no Dad."

"Good, and make sure you lock your doors at night, you wouldn't want anyone residing in your roof."

What the!

Dad gives me a knowing grin and I can feel myself going numb all over. Bloody Rob.

"Oh don't be silly Ian," Mum tuts, "you'll give our girl nightmares. Now I'll just go and say goodbye to Millie."

Mum disappears and Dad and I are left standing there awkwardly.

Mum comes back red as a beetroot.

"Um Lisa dear, tell Millie I'll see her in a few weeks I.. um.. think she's busy."

I watched as Dad fired up the Winnebago and drove off, leaving behind an imprint of a motor home scorched in the lawn. I stood and waved them goodbye until they were no longer in my sight.

I feel kinda strange and a tiny bit sad but have no time to dwell on them leaving, Rick will be home later and Matt and Neroli are due here soon to discuss wedding plans.

I also brought a pregnancy test for Neroli. Okay I can't force her to take a test but if she denies being pregnant then she won't have any issues with taking a test when I suggest she proves me wrong.

After all, I have it from a higher authority that she is pregnant and then I'll insist that Matt tells Pamela that he's marrying Neroli for that reason and not because I planted the silly idea in his head and Pamela won't come after me with sharp objects.

Millie appeared in the office as I was waiting for my laptop to fire up. "Are your parents gone?" she whispered.

"Yeah, Mum came to say goodbye but said you were busy and she will see you when they come back for the wedding."

"Oh god!" Millie exclaimed covering her face with her hands.

"What?"

"Your mum, um, walked in on us."

"Walked in on you and Sid?"

"Yeah, you know...."

"What, shagging? Oh my god Millie."

"I know, the shame," she mumbled in horror behind her hands.

"I mean, oh my god Millie, I can't believe you're at it again! I thought you didn't like sex."

Millie's head jerked up from behind her hands, "I do so like sex," she shot back in defense, "and what do you mean 'at it again', since when do you dictate how many times Sid and I do the wild thing? You're making me sound like a total nymphomaniac."

She hastily turns to depart leaving me dumbfounded at her outburst, but stops at the door.

"I just think you're jealous because you're not getting any at the moment."

I go to open my mouth but she stomps away leaving me wondering what the hell I just said?

Millie's just embarrassed because Mum caught her shagging and until she apologises, I'm not going to look at her, let alone talk to her.

Hee, hee, so funny, wish I had been there to see the look on Mum's face. Millie will no longer be the golden girl in Mum's books.

I hear the sound of a vehicle pulling up outside and can only presume it's Matt and Neroli, so I got my paper work sorted and my pen and paper poised.

I'm sitting waiting for Matt and Neroli, they seemed to be taking an awfully long time. I went out to see why they haven't made it to the office and knocked on my door so I can call them in like a professional business person.

Turns out it's not Matt but a delivery man with the new bed and Sid is out there giving him a hand to unload. I'm very pleased with the speedy delivery even though it cost extra, because delivery was outside the stores 'area'. Way out of the delivery area, in fact when I submitted the order, the salesperson rung to check the order was real.

Matt pulled up in his work ute just as Sid and the delivery guy took the bed from the back of the truck.

"Good timing!" Sid called out to Matt, "we can put this straight on the back of the ute."

Tom jumps from the cab of the ute followed by Neroli holding baby Bailey.

"Hi Aunt Lisa," Tom calls out to me before spying the geese that are happily settled once again on the bonnet of my car.

I went to tell Tom to leave the geese alone but it's too late, geese are flying everywhere as Tom takes to them with his pretend laser sword.

Matt's looking alarmed at the sight of the mattress being loaded onto the ute, so I quickly went to explain.

"What's that?" he asked Sid.

"Your bed," Sid shot back.

"Like fuck it is," said Matt.

"Ah new plan," I said, "Sid's going to give you back your headboard and you get a brand new mattress, what do you think about that?"

"What's wrong with my old mattress?"

"Nothing, it's just that.. err.. this is an early wedding present for you and Neroli."

"So I get to keep my old headboard?"

"Yep nothing changes it will still be like your old bed but with a new mattress."

I feel like I'm coaxing an infant from a cot to a big person's bed.

"But I don't want a new mattress."

"But this one is so much better."

"But it's not my bed."

"*Ahem,* excuse me," said the bewildered delivery guy who nervously stood there with clipboard in hand waiting for someone to sign so he could get out of this rural crazy land and back to the safety of the city.

I signed it off as Sid and Matt continued to argue.

I left them to it as Tom is now running towards me with the flock of geese in tow screaming his little lungs out. "Aunt Lisa… help!"

Back in office

We got the geese diverted thanks to Sid's quick thinking of making so much noise the geese stopped chasing Tom and started chasing him. I'm not sure what the outcome of the bed dilemma was but am so over it that I decided not to get involved. They can sort it out, I mean after all what am I? Supreme diplomat of all things cozy.

Neroli and Matt are now seated and I begin my speech on the type of services I provide. Matt is trying to interrupt me saying he knows all about me and this is a waste of time, but I quickly silenced him by throwing my stapler at him. "Now, what kind of wedding do you have in mind?"

Matt and Neroli look at each other in total bewilderment.

"Isn't that your job?" asked Matt.

"Yes but it's your wedding day so what sort of theme did you have in mind, you know, church, garden?"

Neroli placed baby Bailey on the floor next to her along with a small mountain of toys.

"Well," she begins, "I was kinda hoping to have it here as this is where Matt and I met."

"Mum wants a church wedding," Matt shot back.

"Well you could have a church wedding and hold the reception here," I suggested.

"Yeah great idea, I'll run it passed Mum first."

I look over at Neroli for her reaction, she didn't seem phased in the slightest.

"Neroli is that what you want?"

"Um, yeah I guess," she shrugged.

"Great," says Matt, "then that's what we'll do. Well, if Mum approves."

"Matt what's this got to do with your mother?"

"Well she's paying for some of it."

"Yes Matt but it's your wedding, and Neroli's, what about her and her culture?"

"I don't have any culture," said Neroli.

"But aren't you of Polynesian descent?"

"Yeah" she shrugged, leaving the rest hanging in the air.

"Okay," I sighed, "well I suppose you want to know what my fee is?"

I have been waiting for this, I may have overestimated my fee slightly, but am confident that as soon as they see how much this silly little ceremony costs they may reconsider getting married.

"Mum said she'll pay for you to organise it," Matt said, "so send the account to her, I have her address."

I could feel the colour drain from my face. I know Pamela, she's not the type of person who just steps aside and lets someone else organise anything.

Got to get to the bottom of this.

"Neroli are you pregnant?"

Her head shot up from cooing over Bailey.

"No!"

"Then why are you getting married?"

She looks over at Matt bewildered, "because we love each other."

"Not because you're pregnant?"

"No."

I produced the box, "then take a pregnancy test."

"What?" Matt exclaims. "Man have you flipped your lid?"

"I'm not pregnant," said Neroli.

"Then you should have no objections to taking the test Neroli."

Neroli went to take box from my hands but Matt stopped her.

"She's not taking the test," said Matt, "what have you got against us getting married anyway, after all it was your idea in the first place."

Then suddenly I felt something hit the back of my head, like I'd been slapped from behind. I turned to see but there is nothing or no one there. Very weird.

Oh my god, I just had a sudden thought that it could be Pamela sending me out hurtful vibes.

I had a sudden panic that Matt could have told Pamela it was my idea.

I told Matt again that it wasn't my idea and then also told him again that I thought he was too young to get married. Matt argued back that he *wasn't* too young, so I asked Matt to admit that him getting married had nothing to do with me.

Matt said that indeed it was me who got him thinking about marriage in the first place,

so I grabbed at his wrist from across the table and pinched him until he took it back and admitted that it wasn't my idea. Matt eventually said that no, it wasn't my idea at all and that he was getting married because he loved Neroli and wants to marry her.

I also made him promise to repeat his last statement to his psycho mother.

I got so wrapped up in the little tussle with Matt I didn't notice that Neroli and baby Bailey had gone.

"Now look what you've gone and done," Matt said before leaving to go and look for her.

I looked down at my notes in front of me and had a small joyous moment as that was my very first official appointment as a wedding planner. Okay, it wasn't exactly a scrapbook moment but all the same small leap of joy surged through me.

I decided I'd better go and look for them both and apologise. I'm still convinced Neroli is pregnant but Matt's right, it's his life and I'm just the wedding planning chick.

I found Matt and baby Bailey outside, Matt was chatting with Sid.

 I said I'm sorry for inflicting violence on his wrist and asked the whereabouts of Neroli. Matt said Neroli is taking Tom to the toilet and he also apologised for the misunderstanding over whose idea it was to get married. After an awkward hug with Matt I went to find Neroli. Neroli was heading back from the bathroom and looked startled when she saw me.

"Hi, is Tom still in the bathroom?" I asked.

Neroli stared at me like a possum caught in headlights as I stood there waiting for her to answer the simple question. Tom shot past us at roadrunner speed.

"Oh, there he is, err thanks Lisa."

I grabbed Neroli before she pushed past me to join Matt.

"Err Neroli, sorry about before, I just wanted to um, make sure you're doing the right thing. You know, it's all part of my service."

"Oh it's fine," she said, trying to brush my hand away.

 She seems really edgy; I must have really scared her before.

"So are we cool then?" I asked.

"Yeah, cool," she beamed as she made a hasty exit.

Back in office

Well, looks like I have a wedding to plan.

I'm so excited and I'm putting my fears about Pamela to one side, I'm not going to let her bother me.

I mean it's not my fault that she decided to have an affair with a man half her age and then that man abandoned her, which led to her marriage breaking down and in turn her having a breakdown, so she's unavailable to organise her son's wedding.

I also have the tiger's eye now, so am protected.

I had a tiny thought about Rick and remembered that he's coming home today with my surprise. I thought back to what the tarot reader said about me not being sure about wanting Rick. I mean, how absurd is that, Rick is the love of my life.

I can feel a presence again, like someone beside me.

So weird.

It doesn't feel like the wrath of Pamela as I'm not being bitch slapped, but a calm presence, almost like it's here to guide me.

Oh my god, it's my guardian angel, it has to be. That tarot reader said I have a spirit guide.

How cool is that.

Wonder if I should say hello.

Oh it's gone now.

Ohhh that's right, better start on wedding plan.

I reach for my notes on my desk and pick up one of baby Bailey's plastic toys from on top of my laptop, am about to run out to see if Neroli and Matt had left when I noticed the pregnancy test box had been opened.

There were two tests in there and one's missing.

I ran back out to catch Neroli but watched as the ute drove off complete with new mattress.

No wonder she looked a little odd when I saw her. Taking Tom to the toilet my arse! She must have grabbed the test while Matt and I were having words. I ran back inside to inspect the rubbish bins, I filtered through the masses of discarded paper until I found it.

And it's got a pink line.

I read through the instructions on the box and sure enough it's a positive one. So Neroli is pregnant! I knew I smelt the presence of a baby. And I bet all the nappies under the sun that Matt suspected as well that's why he was so keen for Neroli not to take the test. Ha! Then it is definitely not my fault that they are getting married. And Pamela has no reason to hate me.

Realising that I'm still holding a stick that Neroli would have urinated on, I quickly threw it back amongst the discarded bits of paper in the bin.

"Right I'm off," Millie said, bursting through the door like a bull searching for a horny cow. I remembered that I wasn't meant to be speaking to her until she apologies for biting my head off earlier, so I folded my arms and glanced at the ceiling.

"Oh would you get over yourself," sighed Millie, "I'm off, I'll see you next Friday." She leaned forward to hug me but I turned away from her and stuck my nose higher in the air. Millie rolled her eyes.

"What's your problem? Is it because I said you weren't getting any before. Okay I'll take it back, you're getting plenty."

I wanted to say that she owes me an apology but Millie's a big girl, it's about time she worked it out for herself.

"I haven't got time for this," she sighed as she pecked me on the cheek. "I'll see you next Friday, look after Sid for me."

"You're not taking your big trench coat with you are you?" I asked, mumbling under my breath.

"Sorry?" Millie asked, cocking her head.

"Ha! So you're sorry, that's all I wanted Millie, an apology. Now can I borrow your trench coat? I'm going to surprise Rick later."

"What, by dressing up as a detective?"

"No," I scoffed, "you know, to hide my semi nakedness."

"Okay well yeah sure, just don't put any stains on it."

Millie's so gross.

Back to organising wedding

I figure if Neroli's pregnant then when the wedding rolls around she still won't be showing signs of her pregnancy but then again we didn't know Neroli was pregnant last time until the night she went into labour. In fact maybe Neroli has no idea how far along she is herself, so I'd better make allowances for a bulging belly when it comes to the dress. Working down my list that I printed off from a 'how to plan your wedding' site on the internet, it says the first thing to do is book the venue.

Matt mentioned a church wedding and I know this lovely charming church just out of town set amongst the backdrop of the hills. I can just picture it now.

The main ceremony in a country church followed by drinks and nibbles on my sweeping front lawn while the guests' children are entertained by the gathering of white animals from my petting zoo and then we guide the guests' to a marquee for the reception. How perfect is that.

2 hours later

God maybe I should convince Matt and Neroli to change their date as it is taking a lot longer then I thought to find a pure white miniature cow.

I'm now trying to find the number for the church in the phone book but am not sure where to start looking. Under churches there is only one and it's the big catholic church in town. I may have to go for a drive and knock on the door, surely priests live in churches don't they? So for now I'll move down the list.

Next is invitations.

Well, I cannot do that until the church is booked. But then again, I can go ahead and order the blank invitations.

I'm thinking of going with the white animal theme as the invitations need to be some sort of country theme anyway so that'd suit.

I got on to this amazing website that does invites and I'm thinking a backdrop of a white horse with a picture of a bride on its back.

Hmm, wonder if I can convince Neroli to ride in on horseback?

This is so fun and it doesn't even feel like work.

Imagine how much fun I'll have when I plan mine and Rick's wedding.

Which reminds me, I'm meant to be making my want list to the universe.

I put the wedding stuff aside and got out a fresh piece of paper.

To whom it may concern.

No, too formal.

Dear universe.

Here is the list of things I want. Hope you can help.

- Rick to always be at my side and treat me like a queen.

- Rick and I to get married and have two – no – three children all with Rick's dark complexion.

- To run a successful wedding planning business.

- A petting zoo filled with white animals (no roosters).

- A new car, I'd prefer a small car that has blue tooth and is environmentally friendly (that's one for you).

- To lose ten kilos, especially around my inner thighs and my lower abdomen.

- And could you arrange the above four requests before 20th May?

There I think that about covers it.

Now I have made the list I don't know what to do with it.

I can't post it, and it seems silly to burn it, I mean what if I want to add to it. I went to find Sid as he's into this stuff.

I found him in the living room looking at the floorboards.

"What ya doing?" I ask.

"Checking for white ants, seems there are signs in this corner that they are active."

Boring.

"Um Sid, you're into the universe and stuff eh?"

Sid looks up from his ant hunting, he seems a little baffled.

"Depends what you mean."

"Well I've done a list of things I want, to the universe and now I don't know what to do with it."

Sid seems amused and is trying not to laugh, so I told him he's big loser and went to walk off in a huff, but Sid pulls me back.

"Okay I'm sorry. Look Lisa, it's not all about just asking for it, you have to take steps to make it happen and use the power of positive thinking."

"So you're saying my list is silly?"

"No, not at all," Sid rubs his forehead, "look, I'll lend you a book of mine. It's all about the power of manifestation okay?"

Sid goes to retrieve the magic book and I suddenly remembered about the mediation class and how I was going to ask Sid to be my meditation buddy. Waiting for Sid to return my phone beeps with a message, my heart drops as Rick's name appears on the call screen. He says that he's home and feel free to drop down anytime unless I want him to come over. I quickly message him back telling him that I'll be down soon.

Sid appears with the book called 'The Secret'. Sounds intriguing but I guess it can't be that much of a secret if they published it and sold it in every airport bookshop across the nation.

I told Sid about the meditation group next Tuesday and he seems keen and praised me for being so open about it. So happy, it's like Sid and I have finally bonded.

Sid went back to his ant hunting and I made my way back to the office.

Back in office

Cannot concentrate.

Now Rick is home I really cannot wait for my surprise.

 But being only eleven in the morning, it seems a little early to be dressing up in tart gear for a big shag feast with soon to be fiancé. I need a major distraction so decided to go and check out the church. Just got another text message from Rick saying he's coming down, I again quickly texted him back to say that I'm not home. He's clearly ruining my plan. I cannot blame him as I'm sure he's just as keen to get engaged as I am.

Arrived at church

I parked my stupid car on the grassy verge. It's still making a funny knocking sound and I feel it would have been quicker if I took the tyre's off and drove it in Fred Flintstone style. I hope the universe hurries up with my new car.

Walking towards the church I'm having a sense of déjà vu. It's like I have been here before, it's very strange as I have never even been past the front gates.

It feels like a dream I had some time ago and I'm only just remembering it.

Very, very strange.

The tiny building was nestled amongst the shade of huge jacaranda and gum trees that surround it. The mid morning rays of the sun lightly filter through the branches and reflect off the church windows. It's almost like God himself is pointing out the finer features of this charming old building. I climbed the old and chipped stone steps that led to the entrance. Turning to look back towards the roadside took my breath away. The stunning view from the church steps would be enough to start any marriage off in peaceful bliss when the bride and groom emerge after their vows have been sealed.

As luck would have it the doors were locked. I walked around the outside of this charming little work of wonderment to see if I could take a sneak peek of what's inside. But I guess the stonemasons didn't plan for any nosey snoops when they designed it or they would have placed the windows down at a level where I could see.

But nevertheless, I'm sure it's just as perfect inside as out and I cannot wait to show Matt and Neroli.

The church has no billboard or any sign of how one would go about hiring this amazing piece of history, so I decided to drop in and ask at the local council on my way home. Turning the stupid car around I headed towards town when my phone beeped and Rick's name appeared on the call screen. I didn't answer it as I drove off down the road, he's probably just asking if he can come round again and then I'll have to come up with yet another excuse as to why he cannot see me until I have put on sexy gear.

If Rick is going to propose to me tonight then I want it to be perfect so when our grandkids gather around us, as we sit on our rocking chairs old and grey, Rick can tell them that grand-mummy looked so stunning in her lace chemise that after she accepted his proposal of marriage we then engaged in a night of passion and shameless sex.

Okay, maybe not a story to tell our grandchildren but all the same, I want this night to be perfect.

That's if Rick *is* going to propose that is.

Now I'm having doubts, what if my surprise isn't an engagement ring. What if he got me a paint-by-numbers set instead?

I mean I think I did mention to him that I wanted to take up painting.

I flipped open the phone, careful as not to take my eyes off the road, read Rick's text message that was all of five words asking when I'm coming down. I sent a text back asking him why. His text come back with a little smiley face that read 'never you mind' and asked if I'd come down for dinner. Now I'm really excited because Rick has never asked me down for dinner except one time when we first met after Rick returned to the family home after Jake left. And then it wasn't really dinner, just Chinese food eaten in front of the TV. Since then Rick had always eaten at my place.

Oh my god there's only one thing for it, that he *is* planning on proposing.

I flipped open the phone again to message him back when suddenly a car beeped its horn. My head shot up, I realised I was driving in the middle of the road and a motor vehicle was heading straight for me.

I turned the steering wheel sharp as a ute swerved around me, honking its horn even louder in an attempt to let me know how angry it was that I almost caused a nasty accident.

I braked suddenly as the ute looks very much like Mrs Crankshaw's battered old ute. But it doesn't stop, just keeps on going and it's not Mrs Crankshaw that's driving. Unless she has had her hair cut and then dyed a mousey brown colour. It's definitely the Crankshaw's ute as it's the only ute in the area that has the bumper sticker across the back window that reads 'Udder Madness' accompanied by a picture of a stoned cow.

But who is driving?

It's not Max Crankshaw, not beady enough, and I'm certain it wasn't Rick as he would have stopped as soon as he realised it was me who was driving in the middle of the road.

Unless it's been stolen.

Oh well, not to worry I'm sure whoever stole it did them a favour.

Anyway, what am I, the police?

Arrived at council office

I'm waiting for the young girl behind the counter as she taps away at her keyboard. It seems the old church is privately owned after being sold off back in 1957 after they built the new catholic church closer to the village.

She eventually stops her flurry of typing and looks up. "Okay I have the name and address of the present rate-payer but because of the Privacy Act I can not disclose that information to you unless I have their permission. So if you would like to fill out this form stating the reason for your enquiry we can forward your request onto the owner."

"Could I not just have a phone number?"

"Sorry, that's our policy I'm afraid."

"But that could take weeks," I argued, "and this is an emergency."

"I'm sorry but if you fill out this form then we will be sure to post your request as soon as possible........ what are you doing?"

I had tried to discreetly slip her a twenty dollar note in exchange for a phone number just like they do in the movies; clearly it's not that easy.

"Ah nothing," I said slipping the note back in my pocket, "if I fill this out do you promise to mail it straight away?"

"I'll do my best."

"No, you have to promise."

A scary looking lady whom I presume is her supervisor must have overheard and is now walking towards me with a stern look on her face so best I don't press the issue. I fill out the form with all my contacts including Millie's mobile number and wrote 'very urgent' across the top of the sheet. Nothing more I can do now. It's in the hands of the Gods or more importantly, a council receptionist by the name of Jo.

Back home

Sid's still ant hunting.

I ordered invitations and am very pleased as yes, they do have ones with a picture of a white horse embossed in the background. I wasn't sure on numbers so ordered about two hundred.

I then rung Jo at the council to make sure she posted my request for the church owner's details as promised and then did a search for more white animals.

I found this really cute white miniature pony on *horsefind.com* and almost choked on my tic-tac at the price. I mean for the amount of money that 'Madeline 888' is asking for the pony, I'm so tempted to message her and ask where the rest of it is.

Which means I may have to have a re-think about large white animals and just stick to small things like bunnies and doves.

I almost pee my pants in excitement as I realise the time and that Rick is expecting me very soon. I have to applaud myself as I have gone the whole afternoon without thinking about my up and coming engagement and I didn't even rehearse my acceptance answer much or think about my facial expressions when Rick gets down on one knee.
Very proud of myself.

As I slip into my white lace chemise I can't help but notice how quiet the house is with everyone gone. Sid and I hardly cross paths unless we need to speak with one another which is not that often, as Sid and I never know what to say to each other when Millie's not around.
I have to be honest, I'm not really looking forward to these days when Millie goes off to work and it's just Sid and I trying very hard to stay out of each others way.
I finish putting on white stockings and wedge my feet into very high white stiletto heels.

Rick is going to be so turned on when he sees me, as I have to admit, I'm looking very sexy especially the way my hair had decided to sit very boffy and wild looking. I put the finishing touches to my make-up and am ready.

I cannot believe that after tonight I'm going to be engaged.

Sid was taking a break from ant hunting and was in the kitchen making dinner when I made my graceful entry in the big trench coat.

"Um going out?" he asked.

"Um yes, just down to Rick's."

"Not staying for dinner?"

"Um no sorry, hope you didn't cook anything for me."

"Um no, unless you know, you want me to make something for you."

"Err no that's okay."

"Okay. Well, have a good night."

"Yes you too."

I'm pleased to be out of there, Sid and I really must work on our bonding if we are going to share the house on a permanent basis. I then had a sudden realisation as I turned the stupid car around and headed off towards Rick's, that I may not be sharing a house with Millie and Sid for much longer.

And I really don't know how to feel about that right now, it's like my stomach all of a sudden is tied up in knots.

Okay, best not to think about the minor details now, I have a big night of dinner and shagging, and I don't want to throw up during either.

I pulled up at Rick's house and checked my face again in the car mirror. I had a hard time driving down here in such high heels so had to take it slow. So slow in fact that a roo hopped alongside the car as if it was on a leisurely stroll.

But I'm here now and feeling very excited. I made my way to Rick's front door wrapping my coat around me and trying to negotiate the path in these ridiculous heels.

I knock on the door and waited with my hands poised on the coat. When Rick answers the door I'm going to open my coat and he will be marveled by my sexiness.

I could hear footsteps coming closer to the door.... I opened my coat as the door swung open.

"Ta-da," I sang, flashing my semi-naked body in shameless fashion

.*Oh!*

That's not Rick..

4

"You must be Lisa," said a strange man with a grin on his face.

Shit!

"Um yes," I squawked like a dodo bird, trying in a desperate attempt to quickly cover myself. I'm so mortified and want to turn around and run, but cannot seem to locate my knees as I have gone numb from the neck down.

And besides, I won't have a hope in hell running in these ridiculous sexy stilettos.

I'm hoping for a tiny moment that the strange man may in fact be blind and didn't see anything, so I decide to act as if nothing has happened and casually ask if Rick was home.

The strange man now had a wicked smirk on face, "Rick!" he calls, not taking his eyes off me, "Lisa's here and she's got something to show you."

Shit!

Rick appears at the door just as Mr Smug Man steps aside to let me in.

Rick, fresh out of the shower and dressed in faded blue jeans and his good striped shirt, bends forward and plants a kiss on my cheek, dragging me inside.

"Hey gorgeous," he beams, leaving the scent of aftershave hanging in the air, "what's with the coat, is it cold out?"

I opened my mouth to answer but Rick is all hyped up like a child on Christmas morning and didn't give me time to rustle up a white lie.

"I see you two have met," he beamed as he reaches in the fridge for a bottle of wine.

I did the polite thing and stuck out my hand. The strange man shot a glance at Rick's back and then back to my hand as if it was the most toxic thing he had ever seen. I lowered it feeling like a total twat.

"Hey," he greeted with as much enthusiasm as a stone sloth. He couldn't have made it more obvious that my presence here was not welcome by him.

"This is the famous Daniel," beamed Rick like a proud otter, opening the wine, "back from the UK. Right mate?"

Daniel grinned, not taking his eyes off me. He looked around the same age as Rick, his thick mop of mousey brown hair shielded his round face. He was a bit short in stature, but very broad across the shoulders.

"You remember me telling you about Dan?"

I suddenly felt the blood in my veins run very cold. I vaguely remember Rick telling me about his 'best mate Dan' and when I say vaguely told me, I mean he wouldn't shut up about him.

Apparently they have known each other since birth, like most people around these parts. Daniel's parents had a farm here for many years and as children Daniel and Rick were inseparable. They went through everything from primary school to puberty and even shared a flat in Sydney for a while until Daniel went to the UK for work.

I got so cross one night at yet another one of Rick's 'Daniel and me' stories that I asked him if he was secretly in love with him, Rick thought I was joking and said yes indeed he was. And now here he is, the famous Daniel in person, ruining yet another night of shameless sex.

"Yeah, so anyway babe," Rick goes on, "Dan rung the other day spur of the moment and said he's coming home, so we spent a couple of days in Sydney catching up with some old college buddies. I thought I'd surprise you." Rick hands me a glass of wine. "So, are you surprised?"

I can barely speak.

Perfect, just bloody perfect! I manage to nod my head. Rick then patted me on the backside and carried on with dinner. Rick had mentioned that Daniel has a store over in the UK or something, can't remember what sort as I wasn't listening, so I'm presuming he's only back for a short time, thank god. I can feel Daniel's eyes on me and wish he would stop staring, not quite sure what to make of his gaze, it's like he's either checking me out to see if I'm suitable for his precious Rick or he's willing me to take off my coat again.

Either way he's being obnoxious about it.

I should make an excuse and go home and put some clothes on as I can feel the beads of sweat forming on my brow and I'm pretty sure you could fry a porterhouse steak underneath this coat. It also does not help that the only night you are half naked under a huge coat is the only night in your whole relationship that Rick has decided on a roaring fire. It would be very romantic if we didn't have a strange man present .

I'm not sure whether this is the whole surprise that Rick had in store for me or this is some weird practical joke and any minute now Daniel is going to point to Rick's display of fake flowers hidden discreetly placed behind the layers of dust on the corner table of the kitchen and say, smile you've just been punked. Unless Ashton Kutcher jumps out, then that would be so cool.

Rick slammed the oven door, which looked to be housing a roast dinner. "What's with the coat?" he asked, twisting the top off another beer.

"Um... oh you know its cold out."

Out the corner of my eye I could see Daniel crinkle his brow; I'm feeling a wee bit cross with Rick for not telling me about Daniel. But that's nothing compared to the devastation I felt when I realised there may be a small chance that there may not be an engagement happening.

Well for tonight anyway.

I located the table which I guessed would be playing host to our dinner and sat down, slipping my shoes off. I can still feel Daniel watching me as I carefully attempted the whole maneuver without tripping over.

Rick, who seemed to skim over my last statement, took another swig from his beer.

Judging by the empties spilling out from the recycling bin it's been quite an afternoon.

"So Daniel's going to take over the lease for the shop you signed," Rick said, smacking his lips together.

Great, it just gets better!

I could see Rick is waiting for me to jump up and go woohoo and be ever so grateful to Daniel. But I have decided that I'm not going to put Daniel on a pedestal just to please Rick.

"So what do you think about that?" Rick asks.

"Fine," I said a little coldly.

Rick leapt from his chair to check on dinner, Daniel shifted uncomfortably in his seat, making it obvious that he doesn't want to be in my company.

"Um, so?" I asked, slightly frosty in my tone, trying to break the tension.

"So?" he shot back, almost making me choke on my wine. He had such a strange sound about him; there was no gruffness to his voice, just a mild tone that was a cross between a strangled chicken and a howling dog.

"I s'posse you want to know what I'm planning for the shop?" he said.

"I guess," I said.

"Well I'll tell you, but only if you ask me nicely," he shot back, taking another swig of his beer.

What the?

"Well then, you'll be waiting a while," I said, sticking my nose in the air. I cannot believe I have only known this guy for ten minutes and already he's crossed the threshold from being on my *'I'll tolerate you because you're my boyfriend's friend'* list, to my *'oh my god, I completely despise you'* list.

"Whatever, I don't care," he shrugged.

Rick bounced back to the table still hyped up on the adrenalin of his best friend being here. He and Daniel delved into conversations about old times, occasionally shooting me glances so I didn't feel left out of the conversation, well Rick did, Daniel didn't look at me again. As I sat listening to them it occurred to me that Daniel and Rick seem like an odd couple.

Rick is more soft spoken and gentle where is Daniel is an obnoxious twat.

The ever present lump in my throat is stopping me from telling Rick how upset I'm feeling and the smells from the roast in the oven are making me nauseous.

"Um I think I might go home," I said abruptly, interrupting their conversation, "I'm not feeling the best, must be coming down with something."

Rick rises from his seat scraping it across the floor as he put his hand to my forehead.

"My god you're burning up," he said with a tone of alarm, "no wonder, look at what you're wearing." Rick makes a grab for the coat.

"No!" I said a little too harshly, tugging the coat from his grasp, "I mean, no it's fine, it's freezing in here, gotta go. Rick, call me," I said as I made a bolt for the door.

I'm outside trying to locate my effing car keys when the sound of Rick's voice made me jump. Even in the darkness his sexy presence is powerful. I have the over-whelming urge to rip more then this ridiculous coat off, but have to appear annoyed.

"Are you okay?" he asks, sounding very concerned.

Oh that's right and I also have to pretend I'm ill.

"Oh fine," I said in a husky voice, "just not feeling the best."

"What's under the coat?"

"Nothing."

"Then take it off."

"No I'll catch a chill."

Rick sighs, "look, are you pissed off because I didn't tell you about Daniel coming?"

No I'm pissed off because Daniel is an obnoxious twat.

"Pff that, no," I scoffed. I should know better then to use sarcasm with Rick, it just washes over him. He stares at me for a long time, I can feel hot tears running down my cheeks.

"I'm sorry," he continues, "it just happened fast, I knew he was coming back but when he did get hold of me he was in Singapore about to board a flight home. I kinda had to rush off and of course when I called the others to tell them, they insisted we stay and...."

"Rick I said I don't care."

"Please take the coat off."

"Why?"

"Because I want to see what outfit would go with those white stockings."

"What the...?"

Rick holds up my shoes, I look down at my feet and realise I have no shoes on. Rick steps forward and gently opens my coat.

"Wow," he whistles.

"Yes well," I sniffed, wrapping the coat around me again, feeling my cheeks burning, "you could have warned me about him."

Rick quickly got his arms around me muttering "I'm sorry" into my ear, the stench of beer wafting from him. He steps back and gives me the once over again. "Damn shame," he said, "that outfit would have been perfect when I gave you this," he reaches into his pocket and pulls out a velvet box.

Back home

I opened the velvet box and pulled out the new gemstone earrings that Rick got me at the little gift shop at the airport. I almost had a small heart attack when he first pulled out the tiny box. Rick was a bit surprised when I flung myself at him screaming 'yes' before he even opened the box, and said that he would have bought me earrings every day if he knew how excited I'd get.

I have to say I was a bit upset when I found out it wasn't an engagement ring, but managed to slap a silly grin on my face and thank him for being such a sweet, thoughtful man all the same.

Rick promised to come down tomorrow and spend the whole day with me. So I guess I can forgive him for not proposing. And besides, Sid is going garage sale-ing in the morning which means Rick and I will have the house to ourselves.
I so wanted to get engaged though.

I was about to go to bed when Rick texted to ask me if I was okay. I texted him back and said I would be better if he was here. Rick texted back and said he was on his way. I then rung him in alarm and told him he's had too much to drink and indeed cannot drive. Rick's now sounding so drunk after he and Daniel's little drinking session, that he starting singing down the phone. It sounded cute to begin with but after the fourth phone call I so wanted to drown the phone in an icy bucket of water.

3.00 am

I told Rick if he phones me one more time to tell me he loves me I will never have sex with him again.

3.15 am

Told Rick we're never having sex again.

3.37 am

Okay told him I *will* have sex with him again as long as he lets me go back to sleep.

3.42 am

Told Rick I love him too and that I think his butt is sexy as well.

4.05 am

Very sleepy and pissed off now, Sid enters my bedroom telling me if I didn't turn my fucken phone off, he will drop it in an icy bucket of water.
Very surprised at Sid's outburst.

Later that morning

I woke to find Rick hovering over my bed. He looks like he's been up all night.

"I left you a message, you didn't reply," he slurred as he fell on top of the covers beside me. Outside I heard the sound of a car leave, I can only presume it was Daniel that delivered a still drunken Rick, as it was too quiet to be Sid's. Sid's car sounds more like a tractor. The smell of alcohol was overpowering as Rick lay like a crash test dummy.

"What are you doing here?" I asked in my sleep induced state, willing him to pass out, "it's too early in the morning for sex."

"I misth you," he slurred, "d'id you misth me?"

My god he's hard work when he's drunk and the stench of alcohol is putting me off. I wonder if Daniel is in the same state, surely he can't be as bad otherwise he wouldn't have driven Rick here.

I started thinking about Daniel and our first encounter yesterday and the look on his face when he opened the door, and call me crazy, but at one part I almost mistakened his obnoxiousness for flirting. Maybe I was a bit hard on him and should make an effort, after all I have to admit a tiny bit, that he is a little good looking and I'm sure if I hadn't flashed my semi-nakedness at him then I wouldn't haven't been so defensive.

Rick's cold hand is now moving up my thigh and all of a sudden I feel very turned on. I wonder if I should phone Daniel up and apologise. But I have nothing to apologise for, after all he's the one lacking in social grace. I still cannot get that look on his face out of my mind when he first opened the door, I'm not even feeling embarrassed about it.

Rick is now nibbling at my neck.

Anyway, if Daniel is back for good then I should make an effort to get to know him. After all he is Rick's best friend. Even though he is a tosser and a smug one at that.

Shit Rick's passed out.

Later that afternoon

I checked my emails to see if there is anything from the council about the church. Nothing. And if I don't hear back by the end of next week I will have to consider a new venue, although I'm sure a lot of the wedding preparations can be made around the venue. Anyway it's only been one day since I made contact.

Rick is still sleeping it off and so far there has been no word from Daniel.

Obnoxious twat.

Not sure where Sid is, I suspect he's in his room catching up on some sleep. I was about to log-on to *livestock.com* to see if I've had any interest in my advert for all things white and fluffy when I heard Matt's car outside. I cannot wait to tell him about the church and how I think it would make a perfect wedding venue and Matt might even know who owns it. Yes, why hadn't I thought of that before! Forget the council and their policies, I shall ask Mrs Crankshaw, after all she knows everybody around here and she has no polices about telling anyone anything.

I went to pick up the phone to dial Mrs Crankshaw's number when I heard yelling coming from Sid's room, sounded like trouble. I ran into Sid's room to find Sid sprawled out in a starfish position on top of his bed gripping onto the sides as if his life depended on it.

Matt's standing over him and not looking happy.

"Give me back my mattress," Matt demanded.

"Nah," retaliated Sid, gripping tighter to the sides of the mattress.

"What's going on?" I asked.

"Hey Lisa," Matt greeted, "just came to get my mattress."

"It's not fucking yours," said Sid.

I groaned inwards, I cannot believe Matt is so obsessed with a flippen mattress.

"What's wrong with the new mattress I got you?" I sigh.

"It's uncomfortable," Matt whinged, "it's hard and smells. I want my old one back."

"That's because it's new," I pleaded, "you need to give it time to get broken in."

"Fine chance of that happening," Sid mumbles.

"Get off," screamed Matt.

"Make me."

Matt grabbed the mattress and tipped it on its side.

Sid continued to cling on.

"Let go," screamed Matt as he shook the mattress, trying to get Sid to release his grip.

I know I should do something to stop them before one of them gets hurt, but it's not really any of my business after all. Think I might leave them to it.

I left the room just as Matt started biting at Sid's hands forcing him to let go, while Sid kicked at Matt, trying to get him to stop. I called Mrs Crankshaw and let the phone ring for what seemed to be an eternity waiting for her to pick up.

Blasted woman, not being home on such a beautiful day like this.

I went back into Sid's room to ask Matt, who now had the mattress on the floor with Sid still attached dragging it towards the door.

"Matt, who owns that old church out on Cannon's Road?"

Matt turned to answer me just as Sid delivered a swift kick to his knee, knocking him to the floor.

"Right, that's it!" Matt yelled, scrambling to his feet and jumping on Sid.

Left them to it.

I have decided to just roll with the possibility that the church will be the venue for the ceremony and work around it until I hear otherwise.

I referred to my wedding planning list for the next item to be arranged. Was about to google 'marriage license' when I heard a tiny faint knock at the door.

Oh my god, it's Daniel.

He's standing there like a shy school-boy. He looks different to the smug, obnoxious twat I met yesterday. I signaled for him to come in and he gingerly entered like he was treading on enemy territory.

Daniel doesn't possess the exotic features or shirt ripping qualities that Rick does, but all the same he's not bad looking, his boyish features seem to be a bit more prominent than yesterday. Maybe that's because I'm not looking at him like he's just inflicted torrential rain on my parade.

Slapping a huge *'let's wipe the slate clean'* and *'let's forget the fact you have seen me semi-naked'*, smile on my face, I greeted him with enthusiasm.

"You must be looking for Rick," I beamed, "I'll just get him, why don't you make yourself at home."

He hasn't said anything yet, come to think of it, he hasn't even looked me in the eye. Maybe he's embarrassed after I flashed myself at him yesterday.

I hurried off to wake Rick, almost tripping over my feet in my haste to find another person that can fill the awkward gap. I entered the room to find Rick sprawled out naked on top of the bed snoring. I attempted to wake him and cover him up at the same time, he wasn't naked when I left him so his clothes must be here somewhere. I'm trying to gently wake, but he's not responding, so now am really shaking the bejeezes out of him. Rick stirred finally, then his arm came up around my neck and he pulled me into his chest.

He's so smelly and sweaty, god, now he's gone back to sleep and I can't get out of his grip.

Shit.

Daniel doesn't smell this bad in fact I have to admit he kind of smelt nice.

"Lisa!!" Matt came screaming through the bedroom door, "you have to call an ambulance."

Ambulance? What the hell?

I'm trying to pull myself out of Rick's smelly grip in a panic but he's just wrapping me up tighter.

"Matt," my panic starts to rise further, "what's going on?"

"It's Sid, he sorta fell over and hit his head, blood's pissing everywhere, call an ambulance!"

Oh great, just bloody great!

I can't really see Matt as one eye is pressed up against Rick's hairy nipple but I can hear Sid swearing as he entered the room.

Thank god, he can't be that bad if he's still walking.

"You little shit," Sid screamed at Matt, "look at my head."

"You fell," Matt said in defense.

"Like fuck I did."

Sid's now charging at Matt, they collide and both land on the bed. I can't see what's going on, but Rick suddenly releases his grip.

That's better, I can see now.

Sid's forehead is dripping blood and him and Matt are swinging punches at each other.

Luckily none are connecting.

Rick now screams profanities at the both of them. Matt aimed an elbow at Sid, but missed, instead landing on Rick's knee and now it's all on.

Naked Rick, a half naked and bleeding Sid, and a mad spotty youth in wrestling mania. I can't believe this is happening, I wonder if Daniel is a fighter?

Oh shit, Daniel.

He's standing at the bedroom door and I'm not sure how long he's been standing there for.

He looks... well, confused.

"Um Rick will be out soon," I said, trying to usher him out the door as I look back to see Rick's naked bottom and Matt disappear over the side of the bed.

"Oh don't worry about that," I said as I pulled the door shut, "like that always happens around here, pff you know, banter. Tch, men huh."

Daniel pushes passed me and enters the bedroom; I heard Matt's protests as he reached down and pulled Matt off Rick.

"Matt Horton?" Daniel said as he pulled Matt to his feet.

Half hour later

Matt and Daniel obviously go way back as now they look really pleased to see each other and Matt's referring to him as Dazza. Sid's also been introduced and they're all sitting on the porch sipping beers.

I'm confused.

After Sid cleaned up the blood, his head doesn't look that bad and thank god, doesn't require stitches. Rick's sporting a sore knee and Matt's lip looks like it has had a collagen injection but the atmosphere is very peaceful.

Don't get me started on how the mattress looks.

Daniel has pretty much ignored me the whole time he's been here. He acts like I'm toxic, I don't think I like him very much, he's so arrogant. I returned to my laptop to see I have a response to my advert for white animals.

And it's from a local source.

My excitement faltered as I clicked on the link to see it's a white fluffy pint-size dog. It's not an ideal start to my petting zoo as everyone has a dog, I mean it's not anything unique.

I logged on to respond to the advert to explain that when I said I wanted 'white and fluffy animals, good home provided', that I meant *unusual* white and fluffy animals. I'm so engrossed in my typing I almost didn't realise Rick's come in and his hand was creeping underneath my top until he spoke.

"I'm sorry for last night," he said all smoochy, "are you mad?"

"No, all good," I said trying to focus on some gorgeous white fluffy guinea pigs to give away.

I could get Sid to build an enclosure, a walk in one even, and if I get rabbits as well then the children can hand-feed them in the enclosure and we can call it rodents-ville.

Did Rick just say 'lets have sex'?

He's standing over me looking really hurt.

"Um pardon?" I asked.

"You are still mad at me," he said all sad and soppy.

God I wish he would shut up.

"No Rick I'm not mad, just trying to get some work done."

Well looking at animals is kind of work.

"The guys are gone," he said, sauntering back in close and nibbling on the back of my neck, "so why don't we head back to the bedroom?"

Daniel's gone? Then why didn't he say goodbye. I mean this is my house and he was a visitor, how rude of him. He's making it blatantly obvious that he doesn't like me, which I can't understand, I mean what have I done to offend him. Matt doesn't always say goodbye either but that's different, Matt used to live here and Daniel was just passing. Well if that's the way he is then I don't like him either. Clearly he's jealous because Rick likes me better.

Shit, Rick's got that rejected look on his face again.

Better log off.

Later

Rick's snoring again.

I have just realised that this is the first time Rick and I have slept together since... well... a long time.

And it was... okay. Not earth shattering sex but Rick's still very hung-over so I'm sure it will be better next time.

But I'm back at my laptop and I have had a reply in regards to the offer of the dog. It says that they also have doves and sheep for sale if I'm interested.

Doves and sheep are white.

I'm so excited I cannot type fast enough; I have asked for an address and will be round as soon as they reply to my message.

Okay, maybe I need to delete the bit where I sound really keen otherwise they may push the price up, but all the same I cannot contain myself. I went to go and find Sid to let him know he has to get a bird aviary organised when the computer flashes a message.

That was quick.

It has the address and says I can call around before dark.

I scribble down the address, grab my local map and scramble out the door. I should have said goodbye to Rick but have no time for such minor things.

Arrived at white animal place

It is so Italian, the way the olive trees line the driveway, overlooking a fabulous view of the valley below, complete with a skinny tanned man with an out of control mustache who met me at my car as I pulled up.

"Ciao," he greeted in an Italian accent, "you come for animals?"

"Err, ciao," I greeted, "um yes."

"Arrr" he said with such passion, "you have land yes?"

I can barely understand him, his accent is so thick.

"Yep," I nodded.

"Ohhh, come, come," he said gesturing with his hand to follow him. We walk down a terrace path lined also with olive trees, no sign of sheep yet, Mr Italian Man is talking to me but I have no idea what he's saying, something about foot rot. He stops at an olive tree and examines a branch.

"Ohhh beautiful huh?" he says, gesturing for me to sniff the branch, "you smell that huh?"

I nod as I inserted my nose to the branch, it smells like... well wood.

"You likea olive?" he asks with a look of hope on his face.

"Err yes," I nod.

"Come, come," he said clapping his hands with enthusiasm as he motions me towards a shed, this must be where he keeps the doves.

What seems like an hour later

Okay this whole communication thing is starting to become a pain.

There weren't any doves, just olive oil, bottles and bottles of olive oil, which he's insisted I sample. Every single batch from his harvest. He hasn't stopped talking and he keeps getting in my personal space. I have quickly become a master at dodging his hands as he waves them about.

I should leave. I keep looking at my phone willing it to ring so I can say I have to leave.

Rick must still be sleeping otherwise he would have rung. Mr Italian Man is now pouring yet another nip of olive oil into a shot glass when the shed door opens slightly and a little white dog runs in.

"Arrhh here he is," Mr Italian Man said as the little dog made a beeline for me, "ohhh he a likey you."

I have to admit the little dog is cute as he dances around my feet.

Not that I want a dog.

I need to move on before I start throwing up olive oil. I tell Mr Italian Man in very polite tones that I must be getting back and can I view the animals.

"He is animal," he said gesturing to the dog.

"Um didn't you say you have doves and sheep?" I asked.

"Agh!" he spat, throwing his hands in the air in disgust, "my wife, she bitch, she tells me she not want me to sell animal but they are hard work and I work and work and she say do this and do that and she won't leave!"

Don't know what this has to do with doves and sheep.

"Um very sorry to hear that," I say in more polite tones, "but....."

"and then she calls police," he continues on, throwing his hands in the air, "I say to them, she is bitch."

Oh god I can see where this is going. And I'm also starting to think there are no sheep or doves. I've been conned by an arm waving skinny Italian man claiming he has white animals to lure me into tasting his oil and offering him marriage advice.

The little white dog seems to get excited and starts yapping every time Italian Man flaps his arms around.

"Twenty thousand dollar I pay her to go and she not go," he continues, as I slowly make my way to the car followed by the yappy dog, "what you do huh?" he said, looking for me to answer, "what you do?"

I had made it to the safety of the car door.

"Well maybe you... um... need to, um, well. You know if you're unhappy need, umm, to think about possibly leaving her..."

Right that's enough marriage advice for today.

Ohh maybe I should offer marriage advice as part of my

wedding planning services.

"Argh," Mr Italian Man spat once again, snapping me out of my business thoughts.

I climbed into the car ready to make my escape.

"Here," he bent down to pick up the little white dog, "you forgot dog."

"Um no sorry, I'm not taking the dog," I said, trying to locate my car keys.

"But he likey you."

"I can't have a dog."

"You came for him, yes?"

"No."

"He good dog, and white see."

Locating my keys I quickly started the engine, Mr Italian Man is now holding the dog through the window where it is licking my face.

"See he does likey you."

"Look I think there has been a misunderstanding."

"But he cannot stay here, my wife, the bitch, dog make her sneeze."

I am not having a dog. I simply will not take this dog. I shall be firm and tell him again I can not take the dog.

Facebook Status Update.

Lisa Collins.

List of things I am over:

 Olive oil.

Boyfriend's obnoxious friends.

Mattresses.

5

Back home

Okay I have the dog.

He does seem sweet and he's only little, how much trouble can he be?

He seems content. He's worn himself out with excitement and is now fast asleep on the sofa.

Hmm, I may have to establish some house rules.

Rick's still asleep and I wish he would go and do that at his place. Even though he seems to sleep through noise, just knowing he is there is distracting me.

No sign of Sid which is a bugger 'cos I need him to start on my dog kennel.

And I need a bowl.

And food and a lead.

The little dog, which I think I shall call Monty, is still asleep so I think I should just nip into town and buy some dog stuff.

In town

I should have left Rick a note but I'm not going to be long. I tried to sneak out of the house without Monty but that dog has super-sonic hearing, not to mention speed, and was sitting by the car before I even made it to the driver's door. He is kinda cute and he can come, but only this time.

I pull the car up beside the little empty shop which was meant to be my wedding planning office. I'd love to get a closer look but there is a rough looking hobo type man squatted in the doorway and I can't see a thing due to a big white sheet hanging in the window with a sign that reads *'New Business Opening Soon'*. So it seems Daniel has already started getting on with whatever it is he is doing. There doesn't seem to be any indication on what type of business it is. Hope it's nothing in customer relations as his relations with people suck.

Locating a shop which sells dog supplies, I told Monty to stay in the car and headed across the road, dodging the traffic as cars pull in and out of the angle parking in the main street.

There seems to be a lot of people in town today and in front of the hardware store is a marquee with some politician cooking sausages.

"Oh hi Lisa," came a voice as I safely navigated my way across to the other side.

"Neroli, hi."

Check for signs of a baby bump.

"Um what are you up to?" I asked as my eyes sneak back from her belly.

"Oh just getting some yarn for crocheting," she said in her daydream voice, while she adjusts something on baby Bailey's pram.

Pft yarn, so obvious it's crocheting for a baby, but fine, will play along.

"Whatever," I said, pretending not to care, "so where's Tom?"

Neroli's face went pale as she looked over my shoulder; I followed her gaze and spotted Tom.

Shit, Tom has spotted Monty in the car.

"Aunt Lisa," he yells spotting me across the street, "look there's a doggy in your car."

How did he get across the road?

"Tom no!!" I yelled, but too late, Tom opened the car door.

Damn, why don't I lock my stupid car.

Monty jumps excitedly at Tom's attention then jumps from the car and runs towards the sausages sizzling on the BBQ under the promotional tent, Tom follows on Monty's heels.

Shit.

I'm trying to run across the road but the line of traffic seems to be going on forever. Neroli is yelling at Tom to stay put. Well Neroli doesn't yell, it's more like a raised whisper that has no threat to it whatsoever.

Finally a break in the traffic.

I can see Monty disappear into the tent followed by Tom. I safely made it to the other side of the road where a photographer is lining up the politician and his supporters for a photo opportunity. I can see Monty as he attempts a jump at the raw sausages resting beside the hot BBQ.

Trying not to raise the attention of the photographer or his posers, I slip into the marquee. Tom's attention was currently diverted by a young lady handing out balloons so thank god no harm has been done, yet. Monty's attempts to poach raw sausages succeed as he lands on the table beside the hot plate.

Thank god no one has seen him due to the posing politician man standing in the way, I discreetly went to grab the thieving dog from the table when I heard Tom's voice.

"Aunt Lisa, watch this."

Tom pulls out a thumb tack and sticks it in the balloon.

Oh my god. Who gave the demon child a combination of balloons and thumbtacks.

Bang! The sound ricochets, sounding twice as loud.

Monty jumps from the table in fright knocking the now rattled politician off his feet. Monty cannot seem to escape from under his feet and I can just see the politician landing on the dog. Making a dive for Monty and pushing him out of the way of the falling politician, all of a sudden I feel myself crash to the floor.

It appears I have landed underneath a sausage cooking politician.

I can hear the gasps and fuss as the supporters pull us to our feet and check we aren't hurt. I look around for Monty but it appears the little canine shit has taken off again. Dusting my dignity off, I went to go and locate the runaway poach when the photographer stops me.

"Look," he says gesturing for me to have a look at the photo taken on his camera.

It looks like I have thrown myself between a falling politician and a hot BBQ, "what a million dollar shot," the photographer boasts, "you saved Mr Dalton from getting burnt."

"Oh yeah, no biggie," I said, desperately trying to get away so I can locate the demon child and demon dog.

"Thank you, thank you," the politician said shaking my hand as his supporters beamed and fussed around me.

"Any time," I said, "okay, gotta um, go."

"How about a photo?" said the photographer as the politician man pulls me closer.

"Okay great, and smile," the photographer said as the flash blinds me.

"What's your name?" asked the politician.

"Um Lisa, Lisa Collins and I really must go."

I made a hasty exit before anyone asks me any more questions or takes any more photos. I spotted Neroli coming towards the tent with Monty and Tom walking happily beside her.

"Where did you get to?" she asks, "and you have a sauce stained napkin stuck to your thigh."

I opened my mouth to tell her but I let it go, am so over today and want to go home.

I unstuck the napkin and located a rubbish bin. As I turned around the rather large homeless looking man that was squatting in the doorway of Daniels 'shop' was standing behind me.

"Excuse me," I said as I went to walk around him.

"You," he said to me in a sharp tone, exposing his discoloured, broken teeth and pointing his beefy finger, stained yellow by nicotine, at me accusingly, "you listen huh."

Rattled by his tone I stared at him before catching my voice in my throat. "Um yes I will." I beamed as I turned to catch up with Neroli.

Strange man.

Back home

"Lisa why do you have a dog?" Rick asks.

God so many questions.

Sid is not happy about building a kennel, says he has enough to do but he does like Monty and those two seem to have bonded so that one will work in my favour when Millie comes home in the weekend.

Millie hates dogs.

But anyway finally Rick has gone home, a little put out that we haven't spent the day together like he said we would due to the fact that I have been adopting dogs and saving politicians.

 But tomorrow's another day and now he's off home I can move on to the next phase of planning Neroli and Matt's wedding.

Number three on the list, catering.

Well there is Tim the baker.

Okay not fancy, but I do need to support local businesses.

And besides, Tim may know someone.

I found Tim's number in the local business directory and waited for him to pick up the phone, god I hope he has snapped out of his doom and gloom mood.

"Yeah um Tim here."

"Tim, Lisa here."

"Oh... hi."

"Just wondering do you do catering for weddings?"

"Um yeah, my aunty does, I help her....."

"What sort of stuff do you do?"

"Um depends. How many are you catering for?"

Shit I forgot that I'd probably need numbers first.

"Um not sure, can I get back to you?"

"Um yep no worries."

"Okay then Tim, bye."

"Bye."

Okay, need to get the guest list sorted first.

Ohh phones ringing.

"Lisa, what's the point of having an answer machine if you're not going to listen to your messages?"

Great it's Mrs Crankshaw. Oh that's right I need to talk with her.

"Eight messages I left on there," she continues.

"Sorry about that," I replied, but the old woman has a point, I have been so preoccupied with Matt and Neroli's wedding I forgot to check my messages. I mean how many other wedding clients have rung expecting my services.

Like this call that is coming though now.

"Mrs Crankshaw," I interrupted her, "don't hang up I just need to take this call."

I didn't give the old lady time to protest, important wedding clients to attend to.

"Good um afternoon, Lisa Collins event planning."

"Oh um yeah, hi, it's Tim again."

Oh that was a fizzer.

"Hi Tim."

"Hi, just wondering if you are still keen to go to um, mediation because I can, um, give you a lift if you want?"

"Tim you live beside the shop where it's being held."

"Um yeah, but it's um like no trouble."

"Oh um, thanks anyway but I should be right, see you Tuesday."

"Um it's been moved to Monday."

"Oh."

"Yeah, so um see you there."

"Okay Tim bye."

"Bye."

Weird man.

"Hello Mrs Crankshaw."

"Lisa have you not heard a word I have just said?"

"I was on the other line."

I can hear Mrs Crankshaw's heavy sigh down the line, "don't forget the CWA meeting this week, remember this is your first meeting since taking over as president."

My stomach did a tiny flip at the thought of chairing my first meeting ever. Must google some information on how to do it.

"Okay thanks, bye."

"Lisa! What did you call me for? You left a message."

Oh yeah.

"Who owns the charming little church down Cannon's Road?"

"Have you not asked Rick?"

"Um no."

Mrs Crankshaw heaved her sigh again, honestly that woman has no patience.

"Daniel does."

"Daniel who?"

"Oh Lisa, Daniel Cannon, you know, Rick's best friend."

You know I should be surprised but given it's me, I'm kinda not.

I hung up from Mrs Crankshaw and proceeded to bang my head against the phone.

Great, just bloody great, it appears that I have to suck up to Daniel.

6

Okay, just when you need to suck up to an obnoxious man he is no-where to be found.

Rick says he hasn't heard from him but that's not unusual as he is busy setting up his business and when I went into town to look through the shop window, it's still closed up with a sign saying 'opening soon'.

Still doesn't tell you what type of business it is.

Must ask Rick.

Anyway finally got some numbers of guests for the wedding, Matt seems to think it'd be around 150 but that depends if his mate Spooner brings a girlfriend, so I have decided to cater for around 200, you know, in case there's more relatives they've forgotten exist.

I've spoken to Tim and he is going to get back to me with prices and a menu. God this wedding planning thing is so easy.

As fun as my business venture is, I've started my shifts at the aged-care home today, it's so boring, but I need the money.

I watch the occupational therapist run through exercises with some of the residents and as I watch their solemn faces, I had a sudden thought that maybe I could start a mobile petting zoo. You know, to bring the pet experience to those unable to have a pet. Hmm it could be part of my event planning business.

"Hi Lisa, how's the new business venture coming along?" Debbie asks as she appears beside me.

Did I just think out loud?

"Oh great," I beamed, "already got my first client."

Debbie seems really happy for me, love Debbie, she's the best boss ever.

Maybe I should mention that I am going to do a mobile petting zoo and suggest that the residents can be my first port of call.

"So what happened to the shop?" Debbie asks just as I was about to put my suggestion across.

"Oh I decided the overheads were too high so I'm working from home. Rick's friend Daniel has taken over the lease."

"Daniel Cannon?" Debbie beams, "is he back? Oh my god I must catch up with him."

"He's a bit obnoxious," I said.

"Obnoxious?" Debbie sounded puzzled. "No, not Daniel, he is the most good natured, polite man I know."

Great, so everyone loves Daniel and I seem to be the only one who thinks otherwise.

He's probably done this on purpose to make me look bad.

"So is he setting up the photography business here?"

"Photography. Who, Daniel?"

"Yes, that's what he does," said Debbie. "He's quite a big shot overseas apparently, photographed for some big time model agency so I cannot imagine he would one to set up a shop in little old hicksville, it must be for something else."

Debbie moved off to attend to one of the residents, leaving me with the sudden realisation that I need to book a photographer for the wedding and once again I am at the mercy of Daniel.

Back home

God I hate Daniel.

I texted Rick to ask him if Daniel is indeed a photographer, Rick seems puzzled that I didn't know that already as he thought Daniel would have told me, after all, apparently Daniel told Rick that he is happy to help me as he has photographed a lot of weddings and may be able to offer suggestions with themes etc.

Pff, as if I need his suggestions.

But this is not really helpful as Rick hasn't heard from him.

Anyway now it's time for meditation class, not really sure what to wear to this thing, Sid said something comfortable, does that mean dressy comfortable or casual comfortable?

So I have some loose pants on with my awesome purple muslin top, very aura attracting.

Sid's excited about meeting like-minded people and his dress sense resembles that of a Woodstock hippie.

Tim greeted us outside when we arrived and handed me a folder of menu options and prices for the wedding.

It's a bit of an uncomfortable situation given that Tim was once sooo besotted by Millie who crushed his heart for Sid, so it's understandable that the atmosphere is a little bitter.

I'll just ignore it and pretend I'm engrossed in this menu.

As we walked into the shop and proceeded to the room at the back blocked off by a heavy drape, we were greeted by a young lady with dyed blond hair pulled tightly into a bun.

A group of woman sat around on chairs and on the floor, chatting amongst themselves. Sid sat down next to a woman wearing a spiral tie-dyed shirt that matched the head band around her dreadlocks.

Trust Sid to pick out the most alternative looking member in the group. I found a seat and sat down, Tim sat next to me, a little too close I might add.

A young shy looking girl sat down on the other side of Tim and next to her was a well groomed lady in dress pants.

"Okay," said the blond lady, entering the room and pulling the big heavy drapes slightly shut, "we have three new ones with us tonight, welcome, it's a big shift in the energy of the group, so if you would like to introduce yourselves."

All eyes turn to Sid.

"Yeah, I'm Sid and I would just like to say it's a blessing to be with understanding, like minded people."

God Sid looks like he's going to choke up, I hope he doesn't, how embarrassing.

Everyone knew Tim so no introductions needed there but I'm pretty sure the young girl beside him blushed when he spoke.

Now all eyes are on me.

"I'm Lisa..."

The lady in dress pants who I found out later is Karen, interrupted me, "you're the one from the paper?" she said.

"Excuse me?"

"Oh yes," said the blond woman, who turned out to be Shelly and who owns the shop. "Your photo is in today's local paper about some heroic act."

Now I'm blushing.

Shelly goes out into the shop and grabs the paper and yes, there I am on the front page under a title of *Local girl caught in heroic act* with the 'million dollar shot' the photographer boasted about, there for everyone to see.

Sid is giving me the 'Millie look'.

Everyone is passing around the paper and I just want to... well mediate into a peaceful place where there are no headlines of me saving politicians from hot BBQ's in president bodyguard, dodging bullet style.

Oh god now Tim is leaning in to me real close.

I think I might move down on to the floor.

"Okay," said Shelly, "if we are all comfortable I would like to begin by closing your eyes and clearing your head, taking all your thoughts and placing them in a box."

I am closing my eyes and imaging myself placing my brain in a big coffin style box.

No wait that's not right.

A square one is better.

"Okay everyone take a deep breath and imagine a white light coming through your feet and moving slowly up your body."

I can hear the soft sound of pipe music playing in the background and I open one eye to see if everyone else's eyes are shut.

Sid looks like he's already left the planet.

Oh that's right, white light.

I close my eyes again and took a deep breath and imagined a white light but it's not as easy as it sounds.

"Now feel that lovely energy pulsing through your body," said Shelly's soothing voice.

Hang on, I'm still trying to picture a white light.

Oh god, there goes the image of that coffin again.

Hope they're not connected.

I'm squeezing and trying so hard but Shelly is going too fast and I can't keep up, I'm also pretty sure Tim has his foot pressed gently against my back.

I opened one eye to see who else is not in the light or going flying down a tunnel filled with flashing colours. Through the gap in the drape I can see out onto the street in front of the shop and that man is there again. The one from the other day, the hobo man that accused me of not listening with his beefy pointy finger. He is looking straight at me, I look around to try and get someone's attention but they are all away in the white light.

Great now he is waving at me.

I should wave back but I don't want to encourage him.

Okay, just a little wave, he is being really persistent.

He gives me a toothless, cheesy grin then closes his eyes and sways from side to side.

Wait, is he mocking me?

I turn to look at Tim who is sitting in the chair behind me, he does indeed have his foot pressed lightly into my back, I moved slightly from his touch to see if he is alert so I can point out the hobo man standing outside mocking me (also very creepy that he was touching my back) but Tim is away with the others in the white light as well.

Oh hobo man is gone.

I close my eyes and try to join the others in the white light but every time I open one eye, hobo man is there again waving and rolling a tobacco cigarette.

Okay this is getting stalker-ish.

Shelly's soft and enchanting voice floats through the room.

"Okay when you are all ready I want you to take a deep, cleansing breath and open your eyes."

The chorus of exhaling breath echo's around the room.

What, is that it??

Everyone is shifting and smiling and I haven't bloody started.

Damn light and hobos.

"Okay," said Shelly, "if you are all ready then who would like to go first and talk about what they have received. We will go around the room."

Sid puts his hand up first.

Trust him.

Sid goes into a tale of medieval times and how he was a knight on a steed and he was fighting a great battle and he died with honour.

The girl beside him (who I think of as rainbow) told tales of how she was left in a house and her mother and brother die from the plague and she was left to stave and rats befriended her.

Tim, all enthusiastic, told of seeing a garden and a chair and someone sitting there with a message.

Oh god I've got nothing.

The shy girl beside him said she didn't see anything but felt the energy filling her.

Oh god I've still got nothing, I'm going to have to make something up.

"Lisa?" said Shelly looking at me with much enthusiasm in her eyes. "Do you have anything you would like to share?"

"Oh well um I climbed up some golden stairs."

"Really?" said the shy girl with an excited look on her face.

"Yes," I said encouraged by her expression, "and when I got to the top I saw, resting on white clouds, lots and lots of um unicorns."

"Really?" said Sid but with a flat tone accompanied by the 'Millie look' again.

"Lisa that's amazing," said Shelly, "you must be multi-level. Unicorns represent a very high spiritual awareness."

"Oh really, um well yes that's me."

"Did you get any messages?" asked Shelly.

My mind has gone blank and through the gap in the drape hobo man appears again and he is pointing and laughing.

"Um, oh, to listen."

"To your intuitions?" Karen pipes up.

Hobo man is still laughing at me.

"Um yes," I said as Tim leans forward and gives my shoulder a squeeze.

Uncomfortable.

Hobo man is still out there.

Shelly has moved on thank god. I turned to Tim.

"Tim," I whispered, "there's a homeless man out there, can you see him?"

"Um no," Tim whispers back.

"Then move down beside me but slowly so he doesn't see you."

Tim slides off his seat beside me and hobo man squats down out of sight.

What the?

"I can't see anyone," whispered Tim.

"Just stay there," I snap, "he has just squatted down out of sight he must have known you're there."

"Still can't see anyone," Tim whispers.

Oh for gods sake.

"Sit behind me so you can see in the same direction and he can't see you."

Tim hovers behind me and presses into my back, a bit too close again.

The hobo man has not reappeared.

Sid is giving both Tim and I a suspicious look.

"Can't see anyone. You sure someone's there?" whispered Tim.

"Well he was before," I snapped.

"Okay well, I'll just sit here until he comes back," said Tim moving in closer.

Oh thank god it's coffee time.

Everyone makes their way toward the supper table.

"Are you sure someone was out there?" he asks again for the fifth time.

Ignoring him, I rise off the floor and head out to the shop to see where hobo man is hiding.

The shy, quiet girl shoots me a glare as I walk past her.

Weird.

"Lisa," said Shelly as I went to go through the curtain, "I would be very interested to work some more with you on a spiritual level. So what do you do, are you a healer or clairvoyant?"

Shit.

"Oh well you know, I just see what I see," I said trying desperately to get away from her.

"Well we do have a lot of healing sessions during the day, let me get you some contact details."

"So, unicorns?" Sid said in a dry tone when Shelly was out of hearing range.

I think it's time to go, I can hear the sarcasm in Sid's voice and the shy girl is glaring at me again.

Maybe she is jealous of my made-up spiritual talents.

After thanking everyone and promising Shelly I will return to the next meditation group, I dragged a protesting Sid to the car, glancing out of the shop as I walked through the door to see if hobo man is out there and make sure he's not going to point his yellow finger at me again.

"Maybe you have a stalker after your new found fame," Tim joked as he appeared beside me holding the copy of the paper, "that's such a nice photo of you by the way," he continues.

God Tim is in my personal space again.

I'm still craning my neck to see if I can see hobo man, while ignoring Tim.

Tim starts reading the article out to me as Sid sulkily climbs in the passenger side of the car and slams the door. All of a sudden hobo man appears again, but this time across the dimly lit street. He seems to be pretending he is dodging a bullet.

Oh shit he is mocking me again.

"Tim," I said grabbing at his arm, "he's there."

Shit he disappeared behind a post.

"Lisa, are you okay?" Tim asks as concern washes over him that I may be, well, crazy.

Am I going crazy?

"You might have seen Larry," commented Tim vaguely, all the while still clutching my arm. "He wanders round here a bit. He's always a bit of a character....."

Oh thank god I'm not going crazy, anyway my attention's wandering now as I am thinking about how long it'll take people to forget about that damn newspaper article.

Back home

Tim talked for ages and I found it hard to get away from him, I didn't want to be impolite as he ended up talking wedding and catering but Sid was rude by jumping in the driver's seat and revving the engine.

Those two really must build a bridge.

Rick was there when we got home and greeted me with the same enthusiasm as Monty, as nice as it was that he was happy to see me, it was a bit over the top.

Sid's engrossing him in conversation about meditation and Rick's telling Sid it's a bunch of baloney.

Hmmm, wouldn't have picked Rick for a sceptic.

Sid looks like he's really offended.

I don't want to get involved in a debate about meditation but am surprised Sid is debating with Rick at all, Sid never sticks up for himself.

Rick is now holding up a copy of the local paper and asks me to explain how I came about saving a politician from a hot BBQ. I'm not really wanting to get into it, so I told him it's all explained in the article and quickly left them and a sleeping Monty to go through the catering menu that Tim gave me.

It's not a fancy feast but they can do platters as well as prepare a three course buffet style meal with a choice of cold meat menu or rotisserie style lamb and pork and it's all reasonable priced.

Okay, it's fancy for a small town catering firm and it's not all sausages rolls and egg sandwiches. And because I'm all about supporting local business I shall present this menu to my client.

Giggled at the word client.

Mind you, I have had a wine since I've been home.

Ooh that reminds me I almost forgot the alcohol.

Heading towards my office to add alcohol to my list and schedule another appointment with Matt and Neroli, I notice Rick taking a call on his mobile.

Wonder if he is talking to Daniel?

I moved closer to listen in and get Rick's attention that I need to talk to Daniel when Matt walked through the door.

"S'up," he greeted, thrusting a plastic bag at me, "Neroli made these for you when you go to fairy group."

"Fairy group?"

"Yeah you know, when you do that airy fairy stuff."

"You mean meditation?"

"Yeah whatever, it's still airy fairy."

Sid looks really offended again.

"What are they?" I asked pulling out an object that looked like something the CWA would put in their underwear drawer to 'keep it fresh'.

"Eye pillows," said Matt, sounding like he's stating the obvious, "they smell, go on have a whiff."

They smell a bit musky but a nice musk, with a hint of lavender. But the material is ugly and it feels like there are dried flowers or something sewn into them.

"You put them on your eyes, it's meant to sooth and relax," Matt elaborated, sounding like he's reading off a script, "Neroli made a whole bunch."

Hmmm sounds like nesting syndrome to me.

"Thanks Matt, but meditation was tonight, I've already been."

"Neroli was kinda hoping you would take some along to sell, I have a whole bunch in the ute," he said looking deflated.

Oh god.

"Yeah sure," I said humouring him, "maybe next week. Now I have a couple of things to go over with you."

As I dragged Matt off to the office to show him the menu for the wedding, Rick was just getting off the phone.

Oh shit that's right.

"Was that Daniel?" I asked and was kinda surprised that my voice sounded squeaky.

"Yeah, he's going down to Sydney for the next few days or so."

"Oh," I said, surprisingly deflated.

Oh that's right, I was going to ask him about his church.

"Lisa when the fuck did you get a dog?" Matt asked as Monty made his appearance and leapt all over Matt.

Ignoring him I turned to Rick.

"I wanted to ask him about his church and can I use it for weddings," I said, sounding desperate, "when is he coming back?"

"Oh," said Rick sounding surprised and slightly cautious "how did you know about the church?"

"I didn't, I discovered it. I want to have it for a venue for Matt and Neroli's wedding. Mrs Crankshaw said it belongs to Daniel."

Matt and Rick are looking at each other with slightly pale faces. Matt starts protesting in profanities that under no circumstances is he getting married there.

"Um Lis," Rick began, filling in the gap left by Matt's outburst, "I don't think that church is suitable for weddings."

"Because..?"

"Because every wedding that's been held there either ends up in divorce or death."

"Yeah," Matt agreed, "something happened there, it's fucken haunted."

Oh for gods sake, *now* they get all hocus pocus on me.

"He needs to be sent back to the light," Sid pipes up.

"Pfff," Matt scoffed.

"But Matt it's a perfect venue," I wailed, "you said you wanted a church wedding."

"No, Mum does, and there is the other church in town."

"But it's ugly and has no character," I pleaded.

"Yeah but it's not fucken haunted," Matt argued.

My vision of the perfect first wedding in the setting of the charming old church was fast fading.

Okay I'm not going to get anywhere with these two, I bet if I showed Neroli she will disagree and will want to get married there.

Yes that's what I will do, superstition or not, Matt and Neroli will get married there and Matt will have no choice but to go along with Neroli's wishes.

"Lisa, what the fuck are you doing on the front page of the paper?" Matt called from the living room.

Ignoring him and trying to think how to get Daniel's number off Rick so I can get the key to show Neroli, oh and get his permission of course.

Maybe I'll just try asking him.

"Could I have Daniel's number?" I asked Rick, surprised at how a lump just rose in my throat. "I need to ask him about photos."

"Sure," said Rick fishing his phone out of his pocket again, "I'll call him shall I, you can speak to him."

"Um why don't you just give me the number."

"Oh I need to speak to him again anyway," Rick said, pressing numbers into his phone.

Shit I'll just have to do this the old fashion way and steal the number off Rick's phone when he's not looking.

It seemed like an eternity waiting for Daniel to answer his phone, finally Rick hung up.

"He's not answering," he said shoving his phone back into his pocket, "I'll tell him you want to talk to him."

I don't know why Rick just doesn't give me his number, but then again why am I afraid to ask him for it again? Maybe it's my sub-consciousness talking because I'm about to go behind their backs and ask Daniel to use his haunted church.

I'll just look the number up after Rick goes to bed.

"Right, outta here," Matt announces, "I'll leave Neroli's stuff for you to take to fairy group, she wants $5 each for them."

Oh god, I'd be lucky if I could give them away, but I have to stay on the right side of Neroli so I can get her to see what a beautiful setting the church is, so I told Matt I'd take them along. After exchanging the catering information with eight plastic shopping bags filled with Neroli's creations, I said goodbye to Matt and joined Rick on the sofa.

Sid must have gone to bed.

"All this wedding stuff must be making you want your own," Rick said, wrapping his arm around me as I sat down.

"Hmmm," I answered, my mind focused on convincing Neroli about the church. I wonder if Sid can find out about removing spiritual attachments, that way it will be a strong point when we tell Matt he is getting married there.

"Ever thought about it?" Rick's still going on.

"What? Oh yeah sometimes," I replied.

Unless Pamela gets involved. Oh god why didn't I think of that before, what if Pamela got married there? After all she did have an affair with Jake and her marriage ended up in the gutter and....

Did Rick just say 'let's get married'?

He is looking at me with anticipation.

"Pardon?" I spluttered.

"Let's get married," he said sitting upright on the sofa like an excited kid.

"I love you, so why not?" he asked.

I'm speechless.

"You do love me?" he asks, slightly alarmed.

"Um... of course," I said.

"Well then, what do you say?" he asks with puppy dog eyes.

I'm shocked and I don't know what to say. I mean I have always wanted to get engaged but now it's actually happening I don't know how to feel.

But then again, looking at Rick's eyes I cannot believe I'm hesitating with my answer, I mean imagine planning my own wedding.

I've always wanted a beach wedding and Rick's such a nice guy.

"Okay," I said, imagining myself telling Mum and Dad the news and finally getting them off my back about grandchildren.

Ohhh, imagine Millie's face.

Rick pulled me into a huge embrace, he sounds so happy while he is telling me how happy he is.

Shit, cannot believe I'm going to get married.

Facebook Status Update.

Lisa Collins.

Lisa is finally engaged to Rick Crankshaw!!.

7

Two nights later

I still cannot believe I'm getting married.

I haven't told Millie or Sid yet as I want to wait until Millie gets home and tell them together, also Rick still has to buy me a ring. We are going to go ring shopping tomorrow so when we do announce our engagement it can be done officially.

So I haven't told anyone yet except the lady that's doing the invitations for Matt and Neroli's wedding but that's only because I was hoping she would give me a discount when it came to ordering my invitations. And I did tell Mr Willard, a client at the nursing home when I did my shift today but he has dementia so no chance that it's going to get out, although I have been tempted to give Mum and Dad a call and tell them.

But that's not a great idea just yet as Mum will want me to describe my engagement ring, so best I wait.

So hard though as I'm so excited.

Still no word from Daniel but Rick said he'll be back tomorrow. Wonder what he is going to say about our engagement.

He'll probably just be arrogant about it all.

Shit, just realised that Daniel will be Rick's best man.

Anyway no time to think about that as tonight is my first CWA meeting as appointed chairperson.

I did google chairperson but couldn't be bothered reading through the one million search results that came back so I'm just going to remember how Pamela used to do it. But without the hoity-ness and bitchiness.

So the 149th monthly meeting of the Country Woman's Association is underway in the back room of the community hall. I have brought a gavel for the occasion. Okay, not a gavel as such, it's more like a wooden hammer that was left at the house by Tom, but still effective if needed.

Taking a seat at the head of the table I feel so official. Gloria is sitting beside me as secretary.

Present members are:

Mrs Crankshaw (life member).

Maggie (also a life member).

Fran, Betty and Mary (also life members but only signing in on a month to month basis due to ill health and old age.)

Tapping my gavel on the desk to get order and start the meeting I frighten the bejeezes out of Betty, who then loses control of her waterworks again, so best I put the gavel away.

After reading out the welcome speech I had prepared we move on to the first item on the agenda which was the up and coming garden tour.

Mrs Crankshaw led the floor. "Okay, once again we have been asked to cater the up and coming garden club's afternoon tea. There is not much involved, we decided to do sandwiches and scones and maybe we could have a little raffle to raise some funds. So any ideas?"

"We could approach local businesses again and get them to donate," said Mary as she clacked away on her knitting needles. Murmurs of agreement.

"Yes," agreed Betty, "which businesses haven't we approached before?"

Deadly silence.

Mary went to say something, everyone turned to her in anticipation, but she stopped. Now everyone is deep in thought again.

The door to the room quietly creaks and in tiptoes Neroli.

What the hell is she doing here?

"Sorry," she whispers when all heads turn to her.

Oh god it looks like she has a plastic bag full of her 'creations'.

"Ahh Neroli, glad you made it." Mrs Crankshaw beamed. "Everyone this is Neroli, I have invited her tonight to sit in to see if she wants to join the CWA."

Since when?

Everyone beams and nods their greetings at Neroli.

I clear my throat.

"Well, welcome Neroli," I said in my official voice, "now back to the agenda item, ideas for a raffle?"

Everyone falls quiet again, only the sound of Mary's knitting needles fill the room.

"What are you making?" Neroli's tiny voice asked Mary.

Oh for gods sake.

Mary looks ecstatic that someone has taken an interest in her knitting and enthusiastically tells Neroli that they are beanies with ear covers, and proceeds to pull out a bunch of finished wares to show Neroli.

I have to admit they are a tiny bit nice, I could see young people wearing them.

Neroli's now fishing in her bag and showing Mary her eye pillows and it seems she has made padded coat hangers as well.

20 minutes later

Okay this is getting ridiculous.

Everyone except me is now wearing a beanie and has Neroli's eye pillows on their eyes.

"Oh this is so soothing," Mrs Crankshaw sighs in pleasure.

"Yes," agrees Fran, "and my head is so warm."

I feel like I'm in a small town craft shop.

"I should show you my knitted bed socks," said Betty, "my family get them every Christmas, they just love them."

I bet.

"I used to make crochet sofa throws," said Maggie, "I should start doing that again."

Right this is well out of hand, I need to show them who's running the show, just the way Pamela used to.

"Ahem!" I said in a loud voice, "if you ladies don't mind we have item one to get through!"

"Oh Lisa, don't be an old prude," Mrs Crankshaw scoffed, "chill out. Have an eye pillow, they're very relaxing."

I'd rather wear knitted underwear then have those ugly things on my eyes.

"Oh I have a brilliant idea," said Fran, removing the eye pillows from her eyes, "why don't we sell all this at the garden tour, we could have a stall to raise money. After all they are lovely eye pillows Neroli."

Murmurs of agreement all around.

I'm convinced the older members of the CWA are all blind and have no taste.

"I also make toy animals," said Neroli.

"Oh you are so clever," Mary said patting her on the knee. "I think that's a brilliant idea. How soon can everyone get their wares made for the stall?"

Oh no, that's sooo not going to work, I mean who in their right mind would want knitted useless stuff. I need to change course.

"Hang on," I growled, wracking my brains to recall procedures.

"We have to move a motion on agenda items."

"I can move a bowel motion," Betty joked causing raucous laughter around the room.

"Yes very funny Betty," I mused, "but have we um voted that we are going to have a stall at the garden tour with donated knitwear?"

"Just don't ask Lisa to make a cake," Mrs Crankshaw joked, "remember that day dear? When you sat in the cake in that little skirt?"

More raucous laughter as Mrs Crankshaw re-tells the story of how I was asked to bring desserts to her dinner party and I slipped and my bum landed in the dessert in front of her nephew Jake.

Now Neroli is in fits of laughter.

Right that's it, where's my gavel.

"Oh which reminds me," Maggie snorted in the middle of her laughing fit. "Did everyone see this?" she asks pulling out the front page of the paper.

Oh god.

Even more laughter and lots of puns, as my photo of saving the politician man is passed around.

Betty is trying her hardest not to wet herself again.

I have no idea what has got into them but this meeting sucks and we still have item two to get through.

Banging my gavel on the table, the room starts to go quiet, everyone is calming down but Mrs Crankshaw and Maggie are having trouble keeping straight faces.

"Okay," I started again, "I move a... mot... proposal that we make um... stuff to sell on a stall at the garden tour instead of a raffle. All for...?"

Argh shit, everyone has their hands up, I'm the only one against this idea.

Well if they think that we going to make money from bed socks and ugly eye pillows then let them, I'm not getting involved.

"Fine, motion passed," I scoffed. The room fills with raucous laughing yet again. "Oh for gods sake."

So immature.

Next morning

Okay my first meeting sucked, I need to work on my assertiveness, and to make matters worse when I left the hall to go to my car the creepy hobo man was there across the carpark, pointing, laughing and pulling faces, pretending he was a court judge with a gavel which means he must have been spying on the meeting. I'm not sure if anyone else saw him as I got in my car and drove away quickly before he started to point his finger at me again.

But no time to dwell on bad meetings and hobos, as I almost forgot that I am now engaged and have not only Matt and Neroli's wedding to organise, but my own.

But first, ring shopping.

I'm sooo excited.

Ohh and Daniel is back today.

Bouncing out of bed after receiving Rick's text message that he will pick me up in about an hour, I met Sid as I bounced into the kitchen.

Sid commented on my good mood.

So bursting at the seams to tell him, but must be poised and keep my mouth shut.

"So the meeting went well then?" he asked, speculating on my good mood.

"No the meeting sucked," I beamed.

"But obviously you're being positive about it?" Sid asked.

"No," I beamed back, unable to hide my smile.

Sid's looking a tad freaked out.

"Um Lisa, about meditation," Sid said but in a Millie manner. God since when has Sid taken on the Millie disapproval.

"Yes?" I asked looking at my fingernails. Shit I desperately need a manicure if I'm going to be trying on rings today, I mean they're not bad, but maybe I should do a quick file and repaint.

"So you made that up about seeing unicorns?" Sid asked.

"Hmmm?" I asked, pretending to pick something out of my nail and avoiding the question.

"Lisa you can't go making up visions like that if you didn't see anything. Meditation, like anything, takes practise. You don't need to be ashamed about it if you're not getting anything."

Since when did Sid get all brave and start lecturing me, Sid used to have worthless opinions. God, ever since he married Millie he seems to be acting more like her.

Hope that doesn't happen to me and Rick, not that there is anything wrong with Rick, I just don't want to be a couple that ends up dressing like one another.

I'm not going to answer him, I've got more important things to do. So I beamed at him and left the room to paint my nails.

In car with Rick

My nails are looking nice and we're on our way to the city. It feels so surreal that I'm going to look at engagement rings. I'm not good at making decisions but according to *Cleo* magazine, if it's meant to be, the right ring will pop out at you. Rick is talking all the way about.... um stuff, not sure what because I'm not really listening. When he arrived to pick me up this morning he said he had been talking to Daniel and gave him my number to call me in regards to wedding photos, so I have been clutching my phone the whole car ride hoping he doesn't ring while I'm with Rick, as I need to ask him about the church.

I could text him but I don't have his number until he calls me.

Unless....

No, bugger. Rick has his phone in his pocket.

Wonder if he is on facebook?

Rick pulls into a car park.

Shit are we here already.

"Ready?" Rick said, reaching for my hand, huge grin on his face.

Ohh let the fun begin.

Two hours later

This is a disaster and I want to cry.

I have tried on dozens of rings and nothing feels right. There's so much to choose from and I can feel Rick getting impatient, even though he said he's not and that I should relax. But Millie's not helping me relax because she has been texting me all morning, as she is at work and bored and every time my phone beeps I keep thinking its Daniel. Rick and I almost had an argument in the last jewellery store over the ring he liked. I told him the skull and cross ring in the tattoo shop window across the street was far prettier, which caused the young shop assistant to side with Rick, (although I think she was into him, going by the way she was looking at him, bitch.) So now I am sitting at a coffee shop while Rick is fetching coffee and I cannot help but feel that me not finding a ring is a sign that maybe I shouldn't get married.

Also Daniel still hasn't rung me about the wedding business, I mean how hard is it to press a button and dial a number.

Rick returns to the table with our lattés, he looks as awkward as I feel.

I want to cry.

As I busied myself with the task of adding the little sachets of sugar to my cup, I could feel Rick looking at me but I cannot look at him just yet.

"Lisa is everything okay?" Rick asks, "we don't have to do this today if you don't want to."

"I do want to," I wailed at him, surprising myself at my outburst, "but it's just so hard."

"Hard to choose a ring?" Rick chuckled, "I thought that shopping for a ring was bred into girls."

Oh god, there must be something wrong with me.

I glanced across the street to avoid Rick's eye again and I can't believe it. It's the hobo, right across the street. He has his back to me but I'm sure it's him. What is he doing in the city? I mean it's at least an hour's drive away. It must be someone that looks like him, all homeless hobos look the same don't they?

I felt Rick take my hand.

"Look," he begins, making me turn to look at him, "the reason I wanted you to pick out your own ring is because I thought you would know what you want."

"I do know what I want," I snapped back at him.

"I meant in a ring."

"Oh."

Rick lets go of my hand and reaches in his pocket. I turned to look across the street again.

Oh my god he has turned around and it *is* him, the hobo, and he's seen me.

His face lights up and he starts frantically waving at me with that toothless grin. But how did he get to the city? Homeless hobo's don't drive, they don't have a car. Shit I hope he doesn't come over.

"Rick!" I said. "Look across the..." turning my head to Rick I see a velvet box sitting in front of me with a beautiful antique ring in it.

Oh my god.

"It's yours if you want it," Rick said, "I didn't know if you would like it, it belonged to my grandmother."

I'm so speechless.

It's absolutely beautiful and I'm so touched that Rick would want to give it to me. I so want to take it out of the box but my eyes keep sliding back to the hobo across the street, maybe because he has his hands over his eyes like he's playing peek-a-boo. Okay, on second thought he's not playing peek-a-boo, it's like he's waiting for a disaster to happen. Now he's on his knees with both hands covering his face shaking his head.

Everyone is walking around him like it's totally normal. Why isn't anyone else seeing this?

The sound of the velvet box snapping shut alerted me to Rick's chair scrapping across the wooden deck, as he got up abruptly, taking the ring with him.

"Going to the toilet," he muttered, slamming the chair back into the table.

I call out to him in total surprise but Rick just keeps walking, what brought that on? I mean I do want the ring, Rick didn't give me a chance to answer, oh god I have really upset him. The couple at the table next to us must have sensed Rick's upset as they keep glancing over to me. Hobo man now has his hand on his heart in what appears to be panting relief.

What a tosser.

"It's all your fault," I yelled to him, causing the couple to jump at my outburst.

"Not talking to you!" I scoffed at them as I rose from my chair, "it's his." I pointed across the street at the hobo who is now laughing hysterically at me. Giving him the bird I left to go and wait for Rick to come out of the toilets so I can make amends.

Oh god now my phone is ringing.

And it's Daniel. Well I think it's him, I don't recognise the number.

Oh my god, oh my god, what do I do?

Okay I'll answer it.

"Ahem, Lisa Collins, um wedding planning."

Shit, I meant event planning.

"It's Daniel," came the abrupt voice at the other end.

"Oh um hi."

Awkward silence.

"Rick said you wanted to talk to me," he said.

Shit Rick is now walking towards me still looking sulky.

I have to spit it out about the church before he is in earshot.

"Can I have your church?" I said almost at a whisper.

"Pardon?"

"Your old church, I want to hire it," I said quickly.

"You want to hide my old shirt?" Daniel asks, completely puzzled.

Shit now Rick is in earshot.

"No, no, never mind." I said, hanging up on him before Rick gets to me.

Feck, forgot to ask him about photos.

"Ready to go home?" Rick asks, still sounded annoyed and not looking at me.

"Can I see the ring?" I asked him.

The couple that were in the table next to us are now listening intently.

Nosey people.

"I thought you weren't interested in an old ring?" Rick said staring at the floor.

"I didn't get a chance to see it," I said gently.

"But you didn't look at it," Rick said, looking up from the floor. I wish he would look at the floor again as I don't like his scornful expression. This must really mean a lot to him.

"Sorry," I pleaded, "but I was distracted. You know the homeless guy that lives in the doorway outside my old shop?"

"Lisa you never had a shop," Rick scoffed.

"The shop that Daniel's taken over," I corrected as the lump in my throat rose when I said Daniel.

Must be guilt over the church thing.

"You mean Larry?" asked Rick, puzzled, almost amused.

"Yeah well he was across the street waving and I didn't get a chance to look at the ring because he was distracting me."

"Lisa it can't have been Larry," Rick said sounding annoyed. "It must have been someone else."

I'm about to protest when Rick's phone rings.

"Hang on," snapped Rick, looking at the call screen.

Rick turned his back on me to answer it and I have a quick look around again expecting to see Larry laughing or doing cartwheels while pointing his beefy finger at me, but I can't see him.

"Excuse me," said the couple, "did you say you're in the wedding business?"

"Oh yeah" I said, looking down the street to see where Larry could have gone.

"Do you have a card?" asked the lady.

I flick them one of my business cards, my eyes still fixed across the street, trying to catch sight of Larry again.

"So where are you based?" asked the man.

Then I spotted Larry, he has appeared from behind a street pole, wait, is he attempting to pole dance?

"Excuse me again," said the lady "But can I.."

"Look," I turned to the lady, "I'm a little distracted right now, in case you haven't noticed there's a homeless man across the street climbing a pole."

The couple glance across the street at Larry who seems to have fallen on the ground in his failed attempt to climb the street pole. Everyone seems to be walking around him.

"Tch, look at that," I scoffed, gesturing across the street, "has anyone stopped to see if he's okay, I mean what is with people?"

The couple get up to leave.

"Um maybe you should take our number," the man said, handing me his card while the lady looked at me with sympathy.

"Fine," I said, as I crane my neck to see Larry, oh it seems he is okay, as now he's walking off down the street.

"Don't hesitate to call us," said the lady, resting her hand on my arm as she and her partner left the café.

I glance down at the business card, it read *Wayne Blythe Psychiatrist.*

Huh? Well that's weird, that's got nothing to do with weddings.

"Lisa," Rick turns around looking puzzled, "what do you want with Daniel's shirt?"

Back home

It's dark when we got home and it's been a long afternoon. I managed to divert the misunderstanding about the shirt by telling Rick that I meant to ask Daniel if he does 'prints on shirts'.

Rick scoffed immediately that of course Daniel doesn't do prints, he's a photographer. Daniel who was on speaker phone and overheard, said of course he can do shirt prints. So now I have ordered 150 tee-shirts in assorted colours that say 'Congratulations Neroli and Matt' with the wedding date as a memento for guests to wear after the ceremony.

Lucky I had Daniel's number. As soon as Rick got distracted I texted Daniel to tell him to cancel the shirts and asked can I rent his church instead.

Then I sent another text to say please don't tell Rick about the church as I want it to be a surprise for, um, Matt and Neroli, as Rick might spill the beans.

Daniel's text back was short and simple saying, yes I can hire the church, but, no tee-shirts no church.

What the hell? I cannot believe he is prepared to blackmail me, I mean what is that about?

He is either the biggest arrogant tosser to ever come out of this side of the hemisphere or he's a very, very good businessman.

I'm going with the first option.

But luckily I'm not paying for the tee-shirts, so I agreed and am picking up the key to the church on the weekend.

So excited.

But what's more exciting is I'm pleased to say that I am the proud owner of a beautiful ring that used to belong to Rick's grandmother.

After Rick and I left the café, we ended up walking through the beautiful botanical gardens where he got down on one knee and proposed with the ring.

I was so happy that on the way to dinner I nipped into the jewellery shop to show the young assistant who had her eyes on Rick, what a real ring looks like and watch her face drop.

I also bought a new fancy touch phone that does email and everything so I can keep in touch with wedding clients on the go.

Perfect, perfect day.

So now Rick is asleep and despite Monty being kicked off the bed by Rick, he has managed to crawl back up and is asleep at Rick's feet. I cannot sleep, as I'm imagining how I'm going to tell Millie and everyone else, shall I just flash my ring at them or write a speech?

Oh my god, then there's dress shopping!

My head is spinning at all the decisions I have to make. First thing is we have to set a date.

Then there is Daniel, I wonder how he is going to react, not that I care what he thinks.

I started to think about the old church and am getting excited over the thought of seeing inside it. I cannot believe people think it's haunted, I mean a church is God's place, so of course there's going to be some sort of presence there.

Hmmm wonder if Rick will be open to getting married there. Maybe I should wait until Matt and Neroli get married there first. And if they don't separate or die then I'll know that it's good to go.

Okay must sleep now.

Okay sleep not an option.

Also Neroli's ugly lavender eye pillows are not working. Tossing and turning, my head keeps swimming with doubt so I creep out of bed so as not to disturb the sleeping Rick and Monty, and slip into the kitchen.

I'm sitting in the dark, nursing my hot chocolate when the moonlight streams through the window, catching the ring and producing a sparkle. I sit and stare at it for the longest time in a state of surrealism. I mean I don't feel like I'm engaged to anyone, it just feels like I'm wearing a really nice ring.

There must be something wrong with me, after all I've just got engaged to an awesome, hot guy who comes from a good family (apart from his bastard brother Jake) and wants a family of his own. *And* he thinks the sun protrudes out of me, he's even prepared to put up with my 'ways' as Millie puts it.

Okay not so much me and *my* 'ways', as half of the time it's more like my friends 'ways', but Rick tends to like my friends and their 'ways' too. So to find someone who is prepared to accept that, then I must be crazy not to embrace this ring and what it symbolises.

I'm starting to feel a bit sleepy now so better go off to bed.

Collecting my half drunk cup of hot chocolate, I proceed to move from the chair and then almost pee my pants when the room fills with the sound of the annoying standard ring tone that came with my new phone. I have yet to work out how to change it.

Oh, I did wet my pants.

Oh no, that's just the left-over hot chocolate, I must have spilt it.

I look at the call screen but don't recognise the number, I quickly cut it off before the tone wakes up the entire house.

I did put Daniel's number in my phone so if it was him it would have flashed up with 'That Twat Daniel'. Unless it's a wedding client.

At 2.24 am?

Okay not a wedding client.

I decided to ignore it, if it's important they would ring back.

Shit, they are ringing back.

I quickly answered it before it wakes Rick up.

"Hello Lisa Collins err, marriage line."

Shit wrong name again.

"You're not listening," the gruff voice said down the line.

"Um yes, I can hear you," I said in polite tones.

"Yeah but you're not listening," it said again.

Not sure what to make of this so I asked in further polite tones what the caller wanted.

"You were in the paper, saved that man I saw."

The caller sound a bit simple minded and.... oh my god it's Larry.

His familiar laugh appears down the line confirming this.

"How did you get my number?" I barked at him, "also it's 2.30 in the morning."

Oh my god, I think I have a stalker called Larry.

"You with dat man," Larry said.

"Okay I'm hanging up now Larry," I said, "goodnight."

I disconnected, feeling a bit shaky as Larry seems to be playing games. I know Tim said he's harmless but phoning me is crossing the line.

Oh god, it's ringing again.

I pushed the button to disconnect it and go to switch it to silent mode, but cannot work out how to do it.

Shit ringing again.

Okay, I'll just answer it again, "um... hello."

"You're still not listening."

Okay hung up again.

Shit ringing again!

How do I turn it off?!

"Who is that?" Rick's voice appears in the dark almost causing me to almost wet my pants again.

"It's Larry," I said, trying to turn the phone off, "he must have gotten hold of this number."

Rick takes the phone from my hand with a look of concern on his face.

"Lisa, are you sleepwalking?"

"No, no, wide awake."

Rick answers my still ringing phone and has a look of surprise on his face. After a brief but polite conversation about wrong numbers, he hangs up and looks at me with caution.

"So what did Larry say this time?" I asked, "that my ears are painted on?"

"Lisa, that was a woman. She was after a Melanie, I told her she has the wrong number."

Typical.

"Well obviously that time it wasn't Larry, give it a minute, he'll ring again."

Okay a minute has gone by and no call back, Larry must have gotten the hint.

Bloody typical.

I snatched the phone off Rick, who now has a look of utter dismay on his face and announces that he going for a slash.

Finally after much frustration I found the call log.

What the..?

It's been the same number throughout. Even the last call that Rick claimed was a woman with the wrong number, was the same number Larry had called me from.

Rick returns.

"Lisa, have you been to sleep yet?" he asked, taking my phone from my hand and switching it off easily.

"Um no... why?"

A look of relief comes over his face as he gently coaxes me back towards the bedroom.

"I think you need sleep, that's why."

I'm too tired to argue about Larry anyway.

Day of announcement of engagement

Okay, I slept in and had better get up as Millie will be home soon.

Rick suggested everyone come around for a BBQ lunch so he's busy texting invites.

Okay, everyone only includes Mrs Crankshaw and Max, as well as Matt and Neroli.

So now Rick's has gone to buy sausages.

I have taken the engagement ring off for now, I don't want Sid to see it, otherwise he might tell Millie before she gets home.

I'm so excited about seeing Millie and I can't wait to show her my ring. I know she will be so proud of me and I know she will say that this will be the first grown up thing I have done, ever.

I'm still feeling a bit freaked out by Larry's phone calls last night but it's such a hazy memory that I must have been in a vague lack-of-sleep induced state.

Which may explain why the crotch of my pj's smell like hot chocolate.

I really need to get up, Monty wants his breakfast.

I'll just have ten more minutes.

I'm trying to drift off but the thumping coming from Sid and Millie's room is driving me insane, not sure what he is doing, sounds like he is rearranging furniture. Probably trying to clean up before Millie gets here otherwise he will get into trouble.

I must get up, before Millie gets home.

Sauntering towards the kitchen with Monty on my heels, I meet Sid coming out of his bedroom.

He looks freaked out.

I was going to ask him what was with the freaked out expression when I heard the sound of Millie's car pull up.

That'll be why.

"Oh shit," Sid exclaims, running towards the linen cupboard and pulling out a pile of bed sheets.

Ha, ha, he obviously got 'told' to change the bed.

Forgetting Monty's hunger pains, I ran out to greet Millie.

I'm so excited to see her.

"You got a fucken dog!" Millie exclaimed as Monty proceeded to beat me to the car to greet her.

"Um, just a small one."

"Did Sid agree to this?"

"Um?"

"Oh god never mind," Millie sighed, "just keep it away from me."

Phew, that hurdle's over with.

Millie looks tired but I guess with the change in her hours and having to work the seven days she would be.

"So everything okay?" she asked after giving me a hug.

I'm sooo dying to tell her, I'm bursting at the seams. Okay, mustn't say anything that will give it away.

"Everything's perfect," I beamed, "in fact I have some great news, but you have to wait until everyone gets here, we are having a BBQ lunch."

"Why don't you tell me now?" Millie asks, fetching her bag from the back seat of the car.

I grabbed Monty by the collar before he jumped into the car, he seems obsessed with cars.

He is also a good distraction from Millie's question.

I pulled Monty inside while Millie went to see Sid. I completely forgot about my phone until I was making my morning coffee and spied it sitting on the bench, still plugged into the charger. Rick had turned it off last night and it's now 10 am.

Okay more like 10.45 am, I mean what if I missed calls from wedding clients?

I switched the phone on and poured the water into my coffee, enjoying the aroma as the steam rises.

My stomach seems to be tied in a knot today, not sure if it's nerves or excitement.

My phone starts to beep, so I go to fetch it off the charger. I hope it's another wedding client, especially since I have a wedding of my own to pay for now.

Oh god, now my phone is beeping out of control. It seems I have eight missed calls from the same number that Larry called me from last night.

So it wasn't an illusion after all! Right I'll get him back.

Pressing voice call, I wait until the number connects. When it does, a recorded voice appears, telling me that this number is not in use.

Okay he must have stolen a phone, I mean it cannot be out of use, the evidence is on my phone.

I'm going to show Rick.

I looked up in time to see Sid bolting out the back door.

Ha, ha, he must be in trouble.

"Lisa!" Millie's angry voice rings out from the bedroom almost causing me to spill my coffee.

"What the fuck happened to the mattress!"

Later at BBQ

The sausages are cooking and everyone's in relaxation mode.

Except Sid, Matt and Monty who are sitting well away from Millie.

I cannot believe Sid told Millie I was responsible for Matt and his little fiasco over the mattress.

 I told Millie that it wasn't my fault Sid got hurt when Matt tried to claim the mattress back and Millie responded by narrowing her eyes and asking 'what do I mean Sid got hurt', so I told her it was best I stay out of it.

But all is good now as Sid has promised Millie he will sort out a new one.

Apparently he has one week.

Millie also asked me what the hell I was doing in the paper.

God she's not even home for one day and already she's putting everyone on edge.

Rick is so thoughtful, as he bought everything for the BBQ lunch including salads so I didn't have to make anything. I want this announcement to be perfect so I have been practising how I'm going to do it. Just after we finish eating and everyone is still together, I'm going to slip on my ring and then Rick will take my hand and tap his wine glass (well, beer bottle) so it makes that ding sound to get everyone's attention. Then he'll say we have an announcement to make and blah, blah. Then after he tells everyone and they clap and cheer and tell us how happy they are for us, we'll go and grab the bottle of bubbly that Rick picked up while buying sausages which is chilling nicely in the fridge.

He's so thoughtful.

I'm very surprised Millie hasn't spied it in the fridge yet.

If fact, she has been very tired and looking very pale since she's been home.

Definitely must have had a hard week.

Mrs Crankshaw and Neroli are frantically knitting wares for the stall. Well, Neroli is crocheting something and Mrs Crankshaw is knitting.

I'm not going to ask what they are making, they will only encourage me to make something ghastly. I managed to pull Neroli aside when her and Matt

First arrived and said I wanted to take her to see a 'special' venue but not to tell Matt as I want it to be a surprise for him and I want her approval first. She agreed not to tell Matt. Neroli's not always in the land of reality but since she kept her last pregnancy a secret until she gave birth, I know she's good at keeping her mouth shut.

Baby Bailey's asleep in the pram beside Neroli.

No sign of Tom, that's a worry.

I'm getting nervous about announcing the engagement but I think that's due to the fact that Rick has just told me he wants to wait until Daniel gets here as he was going to ask him to be his best man. And I'm worried that Daniel is going to let slip about the church, I wouldn't put it past him to do it on purpose, he's so obnoxious that way.

I'd better go check my make-up to make sure I'm looking the part, as I'm sure Mrs Crankshaw and Millie will want to take an engagement picture.

Which is great because then I can upload it to Facebook.

Rick has almost finished cooking lunch and there's still no sign of Daniel. I wish he would hurry up as I have my engagement announcement all planned to coincide with the last sausage eaten.

I went to go and freshen up, then was helping with the food when Tom comes running out in an old hessian sack.

Did I mention Tom is into *Lord Of The Rings* now, since Sid loaned him his trilogy DVD box set.

"*Precious,*" he mimicked that bald elf thing from the movie, holding up something shiny.

Oh shit, that looks like my ring, he must have found it in my bedroom.

"What have you got there Tom?" Mrs Crankshaw asked, taking the ring from the tip of his pretend sword before I had a chance to intercept him.

She studied the ring for a moment and I look to Rick for support, but he's too busy talking to Max to notice.

"This looks like Grandma Crankshaw's ring, where did you get this from?" she asks Tom.

"Ohhh, it's nice," Millie comments taking it from her for a closer look.

"I got it from Lisa's room," Tom said with a proud look upon his face before I can offer an explanation.

Everyone, including Sid and Matt, went silent and all eyes turn to me.

"Lisa?" Mrs Crankshaw asks, puzzled.

"Um… Rick?" I squawked.

Thirty minutes later

Okay so that was a fizzer.

We are all sitting around the table now and the excitement of the engagement announcement is over with. Don't get me wrong, everyone is so happy for us, Millie especially, as she said this is the most grown up thing I have done, ever, but I guess it wasn't how I planned my announcement to be.

After Tom had brought the ring out and Mrs Crankshaw recognised it, I looked again to Rick, who had finished talking to Max and abandoned his station at the BBQ to go and greet Daniel who had just arrived.

So I said nothing while everyone sat there and continued to stare at me, waiting for me to say something, until Millie who had a hold of the ring, suddenly gasped when she realised what the ring was for and announced to everyone that I am engaged. So when Rick and Daniel returned to the BBQ, Mrs Crankshaw already had the bottle of bubbly opened and handed a bamboozled looking Rick a glass of bubbly and congratulated him.

Luckily I managed to quickly explain that for once it wasn't my indiscretion that spilled the beans but one of a five year old child who odds are, will be very lucky to make it to his sixth birthday.

So Rick's cool with it.

Now we are all sitting eating and Daniel hasn't really said much, he shook Rick's hand but doesn't seen overly keen about being best man, even though he said he 'would be honoured' when Rick asked him.

Rick looks happy and Mrs Crankshaw almost cried through lunch saying that it was so beautiful how she had set me up with Jake, but it turned out it was his twin brother I fell for.

But I think she's been a bit too hard on the bubbly so that may explain some of it, not to mention she reads too many romance novels.

And of course everyone is asking us when the date is and blah, blah, Rick said that he would like to get married in the spring, which is a few months after Matt and Neroli's wedding, so that will fit in perfectly as I should know by then if the haunted church is jinxed or not.

Speaking of the church, everyone is scattered into their groups and with Rick gone off to construct Tom a *Lord of the Rings* replica ring out of a beer tab, it gave me the perfect opportunity to ask Daniel about the key to the church.

Spying Daniel heading off towards the kitchen to get another beer, I followed him like I was on secret squirrel business.

"Um, did you bring the key?" I asked.

"Yep," he said in his obnoxious tone, grabbing a beer from the fridge.

"Great."

Daniel twisted the cap of his beer and took a swig, observing me standing there with my hand outstretched.

"So, how is the wedding business going?" he asked.

Oh my god, does Daniel want to have a conversation with

me?

Okay his question sounded very patronising but all the same its progress.

"Going well," I said, "need more clients but I just want to see how I go with my first wedding before I really get aggressive with advertising and all, you know, get a feel for the ropes first."

Well that's what I told Mum the other day when she asked if I have had any more response from potential clients, to stop her from tuttering at me.

Daniel looks like he hasn't taken in a thing I said.

"So may I have the key to look at the church?" I asked.

"Sure," he said placing his beer on the kitchen top and reaching into his pocket pulling out a set of keys, "and I'll put an order in for a banner, I just need recent photos of the bride and groom."

"Pardon me?" I quizzed.

He pulls a brochure from his other pocket that shows a photo of a huge banner that is displayed across a church step. The banner says 'Welcome to the wedding of..' blah, blah, and a photo-shop picture of a bride and groom.

It's just a paper flyer with no company logo, just the name of the product.

"No I don't think so," I said politely, handing him back the brochure.

"Suit yourself," he said putting the key back into his pocket.

What the…

"Hang on!" I said as he goes to walk off, "are you saying that if I don't order this stupid banner you won't give me the key to the church?"

"Do you think the banner is stupid?" he asks.

"Yes!"

I don't really, I think it's a brilliant idea but I'm not telling him that.

Daniel shrugs like he doesn't care and goes to move off.

"Okay, okay," I scoffed, "I'll have to run this past my clients first as they are on a tight budget, I can't just be ordering them stuff, so give me the brochure."

"Its $150, I'm sure you can work it in to a budget," Daniel said.

Clearly he is not going to back down.

And neither am I, I mean who does he think he is? He can't go around waving keys to a potentially awesome wedding venue and then force people to buy stupid stuff before he hands them over. I mean what is up with that? I'm sure there are other potentially awesome wedding venues out there so he can go bonk himself.

"Not buying it," I said, standing my ground.

"Okay again, suit yourself," he said grabbing his beer from the kitchen top and moving away.

"Fine. I will suit myself," I scoffed.

"Good," he smiled as he walked away.

What a tosser. Well as I said, I'm sure there are other wedding venues out there that are way better and not haunted. And I'm going out there right now to tell him I'm not buying those stupid tee-shirts either. He can shove his haunted church, I mean no one wants to go near the place anyway so he should be thankful I even thought about it. Tosser!

Facebook Status update.

Lisa Collins. Anyone got a church?

Lisa Collins is now "officially" engaged to Rick Crankshaw.

8

On secret squirrel business with Neroli

Yes, yes, okay I gave in and now Neroli and I, along with baby Bailey, are on our way to Daniel's church.

I told a smirking Daniel when I approached him about the key, that I would not order the banner until my clients have approved the venue.

He said that's fine and what colour would I like the banner in.

I said purple.

So we pull up at the church gates and Neroli comments on the big Jacaranda tree outside and how charming the setting is.

Yes! So far, so good.

She's not even fazed about the old cemetery that's tucked away in the corner of the grounds.

Mind you, Neroli's not fazed by much.

But no time to take in the scenery, as I'm dying to see the inside.

Collecting baby Bailey from her car seat we make our way toward the entrance and I can barely contain myself. We pause at the church steps so Neroli can take in the views. "It's got such a nice feel to it," Neroli said.

"Hasn't it," I said feeling very pleased with myself.

I go to slip the key into the padlock on the door and the lock falls open.

Grrr, typical, all that effort to get the key and it wasn't even locked properly.

The door was surprisingly heavy considering its light appearance and I can smell the emptiness as soon as we step inside.

Tears are welling up in my eyes as it is every bit as charming as I imagined it to be, with its stained arched windows and timber floors. But the biggest surprise is that it has a mezzanine floor with a beautiful stained window in the background of Noah's Ark.

Considering the whole wedding theme is going to be based around animals, how perfect is that.

It's obvious it's meant to be.

"Oh my god Neroli," I gasp clutching her arm, "imagine the congregation sitting down here looking up at you and Matt throughout the service."

Oh how perfect is this.

Neroli shared my enthusiasm by saying she can just picture it now.

The church is a bit dusty, which is to be expected, most of the pews are gone and the bird's nests definitely need to go. But that's minor stuff and I feel I have stumbled on to a potential goldmine for a wedding venue.

Ha! That will shut Mum and Dad up, not to mention Millie and Daniel, when this old church is pumping out one wedding a week.

That's if I don't go broke in the process, having to give in to Daniel's bribes of buying shit just to use his building.

Tosser.

The church does seem to have a nice feel to it, I don't know what freaked Rick and Matt out and has them saying it's haunted. If it was haunted, wouldn't it have a cold and freaky feeling to it?

Better ask Neroli.

"So what do you think so far?" I asked her with bated breath.

Neroli nodded, "it's really nice," she said in her daydream voice.

Okay that's not enough to convince Matt, I'll try again.

"Do you think Matt would like it?" I asked.

"Um, yeah I think so," she said again in that irritating dreamy voice.

"On a scale of one to ten?" I plugged again.

"I can smell lard," Neroli piped up, crinkling her nose.

Ha! That's more evidence that she's indeed pregnant.

Actually I can smell lard too.

But she is changing the subject.

"Neroli, do you like the church?" I asked her in my stern voice.

"Oh yes!" she said, a bit too enthusiastically.

Hmm, I think she's lying.

God that lard smell is getting stronger.

"I think its Bailey," she said reading my thoughts and putting her nose up to Bailey's nappy area. "I think she may need changing."

"Well while you're doing that I'll go check out the upstairs area," I said.

My hopes are pinned on the area upstairs as the final clincher that will seal the deal with Neroli so she can put up a good argument when it comes to telling Matt.

Neroli disappeared out to the car to change Bailey and I made my way towards the stairs.

There is a staircase at either end of the mezzanine floor which is so cool, as I can just see the wedding party going down one side and Matt and Neroli the other.

I cannot fathom why Rick and Matt believe this place is haunted. It doesn't feel like anything bad happened here at all, if it had then it would have an angry feel to it you would think.

My footsteps click along the bare floorboards, echoing though the building as I make my way towards the stairwell. The smell of lard is getting stronger.

Wait, now I can smell bacon.

Suddenly I'm not feeling very relaxed at all, in fact an eerie feeling is coming across me and my skin has gone all goosepimply.

A loud clanging noise from upstairs echoes through the church.

I let out an involuntarily scream.

Okay, I'm paranoid with fear, it could just be a rat.

Yes that's it.

Doesn't explain the lard smell though.

Spying a broken piece of timber that looks like it came from a podium, I grab it and make my way up the creaky stairs.

It flittered through my mind that I should wait for Neroli, but I need to know it is just a rat and not an angry ghost. Rats can be removed with rat bait but if it is a supernatural being then I'm going to need something a bit stronger. I don't want to freak Neroli out and have her tell Matt I tried to talk her into getting married in a poltergeist infested church.

I reached the top of the stairs, which was a miracle in itself considering my legs were shaking so much, but all the same I was impressed that the stairs seem to be in great condition, I poised to listen again. The smell of bacon was now so strong and if I'm not mistaken I can hear it cooking, it seems to becoming from behind a petitioned off room.

Now I can hear something moving.

My fear is gone and is replaced by curiosity.

I mean ghosts or rats don't cook up a feed of bacon.

I think Daniel may have a squatter.

What is it about this town and squatters?

It's a good thing I'm experienced with strangers living in secret places.

Not thinking of murderers, squatters or rats, I leaned towards the makeshift wall and put my ear closer.

"BOO!!" said a head that appeared from around the side of the wall, causing me to scream again.

"Larry?"

Larry starts laughing as I put my hand to my chest to feel if my heart is still beating.

Should have known.

"Lisa?" Neroli's concerned voice appears from below.

"Stay there," I hissed quietly at Larry.

"Up here," I call to Neroli in my 'everything's fine and dandy' voice.

"Did you just scream?"

"Um yeah, just um, stubbed my toe."

I can see Larry out the corner of my eye laughing. I gave him a warning look.

"I'm coming up," Neroli said, unaware there is a homeless man cooking bacon up here.

Okay, thinking quick, should I tell Neroli there is a homeless man here?

I'm going with no. Not that I think it would put Neroli off or scare her, it's because Larry has his fingers to his lips willing me to be quiet.

Although it might explain why people think this church is haunted.

It would be good to be able to explain to Matt, when the time comes to tell him about the church, that it's indeed not haunted, it's just Larry. And all that other superstitious stuff about people dying and marriages ending is all down to bad health and not enough romance.

I mean it's Larry that's doing the illegal thing here that's why he's insisting I zip my mouth, well that's the gesture he is giving me now.

So now I'm going with yes.

"Ohh, this is nice," Neroli said as she made her way up the staircase taking in the view as she climbed higher.

I shot Larry a glance but it seems he has disappeared back behind the wall.

"Yes, can you imagine walking up those stairs in a wedding dress?" I said, running with her enthusiasm.

We both pause for a moment, taking in the floor below.

I think I have Neroli hooked.

"What is that smell?" she asks again, "it smells like pork."

"Shhhh," I said putting my fingers to my lips. "There's a homeless man behind the wall," I mouthed to her, pointing to the petition.

Neroli looks puzzled.

I leaned in closer to whisper.

"There is a homeless man squatting behind that wall, don't worry he's harmless, he's cooking bacon I think."

Neroli gasps quietly and puts her hand over her mouth. "Behind there?" she whispers back, pointing to the wall.

"Yes, but its okay," I reassured her after a look of horror crosses her face, "I know him, he's harmless."

Neroli is not looking convinced so she started to descend the staircase again, carefully negotiating her balance with Bailey on her hip but trying to gain enough speed to get out of here.

"So what do you think?" I asked her once we were downstairs.

"About?"

"About getting married here," I scoffed. "Jeez Neroli it's only been the subject since we got here."

"Um, I don't think so," she said in her coy way, "not with people living here."

Oh for gods sake.

"It's just Larry," I scoffed at her, "and technically he's not 'living' here, he's squatting, you know the same thing that Rick was doing in my ceiling for all those months."

Okay Neroli's look tells me that didn't help.

"Come and meet him," I said gesturing for her to climb the stairs again, "then you will see that it's just Larry, you know who I'm talking about? The guy that hangs out down the main street of town, the one everyone knows, he's harmless."

Neroli gingerly climbs the stairs again with me behind and then hands Bailey over to me.

"Larry!" I called to him, "come and met Neroli."

No response.

"Larry?"

Rolling my eyes in the air and informing Neroli that he is always doing this, I knock carefully on the petitioned wall as Neroli got her brave on and poked her head around the side of the wall.

"Where is he?" Neroli asks.

What the?

He's not here. There's nothing here but an old broom and a dusty floor.

"Well he was a minute ago," I said.

Bloody Larry, I'm sure he was Houdini's sidekick in a previous life.

"I thought you said he was cooking?" Neroli asks, "is there a kitchen somewhere?"

"Um well, I don't know if he was cooking, it smelt like he was cooking bacon."

"Are you sure you saw him?" Neroli asks, like I'm going crazy, and believe me that's a huge insult given that Neroli is well, a mystery herself.

"Yes of course I did!" I scoffed at her, "I wouldn't just make it up."

"Okay," said Neroli in a backing down manner she does when someone is confronting her.

"He must have gone outside," she said offering an explanation so I wouldn't press the issue with her.

I hand Bailey back to her.

Bloody Larry, wait until I see him.

"Anyway, so what do you think?" I pressed again. "Wedding venue or not?" I asked nonchalantly, hoping reverse psychology will convince her.

Please, please, please.

Neroli looked around again and then nodded, "yep, I think so, once it's cleaned up. I'll have to bring Matt to have a look."

"Of course," I said, with all hope revived in me.

We make our way out of the church pausing again to take in the views from the front step.

It's so perfect and who cares if Larry is living here, the wedding is only for one day.

I go to shut the padlock on the door and stopped, will Larry be able to get out, has he got his own key?

Do I need to inform Daniel that Larry is here, I mean what if there is a fire?

Well I'll just leave the lock exactly the way I found it, I mean it's not my responsibility.

I glanced over towards the Jacaranda tree while trying to figure out my small dilemma when I spied Larry in the distance, behind the old cemetery, waving at me.

There must be another door that he slipped out from. I'm locking this one then.

Gesturing to him that I have locked the door by holding up the key I glanced back at Neroli who was too busy strapping Bailey in her car seat to notice Larry.

Oh he's walking off in the other direction, not that I'm going to offer him a ride to town anyway, not after his stalking phone calls the other night. I didn't get around to letting him know that it's not on.

I should let Daniel know he is here, safety and all that.

And Daniel might just appreciate me looking out for the place, I mean, it's obvious Daniel hasn't been here for a while.

I may even suggest to him that he let Larry stay here for free, in exchange for him maintaining the place.

Yes, perfect solution and it's helping the less fortunate.

But I can't be solving all the world's problems, I have to go home and work on Matt. I just hope Neroli steps up her game, her enthusiasm about this wedding matches that of a dehydrated worm.

Meeting with Matt and Neroli to discuss church

Not going well.

Matt is being a total twat about it all saying that I'm a total control freak and this is his wedding and he is not getting married in a haunted church and how dare I take Neroli to the church knowing that she's a chick and chicks love that old building shit and now has her mind set on it.

I have to say I'm very proud of Neroli, she didn't sound too enthusiastic but she did take a stand and told Matt she wants to get married at the old church because it's pretty and has a lovely romantic vibe to it.

Okay, I told Matt that it was pretty and had a romantic vibe to it on Neroli's behalf, but Neroli was beside me when I told him and she agreed in a stern kinda tone and then when Matt asked her again, she said she has made up her mind and she wants to get married there.

So proud of her.

"But its fucken haunted," Matt whinged again, "and what about all the people who got married there in the past, explain their fate!"

"No, that's just Larry," I said with no hint of concern to my voice, "you know, the homeless guy that hangs around town, we caught him squatting there. He's harmless and I reckon it's been him there all along just trying to scare people so they don't kick him out."

"Larry?" Matt looked puzzled.

"Yes Larry, you know?"

Matt looks to Neroli for confirmation.

Neroli nodded.

"And besides," I continued, "you cannot blame a building for the breakdown of people's marriages. There's no such thing as jinxed," I scoffed.

"What do you mean? Is the place jinxed?" Neroli said sounding concerned.

Oh great!

"Pff, of course not," I said, reassuring Neroli.

"Hang on, so you're telling me you saw Larry, the homeless dude?" said Matt, still on that subject.

"Yeah."

He looks to Neroli again for confirmation

God, talk about déjà vu.

Neroli nodded again.

Matt hasn't said anything for 30 seconds.

Rick enters the office with my cup of tea that he insists on bringing me, honestly since we got engaged he's been all over me.

Not that I'm complaining but sometimes it's a bit much.

"So what's going on?" he asks.

"Well your mrs took my mrs to Daniel's old church and now they're telling me they saw old Larry there," said Matt.

"Daniel's church?" repeated Rick, "I thought we told you it was jinxed."

Neroli's gone pale again.

"It's not jinxed!" I scoffed, "it's charming and romantic and in a lovely location."

"Go on, tell him the bit about Larry," Matt pressed.

"Larry?" Rick said again in a dry but alarmed tone.

"Yeah, me and Neroli saw him, he's squatting there."

"Cooking bacon," Neroli piped up.

Rick and Matt are looking at Neroli and I like we just smuggled heroin into baby formula, a look of total horror.

"And you should see the church," I continued, ignoring their look. "It has a timber mezzanine floor and lovely arched windows and even a stained glass portrait of Noah's

Ark," I beamed.

Not that I think Matt will give a toss over a portrait of Noah's Ark but I'm trying to set the scene here.

"Lisa, I don't give a toss about a window with some dude's boat painted on it," Matt said, "you're telling me straight up that you saw old Larry at the church?"

Oh for god's sake, this subject again?

"Yeah."

"And he was cooking bacon," Neroli's quiet voice pipes up again.

"What did he look like then?" Matt asks again like he's trying to prove us wrong.

"You know Larry, beefy fingers, missing teeth, smelly clothes, wears leather shoes and that old brown shirt, usually seen in the doorway of Daniel's proposed office."

Matt turns to Neroli.

"And you're telling me that you saw him too?"

"Um well not exactly saw him," Neroli said, "but Lisa said she did and he was cooking bacon."

"Well not exactly *cooking bacon*," I added, "but it did smell like bacon, aye Neroli?"

"Yep," Neroli nodded enthusiastically.

Why has Rick suddenly sat down and buried his head in his hands?

Oh god, now Daniel's here. I've gone all goosepimply again, weird.

Well it's all out in the open now so I may as well tell him about Larry. Ohhh then we can negotiate a venue fee while Matt and Neroli are here and get permission to start cleaning up the place. Perfect.

"Are you on fucken drugs?" Matt snapped.

Rick gets up out of the chair gesturing to Matt to calm down.

"Lisa, honey," he starts in a soothing voice, "you can't have seen old Larry it must have been someone else."

God I'm getting really annoyed over the subject of Larry.

"Old Larry?" Daniel asks puzzled, as he suddenly caught up on the conversation.

"Yes," I sighed, turning to Daniel, "sorry to tell you this but Neroli and I caught him squatting in your church, I don't know how he got in but I did lock the door behind us and Larry was walking back towards town when we left and..."

"Can't have been Larry," Daniel scoffed in an almost hysterical tone.

"Neroli didn't fucken see him," Matt starts again, "you're the only one here who said he was there."

Rick again gestures to Matt to calm down.

"Lisa, did you see a man at Daniel's church?" Rick asks.

"Yes of course I did."

"Neroli did you see anyone?"

"Um, no," she squawked.

"Okay then," said Rick. "Lisa you may have seen someone but it wasn't Larry, Daniel and I will check it out."

"Oh for gods sake, I know Larry when I see him," I said with more than a hint of frustration, "I know it's him because I've being seeing him everywhere lately, when we were ring shopping, the other night at the CWA meeting and even outside the crystal shop when we had meditation and remember Rick he even called me the other night. I think he's got some sort of fascination with me because I had my photo in the paper.... what?"

Rick, Daniel and Matt look pale and Daniel has a half amused expression on his face as he exits my office.

"You can't have seen Larry 'cos Larry is fucken dead that's what!" said Matt.

9

Impossible.

Larry can't be dead, he's as alive and real as Millie, whose bold presence has now joined us in my office like it's another intervention.

It also doesn't help that Daniel has returned to the room, as my stomach is strangely churning now.

"Lisa has everything been okay with you lately?" asked Millie.

"Not under any pressure or stress?" Rick asks.

Grrrr, they all are looking at me like I've joined a bowl of fruit loops.

"No, I'm fine and I'm telling you Larry is not dead because I have seen him on a number of occasions. He's even spoken to me, remember Neroli when he came up to me in the street that day I got my photo in the paper?"

Neroli looks at me like a possum caught in headlights.

"Oh never mind," I growled.

"What did he say to you?" Millie said in a soothing but very patronising tone.

Oh god even Millie thinks I have lost it, which means she will find another support group to drag me off to. Instead of *'Impulse Behaviour Group'* it will be the *'Seeing Invisible Homeless Men Group'*.

"I can't remember exactly," I said, "besides he mumbles, something about listening, anyway that's besides the point, Larry is not dead."

"Lisa," Rick starts as he looks at everyone else for support before taking me by the hand. "Larry's a bit of a legend around here according to the stories my mum had told me. He was a local, around my parents' age, who was born and raised here, he had a bad horse riding accident as a young adult, which left him slightly brain damaged. He became an alcoholic Mum said and I'm not sure on the rest, she was always a bit vague about it, apart from he's been dead for decades."

Daniel looked like he was going to add something, then stopped and just nodded in agreement.

"Told ya," Matt piped up as he amused himself by dismantling my stapler.

I pause to absorb this information. I had never seen Larry with a bottle in his hand and it appeared he was never in an intoxicated state when I saw him. Nuts yes, but never drunk.

He is real and I think Rick, Daniel and Matt must be talking about a different guy.

I mean there is more then one colourful local in these parts. Looking at the faces around me tells me I'm not going to convince them otherwise. Which means I'm going to have to find Larry or whoever he is and prove to them that I'm not crazy and he is real.

So I'd better play their game.

"Pff, must have been seeing things," I said in my 'silly me' voice. "Never mind, think I need a good nights sleep. Now Neroli, Matt, since Daniel is here what do you think about getting married in the old church?"

God there goes my stomach again.

"Are you sure you are okay?" Rick asks again. "Maybe this wedding business is putting you under a bit of strain, lots has been happening, maybe you just need some time out."

No, I need Matt to agree about the church.

"Yes, yes," I scoffed, "but I'll rest when Matt agrees to a wedding venue. Matt?"

"I told you I'm not fucken getting married there, it's jinxed. No offence mate." Matt said, addressing Daniel.

"None taken," Daniel said.

"God Matt will you just get over it, you're being selfish,

Neroli like's the place so give it a chance."

Ha, that shut him up.

"Well Matt," Millie piped up getting ready to leave, "no harm in looking before you judge, I'm bored and tired, wake me at dinner."

"Yeah, I'm off as well," Daniel said following Millie's lead, "keep the key for now until you've made up your mind. If it's a yes then I'll go ahead and order the personalised key rings."

Key rings, what the hell?

"I'll see you out," said Rick as one by one they exit my office including Neroli as she went to check on Bailey and Tom leaving me with Matt.

"Still not fucken doing it," Matt said when the last person left.

Right that's it, drastic measures needed.

In car on way back to the church with Neroli and Matt

Too easy.

Matt agreed after short, lively discussion that yes, he will just 'take a look' at the church and his mother will never receive the 'anonymous' letter of how her lovely son laced her prize banana bread with an illegal substance at the 37th annual culinary contest 2 years ago causing her to win first prize (information supplied by Debbie from the rest home, love Debbie, best boss ever).

If he still doesn't like it and can give a good, valid reason why, that doesn't include superstitious nonsense, then it's agreed and signed for in writing that the subject will be dropped and Matt will get married where ever he fucken well chooses to.

We got Neroli to witness it.

So we arrive at the church and Neroli and Matt go in first as I wait outside with baby Bailey snuggled in her pram. Another agreement between Matt and I, that I'm to stay outside due to him calling me a control freak. I can't hear what they are saying so I'm putting all my faith in the gods that they will shine a light on the church and convince Matt that this abandoned church needs to be revived.

Oh my god, just had a thought, why haven't I called on the universe to convince Matt,

I mean according to the book that Sid gave me about manifesting stuff, it says that you have to ask and believe it will happen.

And I believe Matt and Neroli will get married here.

Where's my list to the universe, I should add it to that.

I scrounge around in my bag and retrieve my wallet that has the list in it. Fishing for my pen I smooth out the piece of paper to add to it.

Dear universe.

Here is the list of things I want. Hope you can help.

- Rick to always be at my side and treat me like a queen.

- Rick and I to get married and have two – no – three children all with Rick's dark complexion.

- To run a successful wedding planning business.

- A petting zoo filled with white animals (no roosters).

- A new car, prefer a small car that has blue tooth and is environmentally friendly (that's one for you).

- To lose ten kilos, especially around my inner thighs and my lower abdomen.

- And could you arrange the above four requests before 20th May?

- For Matt and Neroli to get married at the old church located at Cannon's Road, Taromeo, Post Code 2432.

Well, I want to make it clear.

There, that ought to do it.

Putting my list back into my purse I glance over the top of the pram to check that Bailey is still asleep. I wonder how Neroli and Matt are going, they are taking an awfully long time.

I glance off in the distance at the cattle grazing peacefully in the field next door. My gaze is fixed on the scene when all of a sudden Larry appears right in my line of vision.

"Boo!"

And again I let out an involuntary scream.

Having wayyy to many déjà vu moments over this.

"Where did you come from?" I hissed, "do you know how much trouble you are causing me, everyone is telling me you're dead."

Larry shrugs like it's no concern that everyone thinks he is dead.

And the freaky thing is now he's standing so close I can smell his breath, there's no mistaking that his name is indeed Larry, it's embroidered onto his jacket.

Hmm maybe I need to coax Larry into the church so Matt and Neroli can see he is real and it isn't a case of mistaken identity. Maybe it was another simple man called Larry that became an alcoholic and died.

I make my way up the concrete steps to the entrance followed by Larry.

I can hear Matt's footsteps.

"You're friend in there, don't like it," Larry said in his mumbling tone.

"Yes Larry I know he's in there, they are just having a look as they are getting married soon and want to get married here."

"Don't like it," Larry repeated.

"Yes well, we are leaving soon," I said.

I really, really want to reach out and pinch Larry to make sure he's real, I mean, he certainly smells real, but he might take offence if I pinch him.

"Nah, don't like it," Larry says again, like I'm just not getting him.

Matt abruptly makes his appearance slamming the door into Larry as he pushes it open.

"Nah, don't like it!" Matt announces.

I watch in horror as Larry falls over the side of the railing from the impact of the heavy door.

"Matt, what the hell," I growled as I descended the steps to go to Larry's aid. I mean the poor bugger hasn't much teeth left as it is.

"What?" Matt said, "I don't like it."

"No, not that you twat, did you not see..."

Hang on, where is Larry?

He's not lying on the ground in pain like I expected.

"See what?" Matt asked impatiently.

All of a sudden I feel like I have left my own body and my vision goes kinda blurry at the realisation that Larry is now in the old cemetery playing leap frog over the headstones. No-one can get up after being slammed with a heavy door and fall from eight steps high to a concrete pad below and still get up and jump over headstones that quick unless.....
Unless they are a ghost.

"Matt," I squawked, trying not to throw up, "please look towards the cemetery and tell me what you see."

"The dead centre of town," he chuckled.

"Seriously."

"A bunch of fucken old headstones, why?"

"No-one strange?" I pressed.

"Not in that direction," he said.

Okay, going to throw up now.

In doctors office

Bloody Matt. He told Rick that I seriously need help after I threw up and almost blacked out. And when I came right and Matt asked me what brought the panic attack on, I just had to open my big mouth and say Larry.

So now I'm lying on the doctor's couch after he has done a blood test, eye test and that test where they bang your knees with a hammer.

Matt's so overreacting.

I can hear Millie and Rick talking outside the door and I bet you it's about me, it's so unfair.

I don't know what to think about Larry, I know I'm not going crazy and I know what I saw.

I have heard about people claiming they see ghosts and strange lights, then they learn that they have a brain tumour or something that offers an explanation.

But none of that stuff ever happens to me.

And if Larry is a ghost then why does he smell so bad and smoke cigarettes and have his name embroidered into his old, crusty jacket?

I mean ghosts and spirits are normally covered in white light and float.

Larry does cartwheels and pole dances.

Pole dances! That's it, I've got it. The couple from the cafe, they saw Larry, they must have, they certainly looked in his direction.

And Tim the baker, the night of meditation he said that I must have seen old Larry, as he is always hanging around.

Even Neroli said she could smell lard when we visited the church, that must mean he is alive.

Which means I no longer need to be on this doctors' bed. I'm going to suggest that Matt gets *his* eyes tested. The door opens and the doctor enters the room again along with Rick and Millie.

"Right, now I've just sent your bloods off, so we'll see in a couple of days if there's anything in your system that is causing you to hallucinate, as you're currently not taking any drugs or prescription meds.

So all I can suggest is that you have put yourself under a great deal of stress and I advise that maybe a holiday or some time away from your daily activities would be helpful."

"Sounds like a plan," Rick said.

"Hello! I have a wedding to plan," I scoffed, "I can't just be taking time out and besides I cope fine, I do meditation."

"Lisa, you have plenty of time to plan Matt's wedding," Rick said, "Matt even said himself before, that his mum can help out if you need a break. You have taken on too much at the same time."

"Pff, don't worry about that, that's the story of her life," Millie scoffed.

"Rick, I fail to see how Matt's mum can help, given the fact she is in a hospital ward and currently mentally unstable,"

I said in my hoity voice.

"… and you're not?" Millie joked.

Well, I think Millie was joking.

"Pamela has been given the all clear, she comes home next week," Rick said matter of factly. "Matt's already spoken to her and she is happy to help, just give her something to do. So how about I arrange a small break, just us?"

Now I seriously do need to see a doctor, Pamela, my mortal enemy, back out in the world and happy to help with the wedding plans.

Okay it's her son that is getting married and she is paying for it, but there is no way I will let her even close to anything that involves wedding planning or sharp objects.

The doctor is now writing me a referral for some counselling and I can see where this is going, Rick thinks I'm stressed and have imaginary friends and Matt thinks I'm nuts.

I'm not worried about Millie because I overheard her telling Rick that this is normal for me.

Slightly offended though.

So to get out of this and to stop Rick whisking me off for a romantic holiday so Pamela can stage a coup on my wedding business, I need to prove that I'm on top of things, mentally stable, that Larry is indeed real, and that I'm in total control of my actions.

It's the situation that's a little out of hand at the moment.

Back home

Matt and Neroli are there so I ask Matt to give me a valid reason as stated in our written agreement why he didn't like the church as a wedding venue.

"Because you went all freaky on us," Matt said in his sarcastic, youthful twat tone, "which means it is jinxed."

"I had a 'moment' Matt, happens to everyone, doesn't mean the church is jinxed, I mean Neroli has them all the time."

Okay that didn't go down well, but I asked Neroli again if she wanted to get married there and she said yes so Matt just has to suck it up and because I have already put it on my list to the universe, it's going to happen anyway, with or without his blessing.

It also dawned on me when the doctor handed me the referral for counselling that the couple at the cafe were also councillors which is perfect.

I showed Rick the business card to prove to him that I am indeed on top of things and can recognise my own symptoms. I told him I shall make an appointment with this *Wayne Blythe Psychiatrist* and not the one the doctor referred me to. Rick said whatever I'm comfortable with. He doesn't have to know that the only reason I want to see this couple is so that they can confirm to me that they saw Larry that day and I'm not hallucinating after all.

Also I need to see Tim so he too can confirm that Larry is real.

Millie's coming down with a flu bug as she's been throwing up on and off today which is great because I told Rick that I must have the same bug and that's what caused me to throw up at the church.

Rick said that could be a possibility which means I'm half way towards convincing him I'm not crazy or under stress and that there is no need for a holiday.

So I need to get on and plan this wedding.

Matt and Neroli have left and I've managed to go along with Matt's demands about getting married in the big church in town but really I'm making the plans around Daniel's church. That way, by the time I convince Matt he will be getting married there, the church will be all finished and looking fabulous.

So now I better get on with it.

Now I have to call Daniel and negotiate a venue fee.

I shall do that right after the knot that has suddenly appeared in my stomach has gone.

Monty came in to the office. As I gave him a pat, I thought about what a good dog he's been. And he's been staying right away from Millie the dog hater.

Well he is now, after she came out of the shower wrapped up in a towel and Monty started pulling at her towel trying to get it off her.

He has been doing that a lot lately.

Anyway, I'm not sure what happened next but Monty seemed to scurry out of the bathroom very fast and hid under the bed, he hasn't been near Millie since.

Mind you, the mood swings that Millie has been having these days, I don't blame him.

Working full time is really taking its toll on her I think.

Anyway no time to dwell on Millie's moods.

3 hours later

My god I'm so fantastic.

Not only have I managed to arrange flowers, marquees for the reception and order a cake,

I have also brought 3 little white guinea pigs with a tiny bit of grey on them and a lamb.

And because they're local, I have sent Rick off to collect them.

Rick's not complaining about it either. He has been brilliant and asking me every half hour if I would like another drink, or pillow, or is the temperature okay.

Acting like you're crazy actually has its advantages.

I can't do much else however as I need the catering numbers from Matt and due to his psycho mother being released from hospital next week, Matt said she will have an opinion so we can go ahead and send out invitations after that. And Neroli and I are going dress shopping in the city next week.

I think it's a bit too soon, you know with her being pregnant, even though she hasn't actually come out and admitted it yet. But I guess Mrs Crankshaw is handy with the sewing machine so if we have to make alterations we can.

Oh my god I have just realised they haven't told me who is in the wedding party. I mean there has been no mention of bridesmaids from Neroli and not sure who Matt would choose for his best man. Scary thought that is.

I mean Tom can be a page-boy there's no doubt about that, actually on second thought, I can see Tom walking down the aisle with his sword poking things, hmmm I think that may be a bad idea.

Better call her.

"Neroli," I went straight to the point when her voice appeared on the phone. "Who's going to be in the wedding party?"

"Oh, okay, well there is Tom."

"Yes."

"And Bailey."

"Hmm don't know where she can fit in, but okay. And?"

"And that's it."

God Neroli's thick.

"What about best man and bridesmaids, who are they?"

"Tom and Bailey," Neroli said again like I was the one that's being thick.

Oh god, bad, bad idea.

"Neroli can you put Matt on please."

"Yo."

"Matt who is in the bridal party?"

"Tom and Bailey."

Shit!

"Matt, Bailey is 6 months old, she cannot sign the marriage licence or stand up yet, so you are just going to have to ask someone else. Tom can stand but he cannot stand still and like Bailey, is too young to sign, so anyone else in mind?"

"Well you and Rick can sign it and Bailey and Tom can be there for show."

I'm trying to picture how this would look, I'm thinking yes Bailey can be there being held by someone and Tom will have to be restrained in chains or glued to one spot, or both.

No, not going to work.

I tried to reason with Matt but would be better off banging my head against a brick wall so I'm not going to argue. He also said if I don't like his decision then he can always get his mum to organise it, so I said I will think of a way to accommodate it, I mean it's their circus so why should I care.

Rick returns with cute white animals

Monty just loves the guinea pigs, he even tried to pick one up with his mouth.

Okay on second thought maybe Monty needs to stay away.

The little lamb is so cute and is not much bigger then Monty.

Because she has been hand-reared she's so friendly, Rick suggested we put her in next to the two goats, Bonnie and Clyde

It's starting to feel like a petting zoo.

Sid wasn't happy about constructing a cage for the guinea pigs; well he didn't tell me that himself, Millie did on his behalf.

But lucky for Sid, Rick remembered he already has a big enclosure at home that'd be suitable, so him and Sid have gone to get it.

Millie has gone back to bed where she has spent most of the day so far, she is meant to be going back to work tomorrow but she still feels sick.

After settling the lamb in and getting nibbled on by Bonnie and Clyde I feel a bit smelly and need a shower.

Standing under the shower feeling the water trickle down my neck I cannot help but feel like my life is finally coming together. I mean I'm now engaged (and have an actual ring to prove it), run a successful business (well it's definitely showing potential), have celebrity status (well in the local area, but news spreads fast) and have established a petting zoo (minus an alpaca and pony but it's on the 'to get' list).

I turn off the water and wrap my towel around my body just as Monty makes his appearance and tries to grab the towel from me.

Honestly what is that about?

Shit, is that someone at the door? I can hear knocking.

Oh that's right, it might be Daniel, I had text messaged him earlier to ask him what he was going to charge me for the use of the church.

He had messaged back and said he will come around and talk to me about that. And now would be perfect as Rick is not here, Rick overheard Matt telling me that he doesn't want the church and he might start asking questions.

God there goes that knot in my stomach again.

I run from the bathroom towards the front door as I don't have a shit show of Millie getting up to answer it and I so need to talk to Daniel before Rick gets home.

I can see Daniel though the glass and it looks like he's about to walk away.

I call out to him to alert him that someone is home as I dive through the living room towards the glass door. Daniel, hearing my call, waits at the door for me to open it. I reach for the latch to unlock it just as Monty makes a grab for my towel, but it's too late, I cannot rescue the towel.

I push the door open just as Monty runs off with my towel leaving me once again standing naked in front of Daniel.

Later

Dignity restored.

After I ran back through to the bedroom with my face burning red while Monty ran off in the other direction with my towel, I gathered up enough courage to make an appearance again (with clothes on) and see if Daniel has run a mile.

Daniel's still here but hasn't looked at me once since then.

It's even more awkward when Rick returned, not because something was said, just because we are now all sitting together and every time Daniel looks at Rick I just know he is thinking 'I've seen your fiancée naked... twice'.

So embarrassing .

But what is most shocking and what I cannot get over is that Daniel has invited me to the grand opening of his shop. Okay, his eyes were looking at the ceiling when he invited me and it was such an obnoxious invite, but still. And that's not all, when I asked about the fee for the church, he didn't even try and blackmail me into buying shit, he just said not to worry about a fee and to come along to the opening of his shop.

I'm starting to think that flashing my naked body at Daniel may not be a bad thing after all.

Wonder if he has a girlfriend?

Anyway, the guinea pigs are settled in their snake-proof and Monty-proof enclosure, so we're all good to go. The geese however are not so good, due to one aggressive one. Rick has already threatened it with unspeakable things after it chased him.

Which means if I'm going to have a petting zoo, then I'll need insurance and warning signs.

Rick said why don't I just get rid of the bloody problem.

It's the first aggressive thing Rick has said to me since learning of my Larry hallucinations, things are getting back to normal.

Daniel is getting ready to leave and he has successfully avoided saying goodbye to me without Rick noticing. I cannot wait until his grand opening tomorrow, although I can imagine a photography studio wouldn't be something that would hold one's interest for long.

Millie has joined me in the kitchen still looking like death. And I have just realised that she goes back to the city again tomorrow and I haven't seen much of her.

I asked Millie how she was feeling.

"Like shit," she said reaching for some herbal tea.

I told her she looked like shit as well.

Okay, she really must be ill, she hasn't bitten back yet.

"So what's been happening since we diagnosed you as crazy at the doctors?" she asked, taking a seat at the table.

Well I didn't know where to begin, I'm so excited about the new animals but Millie doesn't seem excited about that.

I informed her that I have ordered flowers for Matt and Neroli's wedding and proceed to describe them to her but she just yawned.

I told her that Matt and Neroli liked the church and they have decided to get married there but Millie doesn't believe I have convinced Matt's young, stubborn arse.

So I told her about Daniel and Monty taking off with my towel.

Now Millie's pissing herself with laughter.

I changed the subject and told her about Daniel's grand opening tomorrow and proceeded to tell her about his obnoxious attitude towards me.

Millie stopped laughing enough to answer.

"He doesn't come across as obnoxious."

"Well not to you," I scoffed, "and every time I ask about the church he makes me buy all this merchandise in exchange for it."

"What merchandise?"

"Oh you know, key rings, tee-shirts, that kinda thing and when I first met him he didn't even tell me what he did for a living even though it's him that's taken over the new shop. It's like he took an instant dislike to me. Okay, we didn't get off on the right foot as I mistakened him for Rick and flashed my body at him but...."

"Whoa, you did what?" Millie started giggling again.

"Yes, not once but twice, by accident. I mean he must think I'm an exhibitionist, but given his profession, he should be used to that."

Millie's looking at me like she is scrutinising the situation.

"How did he react when you told him about the engagement?" Millie asked.

I have suddenly realised that he hasn't said a word to me about it, no congratulations or anything, yes he did talk to Rick but didn't seem that happy for him.

"I don't think he cares," I said to Millie, "he doesn't seem to be very keen to be Rick's best man, I mean you were there, you saw what he was like."

"I was too busy pinching myself to make sure I wasn't dreaming," said Millie through a stifled yawn. "But I think you may have a problem."

"Because....?"

"Because I think he may be a tad jealous of Rick."

"Because....?"

"Well, has he got a partner or girlfriend? He doesn't give a lot of information about himself."

"Just because he hasn't got a girlfriend doesn't mean he's jealous, god Millie, not everyone who is single is unhappy."

"I didn't mean that," Millie sighed, "I just mean if his best friends girl is flashing her naked body at him every chance she gets and he's not getting any, then yes he will be extremely frustrated. Combined with the fact that his best mate is now attached and he is not, kinda takes the fun out of it for him."

God trust Millie to make out that I do things on purpose.

"It was an accident!" I pressed again.

"So yes, be prepared for him to hate you," Millie said again through yet another stifled yawn, "anyway better get ready."

"You're not going back to work?" I asked in horror.

"Yes, why?"

"You look like shit."

"I'm fine!" she snapped, "jeez don't you start, I'm getting enough sympathy from bloody Sid."

God if Millie ever has children (which is unlikely because Millie doesn't like children), I pity them if they ever step out of line.

Day of Daniel's 'grand opening'

Okay, I'm here a bit early so am standing outside his shop waiting. He hasn't got a sign up or anything written across the front window yet, I can't see inside again, he's got a white drape across the front, like he's about to set up a window display.

I came in early because I wanted to talk to Tim across the road at his bakery shop about Larry. But due to the steady stream of customers, I have been unable to grab a moment and because of the nature of the subject, going up to the counter and asking the person behind it if the local street hobo is a ghost is not a good option. It's better if no-one is in earshot that will run back to Rick and tell him I've lost it again.

I'll catch Tim at meditation tonight anyway.

I also rung the psychiatrist couple I saw in the cafe the day Rick and I were shopping for a ring and Larry was across the street pole dancing. I left a message explaining who I was and did they recall seeing a hobo man outside the cafe pole dancing, and if so, could they contact me. They returned my message with a message saying that I need to call them and please schedule an appointment.

Pff I haven't got time for that.

Since I arrived in town today, everyone I come into contact with has been asking me if I'm the girl from the paper who saved the local politician. Jeez talk about being hassled, I now know how Liz Hurly feels.

Rick just messaged me to say he's running a little late. God now I'm starting to feel nervous.

Two ladies are pointing to me and whispering amongst themselves.

I'll save them the trouble.

"Yes," I said turning to them, "I am the girl in the paper."

"Oh, okay. Well you have a tear in the back of your skirt."

What? Shit. Bloody Monty.

The shop doors open and Daniel appears, standing aside and welcoming everyone in.

Everyone includes about five people who look like they have just come for a sticky beak.

But I guess that's what this is all about.

I waited till last hoping Rick will run in at the last second as I'm feeling a bit nervous about this. Which is weird, but I guess it's what Millie said about Daniel loathing me because I'm engaged to his best mate, or it could just be the vibes he's sending me.

"You coming in?" he asked.

"Oh yep."

The place is done out in tasteful black and white and out the back it looks like he's set up a studio for portrait taking and I have to say, it looks great. He has little platters of cheese and crackers, with tea, coffee and orange juice set up. Okay, so far I'm impressed.

One of the ladies is asking questions about the images around the walls and I have to admit they are a tiny bit amazing, he must have a little bit of a talent for photo taking, but what really caught my eye were his business cards.

Daniel Cannon Photography and Event Supplies.

Event supplies??

And there they are in a display cabinet; tee-shirts, party hats, champagne glasses. You name it, Daniel has it. Personalised merchandise for every occasion done to suit your event. It's his shit he has been blackmailing me into buying and how rude he didn't tell me.

If this camembert cheese wasn't so tasty I would walk out in a huff, I'm so offended.

I mean, way to get on the wrong side of the local event planner!

Daniel shoots a glance in my direction and looks like he is about to break the conversation he's having to come over to me.

Shit where is Rick?

Never mind, I shall be poised and mature about this.

"So, about the church?" he says when he approached with yet another brochure.

"I'm not buying any more of your crap," I said in dignified tones, "so if you don't want to let me use your crappy church then that's fine, I can use another venue." I snapped.

I really didn't mean that, so fingers crossed he doesn't take it seriously.

Oh god I should have kept shut my mouth.

"You really think the old church is crappy?" he snapped back.

"Um well no, not really," I said in my 'I don't care' voice.

"Good, I think we can work something out," he said in his smart arse voice.

God he grates me.

He moved off to address a potential customer, thrusting the brochure into my hand which I didn't look at, just stuffed into my bag. I go outside to see if I can see Rick coming.

Looking back towards the shop I cannot help but feel I have missed an opportunity, I mean event merchandising, why didn't I think of that. It would have gone nicely with my event planning and the shop is so nice and has a nice feel to it. I shouldn't have given the lease away to Daniel, I mean I can see the success just oozing from him.

Why did I let Mum, Dad and Millie talk me into not taking the shop and setting up from home.I mean if they just didn't interfere and let me get on with it, then they too would be standing here at my grand opening and admiring my shop and telling me how I'm so right and they are so wrong.

It's all Rick's fault for coming to the rescue by telling Daniel about the lease on the shop.

Looking up and down the pavement there is still no sign of Rick, but my heart stops as I can see Larry. He is across the road and is looking through the window of the bakery.

"Larry!" I called to him to get his attention so when Rick shows up he can see Larry is real and not a supernatural being.

I call out to him again and again but it appears Larry can't hear me, I'll have to shout louder.

I mean he must be deaf because everyone else in the street can hear me.

"LARRY!" I yelled louder, cupping my hands around my mouth, so my voice carries over the traffic noise. He heard me that time and has turned around and started waving to me.

"Come here!" I yelled, indicating for him to cross the street. A bus has pulled up out in front of the bakery blocking him from my sight.

"Lisa!" Rick says, startling me, "did you just say Larry?"

Shit.

"Um….." I said, trying to buy time waiting for the bus to depart to see if Larry is still there. The bus roars off and there is no sign of Larry.

Bugger.

"…..um, no I said, um, never mind."

Shit, can't think of what rhymes with Larry.

Tim appears out in front of his bakery with a puzzled look on his face as he shoots a glance in my direction and looks towards his shop window before scratching his head and going back inside.

He must have seen Larry as well.

Oh thank god Daniel has appeared because I don't like the look Rick is giving me.

"Nice shop mate," Rick complemented him as they proceed to engage in conversation.

I went to go follow them back inside when I spy Larry again, he is further up the street looking through the window of another shop.

I go to raise the attention of Daniel and Rick who are focused on some crack in the wall.

Oh bugger it, think I'll let it go. Larry's too far away anyway.

Later

I'm so bored.

Every time I go to leave, Daniel insists I stay (in an obnoxious tone) as he wants to work something out about the church. Rick didn't stay long as he had to go back to work but I'm starting to think Millie may be right about the whole hating me thing because the whole time Rick was here he didn't even look at me let alone talk to me. It was only when Rick left and I announced I was leaving, that he asked me to stay behind.

But again, the tone of his voice was arrogant and if I didn't want the church, the camembert cheese wasn't so tasty and the coffee wasn't so nice and hot, I would tell him where to go.

The shop didn't take too long to empty, well with the few that turned up it didn't take long at all.

Just to busy myself so I don't feel like a total yob standing there, I started tidying up the empty cups and discarded napkins and then suddenly it was just Daniel and I.

The lump in my stomach has come back again, probably because I don't know what kind of 'deal' he is going to make. I have to stay strong and tell him I cannot buy any more of his shit.

"You do that very well," he said as I wiped down the table, "but then girls normally are good at cleaning," he said waiting to see if I would react.

Maybe that's his attempt at humour to break the ice, it's so tense in here. Well he's not very good at it and I think I'll let that comment slide due to the awkwardness.

"So what did you want to talk to me about?" I said, surprised at the way my voice sounded very shaky.

Daniel indicated to me to take a seat, oh god, now it feels important.

"So this is your shit that I'm buying?" I started, after I sat down not knowing what to say.

"Do you think its shit?" he asked.

My face burned red.

"Okay I'll cut out the bullshit," he said sounding offended by my last comment.

God he needs to get a sense of humour.

"You can have the use of the old church for a venue for weddings or whatever as long as you use and promote my merchandise."

"...and your photography as well?"

He shrugged. "Yeah, but I'm not too worried about that, I have enough work on with photography, I mean what do you think is supporting this little sideline enterprise."

I felt like saying well if it's making enough money then why have a 'sideline enterprise'.

But didn't.

I pause to think about it, it's not a bad idea but...

"What if the customer doesn't like your merchandise?" I asked, "I mean personalised banners and key-rings to mark a special day isn't to everyone's taste."

"Well then, why don't you trial it at Matt's wedding, I'll only charge for printing and see what feedback you get," he pressed.

The nerve of him, he's going to only charge for printing, I mean what happened to testing shit for free.

But it doesn't seem a bad idea, I just have to convince Matt, and Matt is a push-over when it comes to things other than haunted churches.

And if I tell him it's Daniel's shit, then I'm sure he won't have an issue, I mean they do refer to each other as Mazza and Dazza.

"Fine," I said, "but as long as I get to put my business cards in your shop and you tell everyone about me."

"Yep seems fair," he nodded.

Oh my god I have just realised Daniel and I are having an actual conversation for the first time

Okay, spoke too soon, the awkwardness has returned.

Ohh I can see Larry again, better go catch up with him.

Meditation

"Okay everyone get comfortable and take a deep breath."

I sucked in air and tried to get in the zone after arriving late due to phoning Millie during her tea break at work. I told her about Daniel's 'agreement', Millie still sounded really tired but not too tired to snap at me again. I tried asking what was up, but she said she is fine so whatever, it's her attitude issue, I'm just going to ignore it.

Also I didn't get to catch Larry.

After running out of Daniel's shop and up the street calling out to him, trying to catch up, I was too late. He turned down another street and I lost sight of him.

Tim is sitting behind me again and the young girl that was at the last class is here sitting next to him. She even glared at me again when I arrived.

Man, what is her problem.

Unless she is jealous of my local celebrity status.

Sid's not here tonight, he has to sort out a new mattress and catch up on washing after Millie's marathon vomiting session over the weekend. He looked really sad when I drove away.

But I have to catch Tim afterwards to ask him about Larry, so it's better if Sid's not here as he has a problem with Tim.

Closing my eyes, I tried to focus on Shelley's guidance but again my head is swirling, thinking what I need to do to get the church ready for the wedding. There is lots of cleaning and I should give those steps to the entrance a bit of a paint job to spruce it up a bit, then there is seating arrangements and maybe some flower pots outside.

I wonder if Daniel can provide these ribbons that you see draped up the aisles, I forget what they are called, oh and then I have to get a microphone sorted and a podium.

Did I sort out a priest?

Shit, better get on to that.

The room is now silent apart from the odd little cough and I open my eyes again.

Oh my god Larry is outside the shop again. Right, this time I'll catch him.

I rose quickly, and Shelley, noticing a shift in the room, opened her eyes. I indicated to her that I'm just sneaking outside, to which she nodded acknowledgement and closed her eyes again to focus.

Shit, just stood on the posh ladies foot.

"Sorry, sorry," I whispered as she let out a verbal *'ouch'* causing everyone else to open their eyes.

"Sorry," I said again to the group.

Larry was still there when I got outside but seeing me coming towards him he turned to run down the street.

"Oh no you don't!" I yelled giving chase. There is no way I'm letting him get away this time, I need to invite him to my place for a hot meal and a shower so Rick and Matt can see that he is real.

It wasn't hard to catch him, he's not much of a runner but he did struggle when I caught his arm.

Great, now he has just thrown himself to the ground and is having a tantrum fit like a toddler on the footpath.

I'm trying to reason with him but he has his hands over his ears. God, can't he see that I'm going to offer him a hot meal, he's acting like I have denied him a puppy.

Right, that's it!

I grab his hands to pull them away from his ears and proceed to tell him that if he comes home with me tonight, I'll feed him and he can sleep in a real bed with clean blankets. But he's now laughing at me and struggling really hard again and every time I go to say something, he laughs even louder.

Okay, now he's going 'lalalalala' every time I open my mouth.

Maybe his state of mind *is* similar to that of a child and I need to bribe him.

"Okay, if you let me talk, I'll buy you an ice-cream," I said.

"No, you're not listening," Larry mumbled.

Now that's the pot calling the kettle black.

"Lisa, what's going on?" Tim appears, looking very alarmed.

"Oh good Tim, you're here, help me with Larry would you? I'm trying to take him home with me but he won't stay still long enough and he's not listening."

Tim's not alone, all of the group are here as well. Tim steps forward and reaches his hand out to pull me up from the ground. I release my grip from Larry's hands and he gets up and takes off down the street.

Oh great. I call after him but he disappears into the night again.

"Thanks, now he's got away," I said to Tim. "I probably shouldn't have done that, I think I scared him."

"Maybe she's still in meditation mode," I heard one of the members of the group lean forward and whisper to Tim.

Wait, is that young girl recording me on her phone?

"Um Lisa, you need to come back to us now." Shelley said like we were still sitting in meditation group.

"I am here," I said puzzled, "I'm not in the zone."

They all looked at each other.

"Um Lisa," said Tim, "maybe you need to come back to the shop for a moment."

Facebook Status Update.

Lisa Collins likes a page: Daniel Cannon Photography and Event Supplies.

Lisa created an event: Matt and Neroli's wedding.

10

Back at meditation room

I think I'm going to throw up again.

The young girl who glares at me has now changed her expression to one of smirking while she has great pleasure in re-playing the whole fiasco she recorded on her phone back to me.

And there it is, I can't deny it, I'm on my knees, wrestling with no-one, while talking to the pavement and waving my arms around at nothing in particular.

Oh god she's even recorded the bit where I'm scorning Tim for letting Larry get away.

Oh my god, oh my god.

Tim is explaining to me that what I obviously saw is a spirit and Shelley's being really nice by telling me it's okay, most people freak out when they see energies like that for the first time.

Everyone else is looking at me like I'm mad.

"But Tim, you said to me last time we were at meditation that I must have seen Larry, so Larry must be real."

"Yeah, but I also then said Larry's a ghost," Tim explained, "he hangs around town a lot, died from alcohol years ago. He's still like a local. Obviously not everyone sees him, but he is there. He's not the full quid but still, a bit of a legend round here."

Shelley nods in agreement.

"Do you see him?" I asked Tim, like I was a child and Tim is reading me a story.

"No, I don't see spirits."

Shit.

"That's great," Shelley said, "it's obviously a gift you have," she said beaming.

I'm pleased she thinks it's great. The past couple of weeks is being replayed in my head over and over and it still doesn't make any sense. I mean, why me? And oh my god, that couple in the cafe!! No wonder he handed me his business card for a psychiatrist appointment. And then left the message suggesting I book an appointment. And what about Rick the night Larry called my phone, no wonder he looked alarmed.

And Matt, when he told me I have serious brain issues after telling him that he knocked Larry from the steps. Oh shit, and even today, when I abruptly told Daniel I have to catch up with Larry and ran from his shop calling Larry's name. And Neroli's bizarre looks.....

No, that doesn't count.

"Larry is obviously one of your guides," Shelley continues like it's no big deal that I've just tried to wrestle a ghost outside her shop.

"You can have more then one you know," she continued "and he's come in because there is something you need to do, but you know this already, you're well connected," she smiled.

She left me to carry on with the rest of the group and Tim asked me if I was okay. Tim's been great, you can almost see the awkwardness in him melt away when he is in a group like this, but I don't understand what Tim and Shelley mean when they say I'm connected. If Larry is one of my guides then why is he here and why all of a sudden can I see supernatural beings? Maybe Larry is here to help me with Matt and Neroli's wedding plans.

No that can't be it.

He did tell me that I don't listen.

Maybe he's trying to tell me I need a hearing test.

Okay, I'll book myself in for a hearing test first thing tomorrow.

The group have obviously forgotten about my little drama as they carry on with their regular meditation meeting, I feel so detached from myself right now I think I need to go home.

Back home

Okay, I really have to find a way to deal with this.

I waited until the meditation had finished before leaving, but when I got home, Larry is waiting for me at the kitchen table and tucking into what looks like a huge bowl of piping hot pumpkin soup.

He also looks like he has had a shower as he smells clean and his hair is damp. He smiles a toothless grin when I walk in and pumpkin soup dribbles down his chin.

Monty is at his heels, snarling at him, but Larry doesn't seem to care.

This is so weird, I wouldn't even know how to begin to explain this to a therapist.

Sid enters the kitchen with yet another armload of washing.

"Don't know what's got into Monty," he said as he passes through to the laundry room, "he's been growling at the wall for over an hour now."

Okay, so it's obvious Larry's been here since I tried to wrestle his spiritual arse outside the crystal shop.

"I made pumpkin soup," Sid calls from the other room. "Had no choice," he continues like he has to justify making pumpkin soup, "Mrs Crankshaw brought down heaps from her garden, couldn't let it go to waste."

I feel like I have left my own body, that's about how weird this is.

"Oh and I think we may need to invest in a bigger hot water system," Sid calls again as I listen to the buttons on the washing machine beep as he punches in another cycle, "we seem to have run out of hot water, which is weird 'cos I haven't done any hot washes."

Larry smiles at me again with his toothless grin before letting out the biggest burp while Monty continues to snarl at him.

"So how was meditation?" Sid asks.

I really cannot answer him, the question seems so distant, I mean who cares about such trivial stuff when you have a spiritual being in your house eating pumpkin soup and using up all your hot water.

I must have answered Sid because he looks like he is satisfied with my reaction and moved on to sort damp washing. I continue to stand there while I watch Larry leave the table with a barking Monty at his heels, place a hat on his head and wave me goodbye.

Then he was gone.

Monty looks confused.

I need sleep, or whisky.

Next morning

I woke up feeling great after a lovely sleep and am convinced the last 12 hours was just a dream. I feel I'm back to being myself.

I don't think I should go to meditation again, I think it screws with my brain.

What the hell is Monty growling at?

Oh feck!

Normal moment over.

I should have known better, should've realised it was wishful thinking that I was dreaming, because there is Larry, sitting cross legged at the end of my bed with his back to me, staring out the window.

Oh shit and Rick is also here.

"Good morning sleepy," he smiled as he pulled on his jeans, "you must have been tired last night," he continued, "I couldn't wake you at all when I came in."

I can only manage a half smile in acknowledgement.

"Are you okay?" he asked in concerned tones as he leaned over to examine me more closely.

Larry's spiritual presence is going to take some getting used to, especially if I'm to convince Rick that I'm fine and completely normal-ish.

So I think the best way to deal with this, is to ignore Larry altogether, I mean it's not like he's a pain, he's just there. Monty however, does have to find a way to deal with Larry as this growling is driving me crazy.

"Monty shut up!" I growled.

"I'll take him outside," Rick said, "don't know what's got into him, he's been doing that all morning. You sure you're okay?"

I convinced Rick that I'm fine and that I just had a migraine, which he seems to buy because he's now left for work without any more concerned looks, taking a very noisy dog with him to give me some peace.

The room was silent, even Larry's presence at the end of the bed didn't seem to disturb the stillness. I had my shift at the aged care home to do today, but to be honest I really don't know how I'm going to fit this into my day, especially with Matt and Neroli's wedding getting steadily closer. And with Pamela's return I really have to be on top of things otherwise she will hijack the wedding plans. And that's not to mention the list of things I have to make Sid do so the petting zoo and the grounds are looking fabulous for the reception.

So far all the animals, apart from the out of control geese, seem to have settled in well and Sid's not complaining nearly as much as he used to about feeding and taking care of things. So that side of things seems to be going well.

"Don't like him," Larry piped up, breaking the silence and startling me.

"Don't like who?" I asked like it was normal to talk back to thin air.

"Don't like him," Larry repeated pointed his beefy finger though the window at the reflection of Rick's moving vehicle as it drove off through the gate.

Great, a ghost that judges people.

"Well you would be the first," I said, climbing out of bed and making my way towards the bedroom door, "Rick's a great guy, everyone else likes him."

Larry seems to be making vomiting noises at my response so ignoring him, I made my way to the kitchen.

I'm thinking ignoring Larry is going to be tough, as I'm now in the kitchen and I can hear his fake vomiting noises from here.

God, I hope it's fake.

Surely it is, ghosts don't physically vomit.

I greeted Sid as I made my way to the kettle. Sid and I seem to be over our awkwardness with each other.

I think our little bonding moment with joining a meditation class together seems to have done it. I wonder if I should tell him about Larry? After all, Sid used to spend his time waiting in cow paddocks for aliens to visit him, so one little spirit isn't going to bother him.

"You must have been hungry last night," Sid said, "I didn't know you liked pumpkin soup."

"I don't," I said, "it was Larry, my spiritual guide."

"Your what?"

"You know, my guide, my guardian angel."

"Your guardian angel ate all my pumpkin soup?" Sid said in a dry tone, holding up the massive empty soup pot.

"Uh ha."

Actually now I say that out loud I think even Sid would think that was strange.

Better brush over it.

I sat down with Sid to go over the list of things I want him to do. He enquired about item one, the alpaca shed, saying that an alpaca is a bigger commitment then a goat or a sheep. Have I really thought this through? I love Sid and his polite ways because if his wife was here, she would tell me where to put my alpaca and then make sure the alpaca shed goes with it.

Anyway, I told Sid that maybe we need to concentrate on a plan just in case I do get an alpaca because I have already put some inquires on the 'net for wanting one. Sid said that maybe we should wait until I have definite plans for an alpaca, then we will worry about a shed.

I told him that sounds like a great idea and now he's going outside to start on item two on the list, which is the mini maze.

I need to get motivated to get to work at the aged care home. Well I shouldn't call it work, it's more like just a giant interference in my plans but as Sid said to me, everything we do has a purpose.

So I guess my purpose would be to go and get dressed for work.

What's that sound?

Sounds like thumping.

I followed the sound which is coming from my bedroom.

Oh I don't believe it.

Larry is jumping on my bed throwing the contents of my handbag out around the room like he is conducting a lolly scramble.

"What are you doing?" I hissed.

"Don't like him, don't like him," he sung as his heavy boots continued to tangle up in my lovely clean bed sheets.

Ducking some of the contents of my handbag, I climb up on my bed to try and retrieve it.

"Give it," I demand as Larry continues to jump around in circles chanting 'don't like him, don't like him'.

Trying to retrieve your handbag from a supernatural being is not as easy as it sounds.

Then all of a sudden Larry stops, like he's seen a ghost.

"Run!" he yells, throwing my bag over his shoulder as he disappears into thin air.

"Lisa!" Mrs Crankshaw's voice snaps, "what are you doing up there, and what's with this mess?"

At work in the aged care home

Mrs Crankshaw didn't press me about the bed jumping which is just as well, as I had no explanation to give her. I must start writing down excuses when I think of them, you know, for future reference.

But what was astonishing was when I was retrieving the contents of my handbag, I picked up the brochure that Daniel had thrust at me on his opening day.

I forgot it was there, but the brochure had a beautiful picture of the old church with the light filtering through the trees like god himself was pointing out the finer features of the charming old building.

Whoa, that felt like another déjà vu moment.

Anyway, the brochure promoting the church as a country wedding venue was amazing and I guess Daniel had it in his plans all along to utilise it.

Nice if he'd told me sooner.

Mrs Crankshaw brought more of Neroli's ugly, smelly, stuffed eye pillows around, as well as her own creations of crochet ponchos and boxes of knitted bed socks that Betty had made for the CWA stall that is being held next weekend.

I tried to protest that just because I was the president of the CWA doesn't mean my house is storage for all things smelly and knitted.

Larry was sitting with the residents when I arrived at work, intently watching a game of chess going on between gentlemen. I'm going to ignore the fact that he is here.

"So how was your weekend?" Debbie asks, as I finished getting one of the residents comfortable in his arm chair.

I had to think about it, it seems like so long ago, especially since I'm in touch with supernatural beings, makes my mind go kind of scrambled.

Oh, now I remember. I proceeded to tell Debbie that Matt and Neroli have decided to get married in the old church that Daniel owns and how Neroli and I visited it and what nice ambience it had.

I left out the bits about Matt not liking it and me ending up at the doctors because I saw a ghost.

"Oh really," Debbie chuckled, "Lisa you do like to stir the pot."

"What's that s'posed to mean?"

"Pamela and her estranged husband got married there. Apparently that church was built by one of his ancestors, but with Pamela being the superstitious type, especially given what's happened to her marriage, I really can't see her liking Matt getting married there."

Oh that's bloody marvellous. Now I really do have a fight on my hands when Pamela gets wind of this. God why don't people just let me decide what's best for them.

"Yeah, good luck with that one," Debbie chuckled again as she exited the room.

I glanced over to the two men playing chess and Larry is still there, sitting between them watching and seems content. I wonder if he had been a resident here, I must ask Tim. I chuckled at that thought, I mean who would have thought that Tim the baker (as he's known around here apparently), would end up being the only one who doesn't think I'm losing it.

I went about my duties with one thing on my mind and that was Pamela. How am I going to get around her and get her son married off in the same church that her failed marriage took place in.

And, if she didn't have relations with a man young enough to be her son, then her marriage wouldn't have failed, Matt wouldn't be a twat about it, Daniel's merchandise would be on display, and my career as an event planner would take off in leaps and bounds.

It's all her fault.

The morning went fast but that's because the more I thought about Pamela ruining my plans, the faster I worked. I haven't gone back to check if Larry is still there but he hasn't made an appearance to tell me I need another hearing test or that he doesn't like Rick, so all must be well.

I was almost at the end of my shift and just rinsing the last of the dishes in the staffroom when Debbie came through to me.

"There's a foreign lady here to see you," she said.

"Foreign? I don't know anyone foreign?" I asked, slightly puzzled.

"She said you have her dog."

"Oh."

Drying my hands, I made my way to the reception area, it must be Monty's old owner, the skinny, arm waving Italian man's wife. Oh my god, I hope she hasn't come here wanting Monty back, I mean he is a pain and completely humiliates people by towel stealing but he has grown on me. Well I'm just going to have to be strong and tell her there's no returns and Monty stays with me.

She turned to look at me as I entered reception, her frizzy short auburn hair and large glasses that seem to frame half her face made it difficult to pick her age. I smiled sweetly at her to soften her up so she doesn't demand Monty back.

"Did you take my dog?" she said in a thick Italian accent.

"Um yes," I nodded, taken aback by her abruptness.

"And you spoke to my husband?" her voice rose.

"Um ...yep."

"And you told him leave me?"

"Ahh…"

"You proposition him?" she snapped.

"Oh no, that definitely didn't happen…"

"And you told him leave!" she spat.

Oh god her voice is getting louder and I can see where this is going, okay maybe offering marriage advice as part of my wedding planning business is not such a hot idea after all.

He did ask my opinion, so it's not like I said anything willingly. I'd never have said anything if I'd known he would run back to his wife and tell her that a young-ish woman took her dog and supposedly propositioned him, before telling him to leave his wife. Surely she didn't take it *that* seriously.

Should have kept my mouth shut.

"Um no, that didn't happen," I said, trying to coax her outside as one of the residents has appeared to see what's going on. "Maybe you need to go back and sort things out with your husband."

She flung her arm from my grip and pointed a finger at me. Oh great timing, now Larry has shown up and is standing behind her pointing his beefy finger at her.

He looks so funny mimicking her with his toothless mouth, I'm trying not to laugh.

"The last person interfered my business," she continued to snap, "never interfered again."

I can't help it, Larry is just too funny and the corners of my mouth start to twitch.

"You stay away from my Pauly," she continues.

Oh god I think I'm going to lose it.

Too late, I burst into fits of giggles and Larry does as well.

Frizzy haired Italian lady purses her lips.

"This is not last you hear of this," she spat as she stormed out the door.

It's not really funny, I mean she sounds serious, as if I would dream of propositioning her skinny, arm waving husband with the overgrown moustache. For a start he is wrinkly and looks about 100.

God I hope she's not in the mafia.

Oh Larry's gone.

Why is Debbie standing there shaking her head.

Back home

"Hey Sid."

"Hey Lisa, a foreign lady was here looking for you I told her where you were."

"Yeah, thanks for that."

"Monty didn't like her."

"Understandable."

Sid has done an amazing job on the back lawn with the preparation of the mini maze, it can't have been easy to plan a maze, not to mention time consuming, but thanks to Google, he seems to have it sorted. And believe it or not Sid is really good with things like riddles and puzzles.
The back lawn is pegged out with white string and taking a closer look, I can see the patterns and dead ends and the path to the middle. Now I just have to order the hedging plants to complete it, although I think I'm going to need something faster growing as wouldn't it be great if it was ready in time for Matt and Neroli's reception.
Okay, maybe that's a long shot, but possible.
Must consult Sid on that one.

I still feel a bit rattled about the Italian man's wife's accusations about propositioning her husband and telling him to leave her. I only went there because he said he had white animals. Did he really take what I said about maybe he should leave her seriously, or was he setting me up? That's the last time I taste his olive oil.
God I hope he didn't think because I went down to his shed and tasted his olive oil, I was propositioning him.

After all I did think it was a little weird the way he spoon feed me at one stage.

Why do these things keep happening to me?

Anyway I'm pleased Debbie thought it was funny because I certainly didn't, even though Debbie said she thought it was a bit rude of me to laugh in her face as that would have only wound her up more.

Of course I couldn't tell Debbie that I was actually laughing at Larry, not the angry Italian lady. Debbie said not to worry, she's crazy anyway and no she's not in the mafia and I should just forget about it.

So from now on I'm not going to worry about it.

But what I *am* worried about, is Pamela. So I really need to put Plan B into action, as Plan A, which is Matt and Pamela agreeing to the marriage taking place in Daniel's church, is not working out so well.

Plan B may require bribery and treachery on my part. I'm thinking that once I get Daniel's church looking all nice and lovely I will show Neroli, in one last attempt to convince Matt. If Matt is still being a twat then I'll just have to tell Matt that the other church is all booked out and what a shame and he has to take the available venue after all.

But I figured I'll leave that last one up my sleeve till a few days before the wedding.

But no time for that now as I have got to get going to Daniel's shop to look over his brochures and order some of his merchandise.

Stomach's in knots again and my palms have gone all sweaty, god what is up with that.

Ohh, phones ringing.

Oh it's just Matt.

"Yes," I answer casually, expecting Matt to tell me him and Neroli have decided Tom is going to be the toastmaster or something ridiculous like that.

"Is this Lisa?" a familiar snotty voice appears at the end of the line.

No. It can't be. No wonder my stomach is tied in knots.

"Um yes, this is she," I answered, praying that it's not her.

"It's Pamela Horton here. I was just wondering if it's possible for us to sit down and discuss how the wedding plans are going so far?"

Oh my god, she is acting like nothing has happened between us and she hardly knows me.

I'm so shocked I don't answer her for a moment, Larry has appeared in my line of vision and is playing with my stapler.

I quickly gather my thoughts.

"Um… sure, let me consult my diary."

My voice is shaky and my heart is pounding in my chest. Not that I'm scared of Pamela or anything, it's just that the last time I saw her she was shagging Jake behind my back.

Shit Larry is stapling all my paperwork together, including the bits that are already stapled.

I hiss at him to stop as I open my diary but he just ignores me.

"What time suits you?" I squawk when I returned to the phone. "Is Friday okay?"

"This afternoon would be much better," Pamela insisted, "I have a lot to catch up on and would very much like to know what's going on. Now how about 4 o'clock?"

This is more like the Pamela I know, snappy and in control, and I just know that she will not let me carry on with the wedding plans without being a total bitch about things. Okay fair enough, she is paying for it, but it's so unfair, why did Matt have to have Pamela as a mother.

Shit Larry is now stapling my post-it notes together.

I reached over to rescue my post-it's, trying to time my grab in between Larry's vigorous stapling. I was way off.

Twack.

"Bloody hell!" I yelled at Larry through my pain, "why can't you leave my god damn things alone!"

"I'm guessing that's a yes then Lisa," Pamela's sharp tone cut through down the line.

"No I wasn't....."

"4 o'clock, at Matthew's house it is then," she confirmed before hanging up.

Feck.

Larry's now pounding the desk in fits of laughter.

Where's my staple remover.

Facebook Status Update. Lisa Collins.

List of things I am over:

Foreign woman who accuse you of husband stealing.

Ghosts.

That is all.

11

2pm in Daniels office

I'm still rattled by Pamela's call and even more so about meeting her in two hours. I should have been more concerned about putting together a report of what's been done towards wedding preparations so far, but instead I surfed the net, slightly tricky with my bandaged finger, on how to remove spiritual attachments, as Larry sat opposite me shoving paper clips up his nostrils.

Sometimes I think he just gets bored.

Daniel hands me a mug of steaming contents.

"What happened to your finger?" he asks, as he sat down opposite me.

"Oh you know, stapler accident," I said.

He nodded as if the very same thing happens to him.

There's such a strange awkwardness between us, I know he's just as uncomfortable as I am.

Mind you that may come down to the fact that the last time I was here I bolted from his shop and gave chase to a ghost while screaming out its name, so it's understandable why he may be a bit ill at ease.

I'm just grateful he didn't mention it to Rick.

"So," he begins, "why don't you look over these products that I have and tell me what ones you would like to use."

Oh, he's actually giving me a choice and not just dictating to me, things are looking up.

I browsed in silence at all the event products he has and I have to say they are all good, there's even little personalised notepads you can order and little gift baskets for the tables.

I want it all.

But no, have to be practical about things.

I'm very aware of Larry standing outside licking the shop window, but even more aware of Daniel staring at me.

And Daniel is the one making me nervous.

I look up at him and he quickly tears his gaze away.

"Have you decided?" he asks. He seems embarrassed that I caught him looking at me.

"Yep, I think I'll go with the banner, the little notebooks and pens for the guest tables, and the little champagne bottles.

I'm thinking about adding in these desk calendars but it may be a bit much."

"What about the tee-shirts?"

"Do I have to?"

Daniel looked at me again as if to say, no tee-shirts, no church.

"Okay so I guess the tee-shirts," I conceded.

"You won't regret it," he says.

Oh god, there's a lady gazing at Daniel's pictures in the shop window and Larry is lying on the payment tying her shoe-laces together.

If I go out there and tell him to stop, she will think I'm mad.

I turned to Daniel.

"So why do people think your church is haunted?"

Hmm, don't know where that came from.

"Probably because there was a suspected murder linked to the church," he shrugged. "The rest of the stories about marriages failing and people dying is just silly superstitions. The church was there when my parents brought the property, they wanted to tear it down but they figured it might be bad luck to destroy a church, so they just let people use it."

"Suspected murder?"

"Yeah someone disappeared, last seen in the church.

That was before my parents had it, so it would be some years back."

"Do you think it's haunted?" I asked.

"No, I don't believe in ghosts," he said in a dry tone.

A slight squeal from outside the shop diverted our attention as the woman who was looking at Daniel's window display suddenly hit the pavement.

I glared at Larry who is chuckling away with his toothless grin.

Meeting with Pamela

Daniel rushed to the woman's aid but luckily the fall wasn't a bad one and she was okay.

Larry was sitting in my car when I left Daniel's shop so I have spent the entire journey to Matt and Neroli's house lecturing a supernatural being on the safety aspects of practical jokes.

Larry's explanation was he didn't like her.

Hmmm, think we may have some social issues.

I think it's about time I get Larry a hobby.

Neroli answered the door and the poor girl looks like she has been judged to bits, even Tom looks a bit put out.

Feeling like I'm stepping into the ring with Mike Tyson. I entered the room. Pamela was sitting at the kitchen table.

Oh my god she looks, well, like she's packed on a few pounds.

"Hello Lisa," she smiles. Not a genuine smile I might add.

"Hello Pamela," I smiled back, as equally as genuine as hers.

I sat opposite her, poised and in control with my portfolio and Daniel's brochures in front of me feeling very professional.

Then Larry turned up.

Okay, no problem as long as he sits here quietly, although I don't know where he got that sandwich from but I wish he would close his mouth when he eats.

Poised and in control.

Matt mutters a greeting in my direction as he joins us at the table. He too looks like he's been judged to pieces.

"Okay," I began when Neroli sat down after strapping Bailey into her highchair, "here's where I'm at so far; the flowers were Neroli's choice as they are her favourite." Well they're not really, but she did say she liked them when I sent her a picture via email, and Neroli doesn't seem to have noticed what I said, actually she's looking for something.

Oh shit, I think Larry has taken Bailey's sandwich.

What the? How does that work anyway, if you're nothing but an energy field?

"Yes, what else?" Pamela asked.

"Also Matt and Neroli have requested that they hold the reception under marquee at *Abby-toir*."

"Oh, the old slaughter yards," Pamela sniffed.

"Yes, at my estate," I said in a completely professional tone, ignoring the snarkiness behind her comment.

Larry's chewing is so loud.

I presented Daniel's brochures and the quote he gave me for the photography, Pamela seems quite impressed and said to run with it so I'm really shocked.

She even thought it was great idea when I mentioned the mini petting zoo for the kids.

Maybe I have misjudged Pamela. Maybe her marriage failure, which caused her to have a breakdown, which landed her in hospital, actually knocked her off her pedestal.

Running with her amicability I quietly slipped the brochure about the church in front of her, on which I had discreetly written 'Matt and Neroli's proposed wedding venue' across the top.

Larry is now playing peek-a-boo with Bailey and the freaky thing is, Bailey's laughing and squealing, I mean can she actually see Larry?

"No fucken way," Matt protested when Pamela picked up the brochure snapping me from my thoughts.

"Language Matthew," Pamela snapped.

"Sorry, but I'm not effing getting married there."

Bloody Matt, wish he would shut his pie hole.

"Why not?" Pamela asked, looking in astonishment at Matt.

Oh my god.

Matt looks very surprised by his mothers response.

"Um, because it's haunted and jinxed."

Pamela rolled her eyes, "oh that's nonsense," she snapped, "superstitious mollycoddle. I think it's a lovely idea, is it available for viewing?" she asks me, fluttering her eyelashes.

I cannot locate my tongue, oh my god, oh my god.

I nodded my head as I can't say much with a numb tongue.

"Excellent," she said, "then I shall have a look as I understand it's been empty for quite a while, but I think it's a perfect venue. As long as Reverend Alistair can perform the ceremony."

Shit that's what I was meant to do.

"Uh huh," I nodded, tongue still not working.

"What do you think Neroli?" Pamela asked her.

Neroli nodded as well, so it looks like I'm not the only one who cannot locate their tongue.

"Excellent," Pamela smiled again, "the old church it is then."

Back home

I'm lying down as am still in shock.

The rest of the meeting went great. Pamela and I got on really well and she congratulated me on my engagement, (Larry made a gagging noise again when she said it), we agreed that she is going to drop by Daniel's church tomorrow while I'm there cleaning and she even thanked me for doing a marvelous job so far.

And the weird thing is, everyone, including Tom and Larry, were on their best behaviour so her presence can only be a good thing. I mean, so what if Pamela had an affair with Jake while I was dating him, it's not like I was *married* to him and Jake was a bit of a charmer. I can't blame Pamela for that, after all she's a woman with needs, if I was married to a Basil Faulty lookalike then I too would look at options.

It seems I may have misjudged Pamela.

Matt rang after I got home and whinged at me for brainwashing his mother and I told him I had done no such thing as his mother is a lovely lady with marvelous taste. To which Matt said that maybe he got it wrong, maybe his mother brainwashed me.

He's just snotty because he has to do what his mother tells him to do.

But now I have to deal with the details of the CWA stall at the garden club (which Pamela said she may attend and if I ever need any advice or tips about my position as president don't hesitate to call). My house is starting to look like a smelly knitting expo with the amount of wares that have been dropped off over the past couple of days. Mrs Crankshaw has done up a roster for the stall and thank god I only have the afternoon shift, hopefully by then people would have gone home and won't associate me with useless knitted goods.

I have a reputation as the local event planner to uphold.

Phone ringing

It's Rick.

I have had no desire to talk to him lately, I don't know what it is, but he seems to be in my face all the time.

And sometimes while I'm trying to plan wedding stuff, he's all over me and asking me constantly if there is anything I need and am I okay blah, blah. He never gets angry at me, just sulks like a child.

But he is a nice guy, everyone likes him, except Larry, but Larry doesn't seem to like anyone. If Larry's like that when he is dead, what was he like when he was alive.

Oh god, phone's ringing again.

I'm just going to ignore it, I told Rick earlier that I would see him later; he doesn't need to call me all the time.

Oh, it's not Rick this time, it's Daniel.

"Hello," I said, quickly picking up the phone before it went to voice mail.

"Hey it's Daniel," he greeted back.

God my stomach has landed in my mouth, "um how are you?"

"Good and you?"

"Not bad."

"That's good."

Awkward silence.

Does he actually want something or is he just calling up for a chat? I mean if he is calling for a chat then that's great as I think he must be starting to accept me as Rick's fiancée and not the bitch who stole his best friend.

"Just wondering if you talked to Matt about the merchandise? As I have to put a deposit down for the printing costs," he said, a little coldly and business like.

Oh, okay, not a friendly phone call then, just business. For some strange reason I feel deflated.

I filled Daniel in on the meeting with Pamela and the fact that she is coming to view the church, before hanging up and sitting here in a bit of a daze. Larry is sitting beside me looking equally as dazed.

Monty is growling at Larry.

"There you are," said Rick as he enters my office.

Larry's now growling at Rick.

"I've been trying to call you."

"Oh yeah, sorry 'bout that," I said, pretending I'm doing something.

Rick moves behind me and wraps his arms around me.

"You okay?" he asks.

"Yes, why?" I said, a little snappy.

"Just wondered, you seem a little, well, off."

"Just busy," I said, a tad coldly.

"Okay, well if there is anything I can do."

I felt like telling him he can leave me in peace but that would sound horrible, I mean after all he's only trying to be helpful.

"Shouldn't you be at work?" I said, as sweetly as I could muster.

"I've finished," he said.

"And there's nothing you need to do now?" I pressed.

"Are you trying to get rid of me?" he joked.

Yes.

"Pff, no," I scoffed.

"Okay I get the hint," he chuckled.

Really? Phew that was easy.

I wonder if Rick can feel that Larry is behind him trying to push him out the door.

"Matt wanted me to grab me a couple of Neroli's eye pillows for his mate at work," Rick said, scratching at his back, "I'm heading over to the garage now for some tyres so I'll take some, Matt said Neroli's run of material too."

Well thank god she's run out of material because there's about a million of them here, I don't think this world can take much more of those ugly things.

I wonder if those poor blokes in the garage know exactly what they asked for.

"You'll be okay?" Rick said with his puppy dog eyes.

Oh god just go.

I nodded sweetly at him as Larry gave him a hefty push through the door.

"Okay then, I'll see ya," Rick said, looking behind him to see what he tripped over.

I didn't get a chance to answer as Larry slammed the door in his face.

"Don't like him," Larry said when I glared at him.

"Yes Larry," I sighed, "I know."

Day of CWA garden tour stall

Okay, it's all set up and soon I can disappear back home before the first of the people get here from their *tour de garden* and see me amongst all this knitted stuff.

Knitted stuff is great for winter but I don't think its going to sell well today given it's stinking hot and the sun is blazing. Besides, the knitted stuffed animals are a bit creepy looking with their button eyes.

The setting is nice, we have tables covered with nice lace tablecloths and garden chairs on the well manicured lawn which belongs to the president of the Garden Club.

And as part of your ticket to the gardens, you can have your choice of either a scone or piece of fruitcake to go with your hot beverage.

The local artists group also have their arts on display and a raffle going for one of their paintings.

It's very well organised.

I didn't bring all fifteen shopping bags of Neroli's eye pillows, just the one, which caused a bit of complaining with the CWA members, as they are predicting it will be their best seller. I'm not sure what planet the CWA members are on but I told them if they do run out (highly unlikely) then just to phone me and I will drop off some more.

Larry has appeared and looks like he has whipped cream all over his face.

Mind you, Tom has also appeared and looks like he has whipped cream all over his face too.

So Neroli and Mrs Crankshaw are doing the first shift at the stall until lunch, then me and Betty take over after lunch. The rest of the ladies are on serving duty for the morning and afternoon teas.

"Okay so I'm going then," I announced after I finished setting up and Matt had arrived to collect Tom, who was currently having his face scrubbed clean by Neroli. I spied Larry who was doing the same with one of the white lace tablecloths.

"Yeah, think Mum wants to talk to you, something about the wedding party," Matt said with a hint of defeat in his tone.

Hee, hee, I think Pamela may be nagging at Matt a bit over his choices.

And fair enough I say, I mean I can't see Pamela even entertaining Matt's outrageous suggestion of making Tom and Bailey the only wedding party members.

Matt just has to suck it up. I went to turn to leave when I almost tripped over Tom as he sprinted past me followed by Larry running as fast as their physical and spiritual legs will carry them as they bolted across the lawn.

Wonder what's gotten in to them.

Mrs Crankshaw reappeared with a rather angry looking woman carrying a cream bowl.

"Sorry to bother you Neroli," Mrs Crankshaw said, looking awkward, "but this lady informs me that Tom has eaten an entire bowl of cream that was reserved for the scones."

Back home

Tom was made to come back and apologise, which he did, and when asked if he ate the entire bowl by himself, he couldn't answer, he looked like he wasn't sure if he was alone or not.

Interesting pair, Tom and Larry, I wonder who led who astray.

Anyway it's a nice, quiet, relaxing day as Rick is outside helping Sid while I'm sitting here in the cool air going over wedding stuff.

I was meant to go down to the church to start the clean up, but setting up for the CWA stall took longer than I thought and besides, far too nice of a day for cleaning. I just had a lovely phone conversation with Pamela after I called her today to say I couldn't take her through the church for a look, to which she replied that she really doesn't need to look as she is aware of what a perfect venue it will be and to just go ahead and book it. She has also had a chat with Reverend Alistair and he is happy to perform the ceremony. She has even gone to lengths to schedule an appointment for Matt and Neroli to have a sit down meet and greet with the reverend and talk about what marriage means under God's law.

Matt is going to be so annoyed when he finds out but that will teach him about getting his mother involved.

Not that I'm complaining about Pamela stepping in, I mean she also agreed with me about the impracticality of having Tom and Bailey as the only wedding party and she assured me she will have a 'word' to Matthew about that.
So things are coming together nicely and I'm starting to feel very pleased with myself.
Next week is dress shopping with Neroli and I have made mention to Pamela that it would be nice to know who was in the wedding party so I know how many dresses to shop for, to which she replied 'leave it with me'. She also agreed when I told her what the CWA was selling in their stall by saying she too does not think knitted home wares were a good fundraiser and it's completely the wrong direction for the CWA.

We are so like two peas in a pod Pamela and I. I mean we even have the same taste in men – well apart from her Basil Fawlty ex husband, he not my type, wonder what star sign she is?
Larry has appeared and seems to be trailing a long piece of white string which is stuck to his boot.

I was going to talk to him about getting wee Tom into trouble and eating whipped cream but he's now discovered the string and is preoccupied in winding it up. I don't think he will listen, and besides it was probably Tom who started it anyway, Larry would have just gone along with it because Tom was doing it.

I just realised how disturbing that sounds and need to remind myself yet again, that Larry is a spiritual being and not a physical child running with the wrong crowd of friends.

Think I need to be on medication.

Nah.

No sign of Monty which means he must be outside with Rick and Sid.

Ohhh, phones ringing.

Oh, just Mrs Crankshaw, I thought it may have been Daniel, don't know why I thought it would be him.

"Lisa dear," Mrs Crankshaw said with slight urgency in her voice when I answered, "we need more eye pillows and quick."

What the hell?

"You can't have sold *all* of them," I scoffed.

"Of course we have," Mrs Crankshaw snapped, "and now we have a queue of people waiting for more, so we need them now!"

Queue of people, yeah right.

"Now, Lisa," Mrs Crankshaw said again, to remind me of the urgency.

Which I'm finding very hard to believe.

"Okay, fine. Give me half an hour."

"No, now!! We don't have half an hour to wait," Mrs Crankshaw snapped.

"Okay, okay," I said, "I'll come now."

Jeez obviously someone doesn't have any patience, mind you she has been sitting with Neroli for…. oh my god it's only been an hour and they have sold out??

Odd.

Grabbing another two shopping bags full of ugly eye pillows I glanced at Larry who is still occupied in winding up the string, which I may add is in a tangled pile on the floor and seems to be getting bigger, he looks happy so hopefully he won't feel the need to follow.

I can hear Sid calling my name to locate my whereabouts when I made my way to the car, he doesn't sound that happy, but I can't stop as I can still hear Mrs Crankshaw's exaggerated urgency ringing in my ears.

At CWA Stall

There seems to be a lot of people here, most of them look around Matt's age.

Hmmm seems young people must be into gardens around here.

Mind you, nothing else to do.

Oh my god, there's a huge line at the CWA stall.

And Mrs Crankshaw is all red in the face and flustered looking.

"Is that all you brought?" she said in a frazzled state as Neroli snatches the bags off me and starts unpacking them onto the table. The first bunch of youths in the queue start handing over money and they don't even seem to care what colour they receive.

"Quick, go back and get more," Mrs Crankshaw's instructs me as she busies herself with unpacking the second bag.

I'm in a bit of a surreal state over these young people's fondness for ugly eye pillows, it must be a new trend, I guess whatever floats your boat.

"Now Lisa!" Mrs Crankshaw snaps.

Okay, jeez.

I don't feel like doubling up on another trip so I'll phone Rick to see if he can bring them down.

Oh that's right, I forgot, Rick's phone ended up down the toilet last night (am guessing Larry may know something about that), I'll try Sid's phone.

"Where are you?!" Sid's voice appeared on the end of the line.

Okay, Sid's sounding a bit snappy.

"At the CWA stall, is Rick there, could you put him on?"

Did Sid just hang up on me?

Can't have, I'll try again.

"Sid, me again, could you tell Ric....."

"Lisa, sometimes you're just so fucken self centered."

"Pardon me?"

"You heard."

Oh my god, I have never heard Sid talk like that to... well anyone, before. Must be the Millie thing rubbing off on him, I'll try the P word, it works with Millie.

"Okay, *please* could you put Rick on?"

Dead silence on the line and I thought Sid had hung up again, wonder why he's so anti today?

God I hope Monty hasn't done anything.

"Hey babe," Rick's voice appeared on the line." I think you better get back here, Sid looks like he's about to explode."

Really? Sid explode. Wow this day is getting strange.

I asked Rick to bring down the ugly eye pillows, which he said he would, but I need to get home as Sid is not happy with me.

Rick wouldn't say why but I have a feeling Sid is still standing there, now I'm curious as to know why.

He was working on the yards for the petting zoo and even checked the timber I ordered off the internet when it arrived so I don't think he could be mad at that.

I think Monty must have done something.But that's no reason to get mad, after all he's only a dog, he doesn't understand.

I hung up from Rick and went over to inform Mrs Crankshaw that Rick is coming with more eye pillows.

Oh my god, they have sold one bag already and there are more youths arriving. It's like the word is getting out.

Mrs Crankshaw's now informing Neroli that from now on only one eye pillow per customer as some were buying two or three.

Okay, people around here certainly need to get out more.

Two hours later

Okay, haven't been home yet.

Rick arrived with all but one bag saying he too didn't think we needed them all and we were so run off our feet I couldn't leave. Betty arrived just as the last of the eye pillows were sold. Neroli is promising she will make some more soon and handing our contact details to the last of the disappointed spotty youths that missed out.

Rick has been hovering at my side all afternoon, so annoying.

I'm exhausted.

Betty's a bit put out because not one of her knitted bed socks sold. Mind you, neither did the ugly stuffed animals, or any of the other stuff.

Neroli is still looking dumbstruck and Mrs Crankshaw can't keep the grin off her face as she counts the day's takings.

"This is the most money the CWA has ever made in a single fundraising event," she said, "not even our little sex toy party brought this much in, I'm so proud of you Neroli."

Betty leaned over and gave Neroli a well done pat on the arm.

God I can see the next CWA meeting is going to be all about Neroli.

Wait till I tell Pamela.

Back home again

Sid is standing in the driveway with his arms folded tightly across his chest.

Oh that's right; Sid needs a 'word' with me.

Wonder how long he's been standing like this for.

"God what a day," I exclaimed as I climbed out of the car. "Who would have thought Neroli's ugly eye pillows would be so popu..."

"Notice anything different?" Sid's voice stung like a dagger.

I can't see anything off hand, he looks the same.

"Um... could you give me a clue?"

"What used to be over there and is not anymore?" Sid snapped again pointing to where the... oh my god.

"What happened to the maze?" I exclaimed.

"Don't give me that shit Lisa."

Sid had spent hours pegging out the maze with string and now all that is left is a few knocked over pegs.

Well it's salvageable, I mean some of the pegs are still there, he could pick up where he left off.

"It's not as bad as it looks," I soothed, "it's fixable."

Wonder where Monty is.

"Why did you do it?" Sid scorned.

"I didn't."

"Don't lie."

"I'm not."

"So you are saying you don't have anything to do with this?"

"Of course not!" I snapped in horror, "what warped and twisted person do you think I am. I wanted that maze, I'm not about to destroy it."

"Really?" said Sid, sounding sarcastic, "well then, come with me."

I rolled my eyes as I followed Sid, trying to keep up with his stomping footprints, I noticed a car slowing up towards my front gate, it could be Rick.

"So explain this," Sid said victoriously opening my office door.

Oh my god.

There is white string draped all over my office. That will explain why I haven't seen Larry, he's been entertaining himself with an enormous piece of string.

Shit, that's right, it was on his boot when I left.

Why oh why did I not realise.

Sid is glaring at me for an explanation and really, what can I say?

I open my mouth, still unsure where to begin, seems I'm saved by a knock on the door.

"I'll get it," I jumped, sprinting to the door.

Oh it's a long haired youth, wearing a black tee shirt with words on it I can't understand.

"Um, may I help you?"

"Yeah, I was told you're the lady with the eye pillows."

Oh for...

"Who told you that?" I rubbed my brow in frustration.

"Um, the chick at the garden place, she sent us round."

"Us?"

"Yeah."

Bloody Neroli.

"Okay," I sighed, "how many?"

The spotty youth doesn't seem too concerned what colour or anything as he pulls out five ugly pillows from the bag, he also seems very happy with the price.

Strange.

I closed the door slowly after the youth left as I know Sid is behind me, I guess I could start by apologising.

20 minutes later

Okay Sid's all weirded out.

I had to explain about Larry, I mean what else could I have said on such short notice. I did write some explanations down for future reference to explain Larry's behaviour but I couldn't find a good one on my list to explain sabotaging carefully laid out string.

"I didn't think it was Monty," Sid said looking as pale as Monty.

Shit that's what I should have said, it was Monty.

I need to put that on my list, 'blame dog'.

Sid shakes his head as if he is trying to clear it. "No Lisa that doesn't make sense," he snapped, "I believe in spirits but they can't physically do anything, it's impossible."

"Well he can," I said, "he even ate all your pumpkin soup."

Okay I don't like the way Sid's looking at me.

"Well you can forget your maze," Sid snapped as he scraped his chair along the floor looking like he is about to cry.

"That took me a whole day, not to mention the planning, that's two days from my life I'll never get back."

Sid storms off as I apologise to his back. I mean jeez, I don't think I need to apologise that much, after all it wasn't me.

God I hope he doesn't tell Millie.

Monty is sitting at my feet looking equally disgusted in me.

So I apologised to him too, but that's it, no more apologies.

Oh god another car load of spotty youths just pulled up.

Dress shopping with Neroli

Someone shoot me now.

She doesn't like any of the dresses I have picked and wants to go with a style of dress that was in the Bon Jovi September Rain video.

As if!

I was so looking forward to this being a fun day. Well that's what the 'how to plan your wedding day' book said, that it should be fun.

Clearly they haven't been shopping with Neroli.

But the good news is that Pamela has convinced them to pick more people for the wedding party, so Matt has chosen Rick and Neroli has chosen me.

But because I have to co-ordinate the wedding I suggested that it should be Millie, to which Neroli said she doesn't mind who it is. Millie wasn't *that* honoured to be asked but she agreed as long as she picks her own dress.

So the boys are trying on their suits today and Millie is on her way to try on bridesmaid dresses.

An hour later

Someone really needs to shoot me now.

Millie is so painful to dress shop with, she doesn't agree on any of the ones I like.

Two hours later

Neroli has picked her dress and I think I want to gag, I told her it's a little tight and impractical given the fact she is pregnant and will be arriving at the church on horseback.

Oh that's what I have to do, find a white horse.

Neroli scoffed and said she's not pregnant.

I can't believe she is in denial again.

I told her not to deny it.

She said she's not and is currently in her time of the month.

Not convinced.

But if she wants to spend her wedding day in discomfort then I'm not to blame.

Millie is snappy and said she's too tired to do this.

Man she's been a ball of fun lately.

Three hours later

Never, ever going dress shopping again.

Four hours later

Okay, I'm convinced my friends are deliberately out to embarrass themselves with their choice of apparel.

Millie told me not to be such a fucken control freak.

The shop assistant was not impressed with Millie's swearing.

Back home

And thank god.

The dresses are all brought and I have to say, never again.

Millie's is a simple summer dress made of cotton.

Neroli's dress is tight fitting, short and full of sequins with matching high heels.

Mine is a cream colour, long and off the shoulder.

Not sure I should go with the whole horse entrance now given the length of Neroli's dress.

Rick and Matt fittings took less then an hour.

Going to bed.

Facebook Status Update.

Lisa Collins.

Cannot understand the eye pillow trend, majorly missing something here.

12

One week later

I have been so busy I haven't taken in the fact that the wedding is four weeks away, but am pleased to announce that so far things are running very smoothly.

Pamela and I are getting on well, things got a bit awkward when Neroli mentioned Jake's name the other day after mistakening Rick for Jake but it was soon forgotten about.

Mrs Crankshaw is still not talking to Pamela but told me when I delivered the invitation to her the other day, that she will put her differences aside just for the day. I thought that was big of Mrs Crankshaw considering Pamela had done her friend wrong on so many levels.

But no ones perfect.

I had rung Mum and Dad, who were sunning themselves on the Gold Coast, to give them their official verbal invitation as it's a bit hard when you're traveling in a Winnebago to receive a postal one. I wish Dad and Mum would get internet, facebooking would be so much easier.

I dialed their number again and am now waiting for them to pick up. Oh my god, it's just occurred to me that I haven't told Mum and Dad I'm engaged! How could I have missed that, Rick asked me just last week if I have been in touch with my parents and told them of our engagement to which I recall I think I said yes, (well I was e-mailing Daniel at the time, was a bit busy) and Rick said it was strange that they haven't been in touch.

Oh my god that means I have to tell them.

To be honest I'm not that excited about it.

"Hello," Dad yells down the phone.

"Dad, it's me, I'm just reminding you that Matt and Neroli's wedding is next month and I need an RSVP."

"A what dear? Did you say a raspberry?"

"No, an RSVP."

"RSVP?"

"Yes."

"To what?"

Sometimes I swear to god they do this on purpose.

"Is Mum there? Can you put her on?" I sighed.

"Who?"

"Mum."

"Sorry dear I can't hear you, how 'bout I pass you to Mum."

Okay, deep cleansing breath.

"Hello dear, we now have internet. Dad just brought a computer and we are just signing up for facetime."

"You mean facebook?"

"Yes that's it."

Trying to keep the conversation short, Mum and Dad said yes they can confirm they're coming back for the wedding. I can't bring myself to tell them about my engagement, somehow it doesn't seem right, I think I should wait until they get here and announce it in person. Maybe that's why I feel the need to put it off.

Anyway I hung up and promised to accept their friend request. Really not sure if that's a good thing but at least they are up with the times now.

The church is starting to look great. I have spent the week cleaning and Daniel had organised someone to come and mow the grass and tend to the gardens. Daniel still doesn't say a lot to me unless its business. He and Rick went out on a boy's night the other night and Daniel had to call me to ask me where Rick keeps his spare house key as Rick was too drunk to remember and still he talked to me as if I was ordering a photo sitting.

But that's okay, I don't expect him to like me.

Although I don't see why not. I thought I was a pretty likable person.

Larry has been hanging around more since I have started the church and he seems agitated and obsessed with a locked cupboard underneath the stairwell. Thank god the groundsman that Daniel hired turned up, as it took his mind off it for a while as he rode around on the back of the ride-on lawnmower.

I'm also meeting with Pamela this week at the church to go over the decorations so it's important it's looking the part. The only thing I need to organise is the seats in the church, there is a couple of old pews scattered but no sign of any others so I have decided to drop by Daniel's shop to ask him.

Sid is talking to me again after the misunderstanding with the maze which is great because Millie is due home today and I don't want Sid still grumpy with me when she's home. Then she would ask why and then Sid will tell her the reason is my imaginary friend broke his maze and Millie will send me back to the doctor for medication.

I have been so busy I haven't even had a chance to catch up with Tim and apologise for missing meditation class this week, mind you, after the last little incident with meditation class, I think everyone will probably breathe a sigh of relief that I'm not there.

So I decided I'd drop in at the bakery to see Tim after I'm finished up at Daniel's.

Weird knot in my stomach is back again.

Larry was sitting at my kitchen table tucking into a bowl of dry cereal.

Monty's sitting at his heals, not growling this time but catching the flakes of cereal as they fall.

Weird, so weird.

"Morning," Sid greeted, coming into the kitchen, "thought I might get started on the gardens today, maybe order some mulch, you know start getting it into shape for the wedding."

As I watched him reach for the box of cereal only to discover it was empty, I can't help but marvel at how far Sid has come since taking on his role here. I mean Sid used to be away with the fairies, have worthless opinions and be constantly hen-pecked by Millie.

Now he seems a bit more grounded, had valuable opinions and can stick up for himself. He's still hen-pecked by Millie but even I'm hen-pecked by Millie so I guess that doesn't count.

"We had more people here wanting those eye things," Sid said glancing at the mess on the floor beside Larry.

I sidled over towards the table so it looked like it was me who had been eating and dribbling bits all over the floor for Monty to eat.

"Not again," I groaned, "that's the 8th customer in two days, surely there can't be any left."

"There's not," said Sid, "I sold the last one this morning, the guy seemed a bit disappointed and asked if we're making more."

"Really. And what did you say?"

"I said I'll check with my supplier," he joked.

Well thank god they have sold out, the house was becoming a drive-through with the amount of youths wanting pillows, and not just the young ones either, seems popular with older age groups too. It's a very strange fetish with homemade eye-wear people have around here, and I sincerely hope I'm not missing something.

"Oh and Lisa," Sid said picking up a brush and shovel to start cleaning up the remnants of the cereal on the floor that Monty didn't eat, "you know how you were saying you think a ghost has been here causing havoc?"

"Oh my god, yes?" I said with enthusiasm.

"Well I don't think it's possible that spirits can do anything physical like eat pumpkin soup," he said as he continued to sweep up the cereal flakes that Larry had dropped from the corners of his month, "but it's possible especially if they haven't crossed over, that they'll make other mischief. Sometimes they do it for attention, you know, because there is something they still need to do."

"Oh, err, thanks."

"No problem."

"So you don't think I'm crazy?"

"I didn't say that."

At Daniel's office

I left Larry sitting in the car, where he was behind the wheel pretending he was driving, making appropriate transport noises.

Daniel was busy tapping away on his laptop when I entered his office. On the wall are some of his latest works of some local landscapes including the church and I have to say they are stunning.

Daniel seems pleased to see me for a change, which is a break-through because normally he looks awkward or disinterested to see me. I continue to look at the pictures on the wall as he nipped out the back to make us a cup of coffee.

I move closer to the wall to get a better look at the church picture, he had taken it recently as he had captured the pots of geraniums I had placed on the steps a few days ago (thanks to Sid's green fingers). Daniel has done such an amazing job capturing the light on the character of the building, I have to say he is very talented in that department. There's also a plaque label stating *'time period of a structure'* beside two earlier pictures of the church. One looked like it was taken back in the 1980's and the other maybe back in the 60's. I examined both pictures to compare them with the latest one when something caught my eye in the earliest picture. It seems it has been damaged in the corner, it looks like someone has smeared ink on it, but what really caught my eye is the two figures standing at the back of the church. They look like two men but I can't be sure as they're not a huge feature in the picture, in fact it seems like their presence was never intended to be in the frame.

Daniel appeared with two mugs and handed me one.

It occurred to me that he didn't even ask me how I liked my coffee, he must have remembered from last time.

"Church looks the same huh?" he said turning to smile at me.

I almost spilt my coffee when my heart decided to leap into my mouth, Daniel has never smiled at me before and he has such a nice smile, one that can send a tingle through you.

I cannot locate my voice box, so continued to look like I'm observing the pictures, until I can feel my heart start to beat at a normal pace again.

Looking at the two figures in the picture, it occurred to me one of them is wearing a coat very similar to Larry's, in fact it's almost the same style, except maybe not so tattered. I cannot tell the colour in a black and white photo, but the pair look young, maybe around their late teens, early twenties, but definitely young. I moved closer and squinted to get a better look.

"That one was taken back in 1959," said Daniel, observing my interest. "I got it from old archives kept by the church after my parents brought it, it's a bit damaged but still, it's a nice picture."

"How did it get damaged?" I asked, finding my voice again.

"It was used in police evidence after a missing person and suspected murder case of one of the locals in the area."

All of a sudden I had goosebumps, like I knew what Daniel was going to say next.

"Can you see the two people in the picture?" he continues, pointing to Larry and the figure beside him.

"Ah ha," I nodded as my voice fails me once again."Well this photo was the last sighting of the man that went missing, they suspected the other one had something to do with his disappearance."

Daniels phone started to ring.

"Excuse me," he said as he went to answer it.

I have a sense of dread coming over me as I thought back to what Rick said about old Larry passing away years ago and that he'd been told he was a drunk with simple tendencies, so I know it couldn't have been Larry who went missing, so it can only mean one thing.

It was Larry who was accused of murder.

"Don't like him!" snapped Larry, as he appeared at my side pointing his big beefy finger at the picture, causing me to let out a short scream.

Daniel's head whipped round in reaction to my scream but I really don't care at the moment, I'm more concerned that the ghost I have been hanging out with has murderous tendencies.

"Don't like him, don't like him," Larry continues to point at the picture as he chants his familiar chant of not liking anyone.

I'm a bit freaked, as am not sure if ghosts can murder physical beings and can't decide whether or not I need to be alarmed about that.

"Is everything okay?" Daniel asks.

Larry's chants are becoming louder.

"Fine," I squawked, "thought I saw, um, a mouse."

Larry is really getting upset now. And I think I need to get him out of here before he starts ripping Daniel's portraits off the wall.

Okay how am I going to do that. It's not like I can excuse myself and tell Larry he needs to go sit in a corner quietly and wait for me to finish up with the nice man.

"You really like this photo don't you?" Daniel asks.

"Huh? Oh, just more interested in the two men in the background, you know me, I love history."

God Larry isn't stopping, surely he's getting sick of repeating the same sentence.

"No, I didn't know that about you," Daniel said.

"Know what about me?"

"That you like history."

"Oh."

Daniel goes to say something else but is distracted by Tim the baker coming through the door in a panic.

All of a sudden Larry goes quiet and still.

"Run!" Larry yells as he bolts passed Tim and out the door.

"Lisa, there you are," Tim pants, "you must have left your handbrake off, your car has rolled back into Mrs Lashlie's Astra."

In library with Tim

Okay Mrs Lashlie's Astra only has a scratch, but that didn't stop her from being a wee bit upset. Larry hasn't turned up again but when he does there is no way I shall leave him in the car unattended ever again.

Wait, what am I saying.

After sorting out details with Mrs Lashlie and copping a lecture about handbrakes and how I should always leave my car in gear from Tim, I asked Daniel if he knew the details of the case that concerned Larry. Daniel said only what he'd been told, which was a little more than Rick knew.

Apparently old Larry was cleared of all charges as they didn't have enough evidence to go anywhere with the case. He said the other man in the picture was Bob Early and he was a known thief and troublemaker so they figured he must have done something wrong and bolted from the area, case closed.

But Tim, who was listening intently, suggested that if I was curious to know more there is probably information in the reference section of the library.

So here we are.

We found an article and are sitting at a table. Tim is on a break so he said he will stay.

Don't know why, I'm a big girl.

"Lisa, the night of meditation group where you went running after… you know."

"Yes," I said, blushing slightly at the memories of my 'moment'.

"You called him Larry."

Oh and speaking of Larry, he's now sitting at the table with us.

I'm a tiny bit pleased Tim is here now, I mean if Larry did try and kill me at least there will be a witness.

Or will there?

"... it's just that my mum also used to talk about Larry, she knew him when she was just a little kid. He used to sit around the streets then and she remembers giving him food 'cos no-one really cared much for him. But if you are connected to him, can you please ask him what happened to the old shop bell. Apparently what's now my bakery, used to have a real old time bell that the local kids loved, but it disappeared and she always thought he took it."

"Don't have it," Larry piped up.

"He said he doesn't have it," I said to Tim, feeling like Jennifer Love-Hewitt from Ghost Whisperer.

I read the article out loud to Tim while Larry listens intently.

It read "*the pair were last seen at the church grounds after being sighted at an attempt of breaking and entering the building by a local photographer. The pair went into hiding before the local police were informed. One local man, Larry Fitzgibbons was arrested a day later in his home for destruction of property, but his accomplice Bob Early never returned home. In a statement made by Mr Fitzgibbons to local police, he said he and his accomplice got separated after they were spotted. Mr Fitzgibbons claims he bolted from the scene, he states he has no recollection of where Mr Early went.*

The local photographer claimed he lost sight of the pair after the now famous picture was taken that featured the pair, saying he then left the scene to inform police. Mr Early's family said he was a good lad who may get himself into strife, but he had a good heart and were anxious to know of his whereabouts.

"Don't like him," said Larry after I closed the paper.

No excuse for murdering someone I thought to myself.

But wait a minute, it doesn't say anything in here that points to Larry murdering anyone, there could be a thousand explanations for this, I really want to ask Larry what happened but not while Tim is here.

Or any other people for that matter, it'll look and sound very strange talking to ones self. I glance at Tim for his reaction and he looks like he is pondering.

"Okay then, can you ask him *where* he thinks the old bell could be," Tim asks.

I rolled my eyes.

"So could you ask him?" Tim repeats.

"Smashed it, too noisy, in pieces," Larry piped up.

"Um... he said he doesn't know."

Back home

It's been a long day and I have a CWA meeting tonight.

So not looking forward to it, especially since I know it's going to be all about Neroli and her wonder pillows.

Millie's home, I can hear her bitching to Sid about something.

Think I'll stay clear of her for now.

Monty's pleased to see me as per usual and he is also getting used to Larry. He's still not at that waggy tail stage with Larry, but no snarling and barking, so that's progress.

I tried to talk to Larry on the way home to ask him what happened all those years ago but Larry's not much of a talker. The conversation in the car on the way home went something like...

"Larry what happened to your friend?"

"He gone."

"Where?"

"Don't know."

"What happened at the church?"

"Nuffing."

"Are you sad your friend has gone?"

"Don't like him."

"Did you hurt your friend?"

"Nah."

"So what do you think happened to him?"

"He gone."

So I think I can establish that Larry doesn't know much, he did however get a little agitated after my phone conversation with Daniel to say he thinks the pews are stored underneath the stairwell and did I want to come and meet up with him now as he thinks he may have a key and/or, set of bolt cutters.

And if I didn't have the stupid CWA meeting tonight I would have turned the car around immediately.

Although I wasn't too worried about the pews as they can wait.

I had said to Daniel I would meet up with him tomorrow after I finished my shift at the aged care home.

Larry was still agitated when we arrived home and actually said five words at the same time, "want to go to church."

I reminded him he is a spiritual being and can go anywhere he likes anytime, but I have to go to the CWA meeting. To which Larry then said he doesn't like me.

Go figure.

CWA meeting

I didn't get to stay at home long, only had time to give Millie's grumpy arse a quick hug (to which she responded with an apology for being grumpy and said she was tired) grab something to eat, feed Monty and get back here as Mrs Crankshaw had changed the time to an earlier one on account of lots to get through, as she see's a new business deal happening.

I need to establish boundaries on people changing times, after all, I am the president.

May have to consult Pamela on this one.

I did invite Pamela along for old times sake but she said that may not be a good idea as the CWA members have made it clear they don't want to associate with her. I feel sorry for her, I mean everyone makes mistakes, it doesn't mean she needs to be judged by them forever.

So the 150th meeting of the CWA is underway in the back room of the community hall.

Present are the usual:

Mrs Crankshaw (sporting a victory smirk).

Betty, Maggie, Fran, Mary and Gloria (all with smirks).

New this month, Neroli (sporting a huge victory smirk on her face and accompanied by another 10 shopping bags full of ugly eye pillows).

Also present are the unusual:

Munt, Stumpy, Morkdog and Patrick. Local youths who want to propose a business idea for the ugly eye pillows, invited and introduced by Mrs Crankshaw.

I can see this being the most interesting meeting ever.

I led the meeting.

"Okay, so as you know, big congratulations to all of you on the success of the garden stall. Top effort everyone, give yourself a pat on the back, now moving on…"

"Ahem," Mrs Crankshaw said, looking expectantly at me.

"…and," I sighed, "we couldn't have done this without Neroli and her ug… creations. Top effort, very proud. Please accept this small gift as a token of our appreciation."

God I was dreading that, had been hoping Mrs Crankshaw would forget about it.

Everyone now applauds while Mrs Crankshaw hands over a basket full of bath salts and loofers.

Even the youths with nicknames are clapping and yahooing.

I'll wait for the unnecessary fuss to die down.

Ohh Larry is here, didn't notice him sitting beside Mary.

Oh god, he has spied her ball of wool.

Don't look, just ignore him.

Think fuss has died down.

"Yes okay, well done Neroli. Now item two, Mrs Crankshaw I believe you have a report on fundraising."

Mrs Crankshaw stands up.

"Yes," she begins, "with the success of our recent fundraiser effort and Neroli's lovely eye pillows being so popular, I would like to propose that we have a website where you can purchase these lovely eye pillows and other CWA merchandise."

Enthusiastic murmurs of agreement all round.

Oh for gods sake.

Mrs Crankshaws continues, "these lovely lads here have also brought to my attention that they need to be readily available for purchasing and have suggested that maybe we approach a couple of local businesses like the pharmacy, to stock them on their counters."

More enthused murmurs of agreement.

"I would also like to thank them for coming tonight, they seem very keen to get involved with our fundraising efforts for the breast cancer foundation, to which the profits from these sales have been pledged."

"Yeah, good cause," spotty youth known as Munt agrees.

"Thank you my dear," Mrs Crankshaw muses, "so now, all for the idea of making these available at local businesses."

"Um before you do," I piped up in alarm, "I have a couple of questions."

All eyes turn to me.

Oh god, Larry is now rolling Betty's ball of wool on the floor, no-one has noticed yet.

"Yes Lisa!" Mrs Crankshaw said, sounding impatient.

"Neroli, are you happy to carry on making these? After all it's your time and materials being used. And secondly, why do people like them so much?"

Everyone looks offended at my last comment.

The spotty youths in the back row look guilty.

Hmmm something funny is going on here.

"It's fine," said Neroli in her singsong voice as she twirls her hair around her fingers.

"Well how about this," Maggie pipes up, "Neroli, let us know how much each one is to make and we will put a mark up on that. If they are popular, then no-one will object if we put the price up, that way it will cover costs and profits can go to charity."

Agreement all round.

"Okay how about we put the price up from $5 to $10?" suggested Mrs Crankshaw.

Murmurs of agreement yet again.

"All for…"

'Yay's' of agreement all round.

"Okay, passed."

"That still hasn't answered my question," I pressed.

"Oh Lisa, what question was that," Mrs Crankshaw said.

"About why are they so popular?"

Okay, again getting looks of offense. For god's sake, it's just constructive criticism.

Betty lets out a shriek causing all of us to jump.

Shit, and she has lost control of her waterworks again.

The youths are looking very uncomfortable at Betty's loss of waterworks.

"What is it dear?" Mrs Crankshaw asked.

"Look."

Oh god, Betty's ball of wool is moving along the floor, Larry is kicking it with his foot but of course no-one else can see that.

I hissed at Larry to cut it out as the room freaks out around me at the moving ball of wool.

Meeting over.

13

Next day at church

I convinced the CWA members and spotty youths that a draft of wind was responsible for moving the ball of wool.

But I really need to get to the bottom of these eye pillows, so much involvement by spotty youths over a craft item seems a little strange to me and Neroli is very reluctant to accept help with the manufacturing process saying it gives her time out from the kids and each pillow takes approximately 5 minutes to make as long as the material is cut and ready to be stuffed.

So Betty has agreed to prepare material for Neroli.

Hmmmmm.

But no time to dwell, as Larry and I are on our way to meet Daniel.

God butterflies in my stomach again.

We arrived at the church and Daniel is already there taking snapshots of the inside for his promotional brochure.

"Place looks great," he greeted as I walked in. Larry makes a beeline for the locked door under the stairs again, he seems obsessed with it.

"Err thanks," I said, this niceness towards me from Daniel is new to me, maybe he is warming to me after all.

A little twang of pleasure rushes through me at the thought of that.

But he is right, the place is looking great and I cannot believe the wedding is less than three weeks away now. I have to admit I couldn't have done it without Pamela, she has been great and she even said how nice it was to have a 'friend' to talk to.

Awww, she's so sweet.

"Okay," said Daniel as he looks at his last shot, "lets see if we can track down these pews."

He packs his camera back in his bag and pulls out a key from his pocket.

"Hopefully it's the right one," he said walking towards the stairwell. "It was on a key-ring that came with the church. If not, I have a hammer."

Larry's jumping up and down like an excited child as Daniel approaches the door.

"Like him, like him, like him," he chanted.

Well that makes a change.

"Oh," Daniel said, turning away from examining the lock, back to me, looking sheepish "seems the padlock's not locked anyway," he said with a 'silly me' look.

"Ah well, you weren't to know," I soothed back.

Oh my god, did Daniel and I just have a 'moment'.

Larry's not making gagging noises like he does when Rick and I have a 'moment', well it's more like Rick has a moment, I normally have other things to think about. But if Larry isn't making gagging noises now, then it couldn't have been anything.

Daniel pulls at the door but it won't open wide, he can open it just enough so there is a small gap.

"It's stuck," said Daniel, "like it's locked from the inside."

Shit.

"Poo, certainly smells a bit in there. A bit rancid like no one's been in there for 50 years," he said, getting down further on his knees to have a look though the gap.

Larry looks pissed off.

"Okay, looks like there are pews in there, I'll duck out and see if I have a crowbar or something in the car to force it open wider."

I was too busy looking at Daniel in action to really take in what he said but I guess he is on to it.

Larry's looking really agitated.

But I guess the good news is we have pews for the seating and because the guest list for the actual ceremony is only small (family and close friends) we're not going to need a lot, so I can tick that off my list.

Larry is now sticking his nose through the gap and being a supernatural being, his head has disappeared through the timber. All I can see is his backside sticking up in the air. So funny.

I stand taking in the room and mentally placing where the pews should go. I'm wondering whether to go with the traditional look of all facing one way or go a bit different and have them facing towards the aisle?

I might consult Pamela on that one.

What's that noise?

I turned to look as another supernatural being lunges out from behind the wooden door knocking Larry backwards.

Holy shit!

My whole body feels like it's one big goosepimple as shock comes over me. Larry, who quickly recovers from being knocked over, recognises his fellow supernatural being straight away.

"Don't like you," Larry screams before lunging back at him, knocking him to the floor.

Now it's all on, Larry and fellow ghost are in a wrestling match on the floor.

"I can't find a crowbar," said Daniel making an appearance again, oblivious to the fight happening in front of him. "But I found this," he continues, producing the handle of a tyre jack.

I cannot peel my eyes away from what is happening. And I am strongly suspecting this spirit that has suddenly made an appearance, is indeed Bob, the missing man from the photo. And if he has appeared from inside the cupboard then...

Oh my god, oh my god.

"Can't seem to fit the bar through the gap enough to get leverage," Daniel said, trying to pull at the door.

"Ah never mind then," I said, quickly pulling my thoughts together as Larry and Bob roll past me.

"Don't worry, I will get the proper tools," Daniel said. "I don't want to break the door. It's also probably a good idea that I get some air-freshener or something to disguise the old smell, seems a better idea than me going in to clean it out," he chuckled.

This would be a great moment of bonding for Daniel and I, if Larry wasn't getting the shit beaten out of him beside me.

"No bother," I quickly said, "maybe pews aren't the way to go. I was thinking of maybe hiring some chairs anyway, so no biggie."

"I know of a great place to hire chairs," Daniel said, giving up on the door and heading for his camera case.

"Good, good," I said, shuffling him closer to the exit, "how about we head back to your office and get that organised now."

"Oh... okay," said Daniel.

"Great," I beamed, shuffling him outside the door, "I'll see you in ten. I just have to, err, check something out."

I quickly shut the big heavy church door on him, yes okay, very rude and strange behaviour, but I think I want to throw up.

Sitting in my car outside Daniel's office

I'm pretending to be taking a call on my phone but really I'm trying to unscramble my brain.

Larry is here beside me, his face looks like it's been through a mincing machine, not to mention he has two black eyes.

I did ask Larry if that was his friend, just to try and make sense of what I was suspecting, but the conversation went like this:

"Larry was that your friend that went missing?"

"Yep, don't like him."

"Why were you fighting with him?"

"Don't like him."

"So does that mean he is dead like you?"

"Yep, he gone."

"So you have just found out where he is?"

"Yep."

"Larry, is his body underneath the stairwell?"

"Yep."

Shit that's what I thought. I'm going to dread asking this but I have to.

"Larry did you kill your friend and put him underneath the stairs?"

"Nah."

Phew, I didn't think so.

"But don't like him," Larry said.

"Yeah, I can see that."

I got through the ordering of the chairs which are white and wedding looking but I don't know how I managed to get through the next half hour. I can see now what happened that day all those years ago when Bob and Larry bolted after being seen breaking and entering, Larry headed home and Bob took refuge in the church.

 And what a way for Bob to die, hiding in a cupboard and being unable to get out. I wonder if it was dehydration or starvation that killed him. I shuddered at the thought.

And also, why didn't anyone hear him? Surely the police would have searched the whole of the church.

 Although it's a thick, solid timber door to under the stairwell and if it was locked, maybe they didn't bother.

But now what I'm concerned about is whether or not to tell the police of my suspicions. And really, what am I going to say? I saw the ghost of the missing person and my other ghost told me his body is under there.

No.

And what about the up and coming wedding? If I get the police involved now, Matt is absolutely going to refuse to get married there, Pamela would agree and we would have to find another venue.

Not to mention, what would happen to my reputation as an event planner.

So at this stage I'm not going to say anything until after the wedding. Then I'll figure something out.

Now I do have to concentrate on the wedding, not on the fact there is a dead body underneath the stairwell of the perfect wedding venue.

I'll just keep reminding myself it's no different to dead bodies being buried outside the perfect wedding venue. Okay, it's not quite the same thing.

Think happy thoughts now.

"Lisa, you don't look well," Daniel said, pulling me from my thoughts.

Shit, wonder how long he has been standing here for.

I told him that I'm feeling a bit off and that I think I should go home and lie down.

He went to say something else but my phone interrupted him.

It's Mum and Dad, I'm just going to ignore it.

Shit, Larry's playing with the handbrake again.

Facebook Status Update.

Lisa Collins: Needs a drink (or two).

Lisa is attending Matt and Neroli's wedding.

14

Almost three weeks later

Oh my god, the day is finally here.

Well, not until the day after tomorrow and to be honest it's gone so quick it's like I went to bed and woke up three weeks later. I have not had time for anything else and even Millie has stayed out of my way and not interfered.

Mind you, she said I was a grumpy bitch.

That's the pot calling the kettle black.

And Larry has not helped at all, if fact he has been the biggest pain in the arse ever and I know he wants me to go to the police and tell them where Bob is, but how can I explain to him that it's all about timing. I mean after all timing isn't anything Larry understands now.

But why should he care anyway because every time we go to the church Larry and Bob end up in a fist fight. In fact just the other day, Bob spent the entire afternoon pulling a piece of hardwood that Larry had wedged in, out of somewhere we won't mention. So it's not like they are friends or anything.

Rick is also being a pain in the arse. Not that he is wanting me to report dead bodies or placing hard objects in unspeakable places, but he is being overly affectionate and every second of the day I'm getting text messages saying he can't live without me and blah, blah.
So annoying.

The good news is, Neroli has been too busy producing ugly eye pillows to worry about anything else so she just does what she is told. The ugly eye pillows are still selling like hot cakes at the local pharmacy, thank god I managed to talk Mrs Crankshaw and the CWA out of doing a website, well for now anyway.
So after I get this wedding done with and report the dead body under the stairs to get the supernatural beings off my back, I'm so going to get to the bottom of it all.
Matt is, quote 'over it and just wants to get pissed', so he just does what he is told as well.
But no time to reflect, as Mum and Dad are due here any minute and to be honest I'm looking forward to their visit. Even though they left me a message saying there is something they need to discuss with me in their 'you wait till you get home' voice, but I haven't got time to worry about their wrath.

It's probably because I have been ignoring their calls, but honestly, build a bridge....

I sauntered into the kitchen in my pj's. Millie was sitting at the kitchen table having breakfast, I have to say she's looking a lot better lately and starting to eat again.

"Morning," she said in her bright, cheerful voice and as irritating as that voice is, it's nice to hear her back to normal.

"How's the wedding planner?" she chuckled.

Millie is getting excited about the wedding which is really great, she seems more enthusiastic then Neroli.

"Better when it's over," I yawned, "I have never felt so tired."

"So what's on the agenda today?"

"Well coffee with Pamela first... What??"

Millie pretends to spit every time I mention Pamela's name.

"Oh grow up Millie, she's not that bad, I mean everyone makes mistakes, get over it."

"So all of a sudden she's your best friend?" scoffed Millie, "come on Lisa, she is just waiting for you to screw up.

I mean she can't stand Neroli so what makes you think she is pleased with her son, who by the way is just out of puberty, marrying someone way older then him and who has children?"

"Um the fact she is helping with the preparations."

"So. Doesn't make her Miss Nicey Nice all of a sudden."

God Millie is so negative.

"And where did you get the crazy idea she is trying to sabotage the wedding and has loathing tendencies towards her future daughter'n'law anyway? God Millie, you do like to dramatise things."

"It wasn't an idea, Daniel told me."

"Daniel told you. Really?"

"Yep, the other night. Pamela is friends with his aunty, probably the only person left in this place that still likes her."

I'm speechless.

"Ask Daniel if you don't believe me," Millie said in her smug voice.

"I don't believe it," I said in my smug voice back.

Ohh Mum and Dad are here.

"Yeah, run away from the truth." I heard Millie say as I went to greet Mum and Dad.

Okay big deep breath.

Rick is not here yet and thank goodness, as I need a bit of time to adjust to their presence before telling them about Rick and I.

I haven't put the ring on today, in fact I haven't put the ring on all week, Rick hadn't noticed anyway so I'll leave it off for now.

Dad is the first out of the Winnebago, he looks like he has a tan.

"Hello luv," he greeted, "have you lost weight? I hope you have been eating."

That's Dad's line every time he greets me, I could be as big as a house and he'll still ask if I'm eating enough.

Millie has appeared to greet my parents.

Mum seems a little annoyed and tight when I hug her, can't imagine what I have done, I mean it's not like I have spoken to them or anything.

Anyway greetings over, I turn to go and get dressed for one more meeting with Pamela to go over the final stuff.

"Hold up young lady, we need a word with you," Dad said as I announce my exit.

Oh god.

"Dad, can't it wait? I have a zillion things to do."

Larry's now gone into the Winnebago for a look, god I hope he behaves, that's the last thing I need.

Millie was about to sneak off, but she back-tracked when she found out I was going to get a talking to. She's a bitch like that.

"No it can't wait, honestly, do we have to read on facetime that you're engaged!!"

Oh, shit.

"Yes," said Mum all tight lipped, "why didn't you tell us?"

Oh crap.

Even Millie's not smirking at this one.

"I made it up to err, stop a stalker."

"A stalker?" asked Dad in alarm.

God when am I going to learn to shut up.

"No, not a stalker exactly, just a guy that liked me. Anyway I put that I was engaged to Rick to stop him from fancying me."

"Bit of an extreme measure to stop someone from liking you," said Dad, "why didn't you just say no?"

"You're right Dad, I should have just said no, god why didn't I think of that. Okay running late now, better go get dressed."

I turned towards the house past Millie.

"Yes run, run," she whispers and giggles at me as I bolt past her to the safety of my bedroom.

Phew that was a close one.

8.30 am, with Pamela

Pamela's still being so nice and greeted me with an enormous hug when I panted through the door half an hour late for our breakfast meeting. I quickly ran through the list of last minute things.

Pamela has agreed to be there when the hired chairs get delivered to the church, which would help me tremendously as I have the marquee arriving at the same time. Sid will be too busy grooming the animals to take care of the chairs and Millie will be taking Neroli for her last minute dress fit.

I thought back to what Millie said about Pamela wanting to see this wedding fail; what a load of crap, Pamela is so keen to see this wedding go forward, after all she has put a lot of money towards it, if she didn't want Matt and Neroli to get married, she wouldn't *pay* for it.

I think Millie might just be jealous of the new found friendship between Pamela and I.

No sign of Larry so far. He must be hanging out with Mum and Dad.

God I hope he's being good.

9.30 am, Daniels office

The tee-shirts have arrived and I have to say, they look okay. I checked out the other merchandise that has arrived too and it looks great. Daniel helped me load the boxes into the car to take them home.

Still no sign of Larry.

I informed Daniel that Pamela had volunteered to be there when the chairs were delivered. Daniel went quiet but didn't give any inkling that Pamela may be a wedding sabotager, which proves my point that Millie was just making it up.

10.00 am, in bakery with Tim

The catering is all sorted and everything is on track, Tim has also made the wedding cake and it almost brings a tear to my eye, it's so perfect.

Tim gave me an awkward hug, think it was meant to be a heartfelt one, but it came off all wrong.

Larry's still a no show.

10.30 am

Back home to drop off boxes.

I spied Larry relaxing in Mum's good outdoor arm chair and wearing sunglasses like he is on holiday, well at least he's not causing havoc.

Mum and Dad are busy setting up for their stay so best I don't disturb them.

Monty is loving the extra visitors.

11.00 am

Millie's off to pick up Neroli for a last minute dress fit, I also have entrusted her to pick up the alcohol for tonight's hen's night. It's not a huge affair, just drinks with the girls at my place while the boys are going to Rick's. I can't see it being a huge night with the girls with Neroli being pregnant and the CWA ladies not being big drinkers. I'm guessing we're not going to need much wine, so I texted Millie as an after-thought and asked her to buy more tea-bags and hot chocolate instead.

11.30 am

Shit Rick's here and he is heading straight towards my parents Winnebago to say hello, what if Dad mentions that I told him that our engagement was a fake. Shit, shit, need a diversion, quick.

12.00 pm

"Wow, what was that?!" Rick said, as he leaned over in bed to cuddle me. Yes, yes, okay, I used seduction techniques to divert Rick away from my parents, so what of it.

I convinced Rick that we shouldn't make a big deal of our engagement until after the wedding and maybe we shouldn't mention it at all as it will take the shine off the wedding.
Rick said that was a very thoughtful idea and how that was something he loved about me, the fact that I'm thoughtful and blah, blah.

Now Mum is knocking at the bedroom door asking if I have seen Dad's sunglasses as she was sure she didn't take them out of the motor-home.

12.30 pm

Okay Larry and the sunglasses cannot be found anywhere. Rick's gone home to get prepared for Matt's bachelor party tonight.

1.00 pm

Sid informs me all animals are bathed and all coats are gleaming white and ready for the wedding.

1.30 pm

Sid's washing the animals again.

2.00 pm

Sid's given up washing the animals and said he'll do them again tomorrow. There's still no sign of Larry. Neroli and Millie are back and now Mum is relaxing in the outdoor arm-chair with Neroli's eye pillows on her eyes.

Dad has taken my car into town to buy new sunglasses.

2.30 pm

Am tired, I need a nap.

5.00 pm

Shit!!!!

I've lost half a day and cannot believe no-one woke me, Millie said to chill out and stop stressing, it's just a hens night, there is no need to put on airs and graces.

I informed Millie that the hen's night was her responsibility to organise anyway.

Millie said she has organised it and I'm just being a control freak.

7.00 pm

Sid's off to the bachelor party with Dad, I am a bit worried about Dad going, especially since Rick had informed me that Matt's youthful mates are going to be there, hopefully everyone will be on their best behaviour.

Larry has turned up again, no sign of Dad's sunglasses and when I asked Larry, he informed me he 'don't have 'em'.

I'm not liking the chances of an answer to their whereabouts, so I'm not going to push it.

Larry has settled down a bit over Bob and his whereabouts, I think he is starting to understand that the real world won't get married in a church if they are aware there is a dead body underneath the stairwell. Besides he knows where Bob is now, he's been under there for a while, a few more days isn't going to make a difference.

Although I have been suppressing a lot of guilt with happy thoughts, I mean I'm sure Bob's family would like to know where he is straight away.

Even though Tim informs me he doesn't think any of Bob's family are still alive, all the same I cannot help but feel I'm doing a big wrong.

I promised Larry I will put it right, but right now I shall block it out with this glass of wine.

7.30 pm

Everyone has now arrived and glasses of champagne are being passed around to toast Neroli.

Also Millie's made us all wear a pink feather boa and tutu.

Even Larry has one.

Although Millie obviously didn't make him wear it, that was his choice.

I had asked Pamela to come, as after all it's her future daughter-in-laws hen's party. But she declined on account of the possibility of CWA members using her for a piñata.

Which is so unfair.

Anyway, everyone seems to be having a good time and there are lots of giggles. Millie is being the hostess with the most-ess and we have been having heaps of fun playing games, Millie's taken care of everything including food. Which is great as I have no energy left and a big day tomorrow. I'm also thinking about Daniel, a lot lately, which is really confusing me.

"Skull," said Millie, passing me a nip glass full of black goop.

"How come you're not drinking?" I asked, noticing for the first time all evening that she has been drinking orange juice.

"Well someone has to have a clear head to organise this lot," she said.

Looking around at everyone, including the CWA members who are sipping drinks and talking recipes, I cannot see how Millie thinks she might have to rein in any wild behaviour.

Larry is sitting in between Mrs Crankshaw and Mum, sipping someone's drink and still wearing his tutu.

If it could be a Kodak moment, it would be a perfect shot.

I wonder how the boys are going?

8.30 pm

Neroli's onto her third cocktail and I am disgusted with her behaviour given the fact she is pregnant.

Neroli insists again that she is not pregnant so I said prove it and she said she would if she had a pregnancy test, to which I said that I had, and she said fine bring it (Neroli doesn't get drunk often as she's a really obnoxious person when inebriated) so I said fine and now Neroli's in the toilet peeing on a stick.

Millie's shaking her head at me.

Mum and Mrs Crankshaw are getting on really well, luckily I managed to grab Mrs Crankshaw when she first arrived and told her that I haven't had a chance to tell my folks about my engagement and want to wait till after the wedding.

Mrs Crankshaw patted me on the arm and said 'mums the word dear'.

Fran, Betty and Mary look all flushed in the cheeks and Maggie is going through the music trying to find something decent to dance to, as doof doof music is way to fast for her.

9.00 pm

Okay according to the stick, Neroli is not pregnant.

Well you can't blame me for suspecting, given the fact no-one knew about the last baby until it arrived.

Neroli and Millie are taking great pleasure in saying I told you so.

9.30 pm

Shit, just on my way to the toilet and I noticed Monty's been into Neroli's bag of ugly eye pillows that she brought round to fill an order for Fran's nephew. I managed to stuff them back into the bag before anyone noticed, my god he can be naughty sometimes.

Maggie and Neroli are dancing to Clearance Clearwater Revival.

Larry is also dancing but his technique is coming off more like an airplane.

9.45 pm

Betty, Fran and Mary are almost asleep.

9.50 pm

Betty is asleep with her head between her knees.

10.00 pm

Millie cuts the music as she has written a poem for Neroli and wants to read it.

We're all settled in for Millie's poem when Monty came running in with one of the eye pillows in his mouth, I thought I put those out of reach, honestly.

Mrs Crankshaw grabs Monty as he shoots passed and tries to exchange the eye pillow for a soggy cracker, but Monty is possessive of the pillow and not willing to exchange it. In fact Monty's acting all weird, I have never seen him like this before, it's like he is hyper or something.

Millie announced she'd better go to the loo again before starting the poem and Mrs Crankshaw has given up on Monty and let him go.

"I'm sure we can afford to sacrifice one pillow," she said as Monty bolted from the room again.

I'm thinking someone needs to wake Betty and take her home before she falls off the chair.

"Um Lis," Millie said, gingerly tapping me on the shoulder and discreetly instructing me to follow her.

Oh that's right, she has a surprise goodie bag for Neroli. We were going to stuff it in a hiding place, blindfold Neroli and make her find it.

"How do you want to do this?" I asked when we were out of earshot.

"Forget about that," said Millie, "how many eye pillows has the CWA sold?"

"Oh… I don't know, thousands, why?"

"Well get your big girl knickers on because you're going to need them."

15

In passage way with Millie

Oh no!!!

Monty has been into the bag of eye pillows and torn them to bits, spilling the contents everywhere.

Wait a minute is that...

Oh no, no, no.

My hand flew to my mouth to keep in the shocked gasp, realising the reality of what we have done.

Neroli's eye pillows are filled with dope.

Okay, not just dope, it seems she has mixed it with lavender, but all the same you cannot mistaken the colour and smell.

And we have been selling these like hot cakes.

Oh my god.

Another wave of dread comes over me as I realise the young ones must have known.

"And how much were you selling these for?" Millie asked, reading my thoughts.

"Um, five dollars," I squawked.

"What's going on out here?" Mrs Crankshaw asked as she made an appearance. "Is that our eye pillows? Oh what a naughty dog."

I gave Millie a 'don't you say anything' glare.

"Wots hapin?" said Maggie, staggering through with her wine glass.

"We had a bit of an accident with the pillows," Mrs Crankshaw sighed, "I'll fetch the vacuum cleaner shall I?"

Maggie giggled.

"Well now we know what her secret ingredient is."

"By the looks of that, it's lavender and dried marjoram," Mrs Crankshaw sighed again.

"Are you sure?" Maggie said, "I thought it looked more liked dried basil."

Larry has made his appearance, he looks guilty to begin with, until he realises it wasn't him that made the mess this time. He puts his hands over his mouth and points to the contents on the floor in mock horror.

Millie and I seem to be holding our breath.

Maggie picked up a hand full of contents and held it up to her nose. "Whoa is that...?"

"They're filled with dope," Millie said, blurting it out like she couldn't hold it in any longer.

"She has to know," Millie said, addressing my look of horror at her outburst. "It won't be long until word gets round."

Maggie looks like she has gone from drunk to sober in an instant.

Larry seems to think it's hilarious as he's lying on the floor pounding it with his fists in hysterics .

I should remind him that the only thing funny here is him wearing a pink tutu.

"Are you sure?" Mrs Crankshaw scoffed, bending down for a closer look.

"I can't be here," said Maggie backing away in alarm, "my husband's a lawyer, this is bad, very bad."

"Well lets ask her," said Millie, "but it certainly looks and smells like weed."

Millie went to discreetly fetch Neroli while I discreetly try to stop Larry from rolling in it.

"Shut the door dear, there seems to be a draft," Mrs Crankshaw instructed.

10 minutes later in kitchen

The contents of the ugly eye pillows is all cleaned up apart from a small amount needed as evidence to present to Neroli.

Neroli has also gone from drunk to sober and just confessed that yes, is it dope and she only used it as a filler, not for clever packaging of illegal substances.

"But there were so many," Mrs Crankshaw said in an alarmingly calm voice, "where did you get the... you know, stuff?"

Neroli looks straight at me and it all makes sense.

"It was *you* who took the dope from my ceiling," I cried.

"What dope?" Millie asked in alarm.

"You're growing marijuana!" Mrs Crankshaw asked in shock.

"Oh this is bad, very, very bad," Maggie mumbled behind the hands that were covering her face.

"Pfff, no I wasn't *personally*, it was already there in the ceiling when I arrived here.

I only found it after Matt and I got up the ladder to see what was up there, it wasn't till after we discovered Rick was squatting in the attic and the police were here investigating that I discovered it had gone missing."

"Then why didn't you tell the police?" Mrs Crankshaw asked.

Millie agrees.

"Hang on a minute, I'm not the one that was using it for distribution, Neroli was," I argued.

".....very, very bad," Maggie mumbled.

"Yes Lisa but you should have disposed of it when you found it, it's a bit irresponsible if you ask me." Mrs Crankshaw added.

What?? Never mind that Neroli *stole* it from my ceiling. I'm speechless.

Neroli continues to stare at the floor, like she has been doing for the last ten minutes and taking *no* responsibility.

I cannot believe I'm the one getting lectured, I mean I'm the one that objected to marketing the ugly creations in the first place.

Told them so.

"Okay," said Millie, rubbing her brow, "so the only people who know about this is the people in this room so I think it should stay this way and we pretend this never happened."

"Until when Millie? One accidentally rips open?" said Maggie.

"We could do a product recall," said Mrs Crankshaw.

"But we sold hundreds!" cried Maggie.

Everyone goes into silent pondering, Neroli hasn't said anything and I'm getting very annoyed of the attitude of CWA members (apart from Millie, she's not CWA).

They're quick to lecture me about harbouring marijuana plants in my ceiling but when Neroli puts the whole of the CWA and members into jeopardy by manufacturing it into smelly eye pillows, everyone's okay with it.

"Alright then, may I make a proposal that we say nothing and hope this just blows over, that includes the rest of the CWA members. After all the less they know the better, then they can't be an accessory after the fact. So all agreed?" said Millie.

I wonder if this is a good time to point out that Millie is not a member of the CWA so officially she cannot vote nor propose on matters.

"That means no more eye pillows unless they contain stuff that's not going to get us into trouble, okay Neroli?" Mrs Crankshaw warns.

"Yep, agreed," Neroli said as if nothing's amiss, oh my god she is unbelievable.

"Yes agreed," nodded Maggie, "Lisa?"

"As long as I don't get any more lectures about providing marijuana in the first place," I said.

Millie rolls her eyes. "Fine whatever, so do you agree, not a word?"

"I s'posse."

Shit, Larry's emptying the contents out of the vacuum cleaner bag.

Facebook Status Update.

Lisa Collins.

List of things I am over:

eye pillows,

misunderstood ghosts,

weddings.

16

Day before wedding - 6.05 am

Oh my god, oh my god, the day is almost here.

I should get up as I have lots to do.

I haven't heard how the boys got on at their stag night. If it was anything like ours then they would have all been sipping tea in their pj's and off to bed before midnight.

Neroli's hen's night turned out to be a fizzer after our 'mishap' as Mrs Crankshaw put it.

I cannot believe Neroli would be so stupid, but the worst thing is that when I told her that, Mrs Crankshaw and Millie pulled me aside and said that I should let it go until after the wedding and yes she did the wrong thing and blah, blah, but is a nice girl who didn't mean harm.

I really want to gag.

But okay, fair enough, I'll let it go till after the wedding.

Even though it erk's me that Neroli is walking around like nothing has happened.

Millie reminded me that that's the whole fucking point.

So anyway the night ended up like this:

Neroli carried on like nothing had happened and seemed to have a good time.

Maggie got even more drunk, not for fun but to try and block out any memory of what happened and eventually got carried out to the car to her waiting husband who had come to collect her, chanting 'I know nuffing' on the way.

Fran and Mary went home before supper was served as it was the latest they have stayed awake in like, 20 years.

Betty fell asleep on the sofa and now I have to wet'n'dry vacuum it, due to loss of bladder control again.

Mrs Crankshaw and Mum decided on a game of gin rummy over cocoa and Larry and Monty appeared to be stoned and mellowed in the corner.

But strangely Neroli said she had a great time and I guess that's the main thing.

But right now I have a zillion things to do.

Right after I have another 10 minutes in bed.

10 minutes later

Someone's knocking at my door.

Oh it's probably just Larry, he's been doing that a lot lately, especially when I'm sleeping.

"Lisa!"

That doesn't sound like Larry.

"Lisa wake up, it's nearly lunch time."

Okay nearly lunch time

I raced out to the kitchen in a mad panic throwing clothes on and barking instructions at everyone.

Daniel's in the kitchen making coffee.

Okay, where is everyone?

The house is quiet and it appears no-one is here.

Millie must be still in bed and where is Sid???

"Why didn't anyone wake me?" I said at the top of my voice.

I cannot believe no one woke me, oh my god I'm not going to get anything done before rehearsals at 5pm!!

Even Larry isn't here!

"Well I did, now. And they all had jobs to do," Daniel said passing my cup to me.

"Sid has organised the animals and is down town getting pegs for the marquee, which by the way is erected on the front lawn and looks great. Millie and Neroli have gone to collect the dresses and I've just arrived to drop off the glassware and cloths for the tables, which by the way are here and Sid will put up this afternoon."

"Yes but what about the rest of the things? I still have to pick up the cake and what about the music and the chairs at the church and...."

God where's my phone.

"And where are Mum and Dad??"

"Your parents are having lunch down at the Crankshaws," Daniel elaborated at my outburst, "Pamela's sorted everything else, she is going down before rehearsal to sort the chairs at the church; so sit down, have a coffee and get your thoughts together," Daniel instructed.

All of a sudden I feel calm.

"Okay," I beamed.

Half an hour later

Daniel is so interesting.

He has been all around the world photographing people and he likes poetry and line dancing and is more of a cat person than a dog person.

So, so interesting.

Anyway, I had a lovely cup of coffee with Daniel and now feel like I can listen to him all day, but alas he said he'd better get going and he will pop down to the church later to let Pamela in.

I told Daniel about how great Pamela is and I couldn't have done it without her.

Daniel's not looking convinced as he moved off his chair.

"You could have done it without her," Daniel said as he placed his cup in the sink, "but you would have done it your way, which would be more interesting," he flashed a smile as he went out the door.

Now what's that supposed to mean?

Shit look at the time.

1.00 pm meeting with Tim at bakery

Tim has a new bell.

I picked the cake up and Tim reported that all is ready and organised and he is open to wearing a headset for tomorrow at my request.

1.30 pm

Back home Neroli and Millie return with the dresses, they said all is organised with the make-up lady and they also confirmed their booking with the hairdressing lady in the morning.

Tom's hyped up on sugar.

Great, just what I need.

2.00 pm

Sid has finished putting tables up in the marquee.

Have to say, it looks great.

2:15 pm

I'm rounding up the flock of geese after Tom let them out of their enclosure.

2:17 pm

Still chasing geese.

2:20 pm

Geese now chasing me.

2:22 *pm*

Sid's got the geese under control.

2.30 *pm*

Tom's in the time out room (aka Sid's bedroom).

3.00 *pm*

I think my brain is going to explode and can't believe Millie and Neroli are just sitting around in the sun and not... well, *doing* anything.

Millie said there's nothing to do until rehearsal.

I told her I beg to differ and she said fine, run around and wear myself out like the control freak I am.

There's been no sign of Larry all day, I hope he's okay.

Tom has now emerged from time out and has been given a job by Sid of blowing up balloons.

Sid's kind of good with kids, shame Millie doesn't want them.

4.00 *pm*

Okay, I think everything's sorted, better check my list again. So nervous.

I have organised Millie and Sid's wedding before, but this is different, I mean this is a paid job, my first ever as my own business and it's kind of a big deal and I sooo want everything to go smoothly.

And just to ensure that it does, I'll put it on my list to the universe, I mean some of that list has come true so far.

Although I wish they would hurry up with my new car.

I opened my purse, pulled out the magic list and smoothed it out.

Dear universe.

Here is the list of things I want. Hope you can help.

- Rick to always be at my side and treat me like a queen.

- Rick and I to get married and have two – no – three children all with Rick's dark complexion.

- To run a successful wedding planning business.

- A petting zoo filled with white animals (no roosters).

- A new car, prefer a small car that has blue tooth and is environmentally friendly (that's one for you).

- To lose ten kilos, especially around my inner thighs and my lower abdomen.

- And could you arrange the above four requests before 20th May?

- For Matt and Neroli to get married at the old church located at Cannon's Toad, Taromeo, Post Code 2432.

- For everything to run smoothly with the wedding and everyone to be happy and have a great successful day.

There, that should do it.

Actually on second thoughts, better cover all matters here:

- For the police to find Bob's body and declare that the cause of death was accidental and clear Larry's name formally.

- That no-one be held responsible for the eye pillow saga (except Neroli of course).

I keep thinking I've missed something.

"Nearly time for rehearsal," Millie said as she entered carrying baby Bailey on her hip.

I folded up my paper, I'm sure I would think of it later.

Millie kind of suits babies.

Not that I'd ever tell her that, she would rip my head off like a preying mantis.

Neroli also sauntered in behind Millie.

Neroli's calm and doesn't seem bothered that she is getting married tomorrow.

"Neroli, is Matt meeting us down there?" I asked.

"I don't know, haven't heard from him."

"Since when?"

"Since last night."

"Can you phone him?"

"Yeah I've tried but he has his phone switched off."

Come to think of it, I haven't seen Rick either, odd.

"Never mind, I'll call Rick."

Rick's not answering either.

Okay, I'll leave a voice message.

Oh and finally my parents have returned home after a very, very long lunch at the Crankshaws, can't anyone comprehend the fact there is a wedding to organise.

"Lisa this is your job," Millie piped up, as if she read my thoughts, how scary is that.

Wait, what am I saying? I mean I talk to ghosts. Strange times we are living in.

"You're getting paid to organise an event and it's part of your job to stress and worry so you know, you made your bed and all."

"Yes I know," I wailed, "but people just won't do as I say."

Millie tutted and shook her head.

"Well if you're ready, we'll wait in the car."

"Fine I'll just try Rick one more time."

Ohh hang on, phones ringing.

Hmmm don't know that number.

"Hello?"

"Come now, church help."

Sounds like Larry.

"Larry is that you?"

"Come now, church."

Yes that's Larry, I wondered where he had been.

"We are just leaving now don't panic."

"Come now, come now, come now, come now."

I'd better hang up, this could go on for days.

I tried Rick's number again but there was no reply, I left another message that we are going to the church for rehearsals.

Hope he remembers.

At church

Larry is really agitated and waiting for me when I arrive, Pamela is also here as well as Daniel.

No sign of Rick and Matt yet.

"Lisa," Pamela greeted me, all smiles, "the chairs have arrived and I have to say, they don't work well with the church so I have asked Daniel if we could have those pews after all. He is just getting the door open now, I hope you don't mind, I don't want to interfere but it's just not working," she said fluttering her eyelashes at me.

Shit.

"Ahh no, that's fine," I tried to muster a brave face.

No wonder Larry's agitated.

I hurried into the church to stop Daniel from opening the door, I'm not liking what I'm going to find but I have to stop Daniel from going under that stairwell.

"Find him, find him," Larry was chanting behind Daniel as he gently prised the door open with some tools.

Oh my god there goes that old smell again.

Pamela had moved off to greet the Reverend who had just arrived.

"There, done without damage," Daniel said, dusting himself off, "looks like the inside lock was locked and then the key broke in the lock. So who's going in?" he chuckled.

"Um I will, but not just yet," I said, slamming the door, only to have it bounce back on my leg.

Great, to top it off I'm going to have a bruise on my leg.

Breathing through the pain I explained to Daniel that no need to do this yet, I will come down tonight and set up.

Larry is now really agitated with me and keeps tugging on my sleeve insisting I find Bob.

I can't deal with this right now, Rick and Matt still haven't turned up and Daniel is asking if I'm sure that I want to leave the seats till later since we are all here waiting and blah, blah, so I had to get snappy and insist my way is better.

20 minutes later

God where are Matt and Rick?

"Okay we will give them 10 more minutes," I said to a very inpatient Reverend.

Neroli has once again tried to phone Matt without success. I asked Daniel when was the last time he saw them and he said he cannot recall as he crashed on the spare bed and woke up early this morning and just left. So I phoned Sid and Sid said he'd left (and asked, didn't I recall him coming home) as he doesn't approve of strippers so he bailed early in the night.

I looked at Daniel when Sid mentioned a striper to which Daniel looked a bit sheepish.

Larry's really tugging at me now.

God I have to settle him down.

I excused myself and went outside so I can talk to my imaginary friend in peace.

"God what is it with you?" I scorned as soon we were out of earshot.

"Find him, find him."

"No Larry I can't, not yet, after the wedding okay. If we find him now police will come and then there'll be no wedding."

"Find him, find him, find him."

Oh god I can't cope with this.

"Just leave it alone," I hissed as I walked away.

I met Daniel coming the other way.

"Do you want me to go round there?" Daniel asked, "they're probably still asleep, big night last night."

"Yes good idea," I said, god why is it that when I'm with Daniel everything just seems okay.

Larry is walking off down the road in a huff.

Pamela suggested that we should just get on with it anyway as we don't want to keep the Reverend waiting.

10 minutes later

Rehearsal over, minus the groom and best man but wee Tom stood in for Matt, it would have been so cute if he didn't say 'bum' every time he was asked something

Pamela seems to be rushing this rehearsal and doesn't seem too concerned that her son is missing in action.

Oh god, it's just dawned on me that maybe Matt has bolted because he's got cold feet. If he did then I will hire a bounty hunter to bring his cowardly arse back here.

20 minutes later, back home

Daniel phoned and said he has found the groom and best man and indeed they are both lying on the floor writhing in pain. Phew, I can call off the bounty hunter.

They're not in pain because of a hangover, but food poisoning after alcohol induced hungry men decided to cook a whole chicken on the camp fire last night using a stick and then have a feed.

Just great, just bloody great.

I told Neroli that her fiancé is a dumb-arse to which she replied, "huh?"

I rang Matt and told him that I don't care how sick they are, they better make it up the bloody aisle.

Matt told me not to shout so loud.

Dad in all his wisdom, offered his two cents worth by saying, "I did warn those boys about the dangers of e-coli poisoning."

Sigh.

Anyway, all is calm now and with everyone accounted for, I think it must be bed time as I'm buggered.

I had told Pamela I was going to the church tonight to set up the pews but the truth is I cannot bring myself to do it.

So I have decided to just go down there first thing in the morning and put the hired chairs out,

I mean who cares if they don't complement the church, better mismatching chairs then having to be in close proximity of a long dead body just for a bit of ambiance.

Mrs Crankshaw said she will give me a hand and meet me there nice and early, so not to panic.

Everyone's having an early night, even Tom is co-operating tonight and Neroli seems so organised, she's even packed Bailey's nappy bag, it looks like three days worth, not to mention the baby stroller and pot-a-cot that she has neatly packed in her car.

I wish she had been more organised with the wedding plans.

No sign of Larry so I guess he still has the pip with me.

Rick tried to phone and has left me mushy messages but I'm so angry I don't want to talk to him.

Okay, sleep now.

12.00 am

Can't sleep.

1.00 am

Still can't sleep, wondering what Daniel will look like in a suit.

3.00 am

Okay, this is getting weird, I just dressed Daniel in a thousand outfits in my mind, also thinking about how many girlfriends he has had. I mean he hasn't mentioned any so I presume there isn't one now.

3.15 am

Might go and grab a hot chocolate.

Neroli's in the kitchen when I enter in a dazed state, Tom and Bailey are up as well and Tom is sitting at the table in his pj's sipping from his cup.

Neroli looks like she has been caught in headlights.

"Can't sleep huh?" I yawned.

"Um no, kids woke me up," she said watching me cautiously.

Argh shit, no hot chocolate left.

Oh well, might go back to bed.

"Night Neroli."

"Oh, goodnight."

"You okay??"

"Me? Um yep."

"Okay, night."

"Night."

17

The big day has arrived

I'm not sure how much sleep I got, but it sure doesn't feel like much.

Coffee will fix that.

It's 5:30 am and the house is sooo quiet.

Larry hasn't been back but that's okay, I don't need to be dealing with him and his issues right now.

Think I need to be getting down to the church.

I tiptoed into Millie's room to wake her to remind her to get up at 7 'cos the hair lady is coming at 8.

Sid was awake when I entered saying he going to wash the animals one last time.

Sid is so co-operative.

Shame Millie's not.

I just threw some old clothes on and was ready to go to church when Mrs Crankshaw phones. This early? She is on the ball.

"Lisa you have to get down here quick," she said in a panic.

"Why?"

"The police are here."

"Where?"

"At the church."

Driving frantically towards the church

This is bad, this is very, very bad.

Arrived at church

Arrrghhh!!

There are police everywhere. I raced towards the church to find Mrs Crankshaw sobbing on the stairs.

"I don't want to go to jail," she sobbed when she saw me, "so I told them I had nothing to do with it."

"With what?"

"With what? Lisa, the eye pillows. I've just told them everything. I couldn't sleep and thought I'd get here nice and early and they followed me here." Mrs Crankshaw said in between sobs.

Oh lord above.

A police officer made his appearance, the same police officer that attended to me when I discovered a squatter in my ceiling.

Great, just great, now I'm definitely going to be known around here as the chick who hides people in buildings.

Hopefully he won't recognise me.

"Oh you again," he said with an amused look on his face, "we had an anonymous call that there is a body concealed in this church."

Mrs Crankshaw stops sobbing.

"Oh really?" I said trying to sound shocked and ignorant.

"Body?" Mrs Crankshaw repeated, sounding horrified.

"Yes, the caller seems to think body is 'under stairs'."

"Oh."

"The caller also said he didn't like him."

Bloody Larry, wait until I get a hold of his spiritual arse.

"So until we check this out and pending an investigation, there will be no entering the premises," the policeman continued.

"But we have a wedding today," I panicked, "we need the church."

"I'm sorry," he sympathised, "I can't do anything, it's procedure; we have to take these calls seriously."

30 minutes later

Daniel is here talking to the police while I continue to sit in a highly depressed state.

Mrs Crankshaw has gone home for breakfast and the policeman said he will be in touch to discuss the 'other matter' with her soon.

Larry has returned and is hovering around the policeman inside as they work.

Another two police cars have turned up as well as some official looking car, now they are putting heaps of yellow tape up and it's been advised that we must leave as yes, a body has been found.

Larry's doing cartwheels and I want to throw up.

Back home

Worse day ever.

I have phoned Matt and Pamela to advise them of the new venue. Matt, with victory in his voice said 'I told you that place was haunted', and advised me to suck on his words. Whatever that means.

And I could almost hear Pamela smirking down the phone when I told her and I have the feeling that she is enjoying this.

Or maybe I'm just being paranoid; I'm not in a good place right now.

So Daniel, Sid and Rick have taken Matt's ute to collect the hired chairs and the ceremony is to be moved here.

I can't get hold of everyone so Daniel's also put a sign at the church advising them of the new venue and has offered to stay there until the last person has been told.

Daniel is so awesome.

Mind you, it's his merchandise that we are promoting so I guess it's in his best interest.

Millie is also being supportive and said here is a much better venue anyway as the sun is shining and it's better then inside a stuffy old church.

She's so sweet and not at all saying things like 'why do you attract so much drama in your life'.

I'd better go and tell Neroli, I've been dreading this, I hope she won't be too upset.

Nah.

7.45 am

Shit, also just realised the hair lady is due any moment and Neroli's not out of bed yet.

I pushed Millie into having a shower as she can go first with her hair, and then bolted to Neroli's room, but she's not in bed.

Christ where is that woman?

Actually I don't recall seeing her car when I left this morning.

Bloody hell, where has she gone? It's so inconvenient, honestly, Neroli only thinks of herself.

I tried her mobile but no answer.

Daniel, Rick and Matt are back with the chairs, Matt said he hasn't seen Neroli and 'duh', he's not meant to see the bride before the wedding.

Rick's trying to be loving and supportive but it's just annoying.

It's not his fault, just the mood I'm in.

Hmm she has the kids with her, so she may have shot back home to get something.

Wish she would answer her phone.

2 hours to wedding

Millie's looking beautiful.

Hairdresser has just finished my hair.

Tim has arrived and is starting to set up for the reception.

Still no sign of Neroli.

Millie keeps telling me not to panic there is still time.

I need a drink.

I phoned Rick and explained that Neroli is missing and could he discreetly go round to see if she is at the house, Rick said thank god I have said that, as Matt has also gone out and hasn't returned.

Okay, now is the time to panic.

Rick has gone round to Matt and Neroli's house to find them and I cannot stop pacing.

Okay, going to have a drink.

Just a couple.

Mum and Dad are hanging around offering their two cents worth again about the whereabouts of the bride, saying they've probably eloped.

I wish they would shut up, it's not helping. And besides, Matt wouldn't dare do that to his mother.

Ohh speaking off...

"What's going on?" Pamela insisted, "I just talked to Millie and she said Neroli isn't here."

"Um… no, not yet."

"Well when is she getting here?"

"Oh um... soon."

"Well that's bloody inconvenient," she said, "I have the children's clothes here and need to start dressing them."

"Well I'm sure she's not far away."

Oh thank god Tim is calling me.

1 hour before wedding

Rick has arrived back with no Matt or Neroli.

Everyone has gathered in the kitchen while he reassures them that they can't be far away and we will just keep trying their phones.

God I'm going to be sick.

Pamela's not happy with me and said how could I possibly lose not only the wedding venue, but the bride and groom as well.

Mrs Crankshaw who had been very tight lipped around Pamela so far, insisted that it was not my fault and how dare she talk to me like that. Pamela retorted by telling Mrs Crankshaw that her tongue isn't always golden. And now it looks like it's going to end up a full-on bitch fight if I don't say something.

Oh, no need, Millie's putting her opinion in too.

So are Mum and Dad.

"Um Lis, I need a word," Rick said quietly, "tell Millie too."

In bedroom with Rick, Millie, and Daniel

Oh, didn't know Daniel was here.

"Okay," said Rick, "we have a problem."

He unfolded a piece of paper.

"I found this at Matt and Neroli's," he said, handing me the piece of paper.

It read:

Yeah hey.

If you are reading this then you would have guessed we're not coming to the wedding. Big of you to organise it Lisa and you rock, but Neroli and me don't wanna get hitched and are probably going to break up anyway, Neroli reckons she's in love with some other dude in Perth, so she's leaving later and I'm cool wif it.

Gone into city to get Maccas and take kids to Luna Park.

You can have a piss-up on us, enjoy.

Peace out.

P.S. Tell mum I haven't gone mental or nuffing.

"What the fuck??" said Daniel.

"Holy shit," Millie exclaimed, grabbing the note from me to read it again.

"Yeah, he kept that quiet, why didn't he just say something when we were getting the chairs from the church earlier?" said Rick.

"Well that's just great," I mumbled into my hands so Daniel won't see I'm about to burst into tears, "we have a wedding in 45 minutes, no bride or groom and a dead body in the church, someone shoot me now!"

I can't see anyone's expression but the room has gone silent. I hope everyone is thinking the same as me and is trying to figure out how to get out of this.

In fact, Maccas and Luna Park sound bloody good right now.

God I just want to run away.

"Well why don't we get married instead?" Rick said, sounding like Newton must have when the apple fell on his head.

Okay, my skin has gone all cold.

"What! You two get married? Now?" Millie said, sounding excited.

My head shot up.

"Well why not?" said Rick, taking my hand, "I mean Lisa, you look beautiful and we were going to get married in a few months anyway. I'm dressed, caterers are here and most of the guests are mutual friends so why not?"

I'm speechless.

"You do want to get married don't you?" Rick asks, looking all puppy dog-ish.

"Of course," I said, mustering up a smile.

A smile comes over Rick's face, "then let's get married!"

Half an hour later

After dragging Mum and Dad into the room to announce to them that not only were Rick and I actually engaged but are getting married in 20 minutes due to a runaway bride and groom, Mum is now sobbing (in a good way) and has offered me her engagement ring as a stand-in wedding ring until we can go and buy one.

Dad couldn't be happier although he did say that more notice would have been good as the suit he has on is not appropriate for walking me down the aisle.

Mrs Crankshaw is also happy.

Pamela's not happy and Rick has offered to reimburse her for the wedding, minus the Matt and Neroli merchandise, to which she said she doesn't give a toss about the money and she knew this wedding was going to fail anyway, and paybacks a bitch.

I decided Pamela and I aren't friends any more and she can just leave.

Everyone seems pleased about our announcement.

Except Daniel, which is bothering me for some strange reason.

So now everyone has been informed of the change of bride and groom, I'm sitting alone in my room trying to freshen up but I keep staring at myself in the mirror.

God do I really, really want to do this?

A gentle tap on the door and Millie comes in.

"You okay bridey?" she said in a joking manner. "You want a drink?"

She didn't give me a chance to answer before she poured a glass of champagne and thrust it in my hand before pouring herself a tiny splash into a glass.

"Cheers," she clinked.

I knocked back half a glass, god I needed that.

Millie took tiny one sip and her glass was empty.

"Millie, that's hardly a mouthful, I mean last time we sat here was for your wedding and you drunk the whole bottle, so come on, pick up your game."

"No it's okay," she said, "so now bridey, how you feeling, excited?"

I went to say of course I'm excited, but the truth is, excited is far from what I'm feeling.

In fact I don't feel anything.

"You do want to get married?" asked Millie, topping up my glass.

"Of course," I said feeling my cheeks burn red.

Maybe it's just nerves.

"Would it make you feel better if I take your mind off it," said Millie, producing one of Neroli's eye pillows.

"What!! Millie please tell me you're joking."

Millie giggled, "yeah, I am joking," she said throwing it into the bin, "but at least I got a reaction. I do have some news that will make you laugh your tits off though."

"What? Sid's discovered a fourth nipple?" I chuckled.

"No, better, he has had an enlargement," Millie joked.

Giggles all round.

"Where in his head?"

More raucous giggling.

"Yep and not the one down below either."

Okay, out of control laughter.

So funny.

"But seriously," said Millie, "I'm pregnant."

"You're what??"

Oh my god.

I flung myself at her in one enormous hug, I mean Millie's pregnant!

I'm so happy and hug her so tight.

"Yeah, yeah, whatever," said Millie when I tell her that's the best news ever, "just don't go all clucky on me," she said.

"Does Sid know?" I asked.

"It was his idea."

"Oh."

I feel so much happier now and it explains why Millie's been sick and acting like a bitch, it also explains the pregnancy test in the bin.

And here I was thinking it was Neroli.

"So on that note," said Millie when Mrs Crankshaw tapped on the door to let me know only another 15 minutes till we start, "better let you get ready so you can hurry up and get married, then we'll have time to analyse what happened with Neroli and Matt."

I think Millie means gossip and bitch about what happened with Neroli and Matt.

Millie exits the room and I'm left with my thoughts again, I pick up the brush and dust it in the powder to touch up my make-up but I can't bring myself to even do that.

I glance at myself in the mirror and the question comes into my head again.

Do I really, really want to do this?

Larry appears in the mirror's refection and I turned to see him looking calm and peaceful.

He sits down in the seat beside me almost squashing a sleeping Monty, who's worn out with excitement.

"Don't like him?" asks Larry.

"It's not that I don't like him," I said to Larry, "it's just that well..."

Oh god I can't say it, I mean that is all I have wanted since, well, forever. To be married to a nice, good looking man that will adore me.

And the man that fits that description perfectly is out there waiting for me at the alter.

But I won't be happy because...

"... well, I don't love him."

Larry reaches out and takes my hand.

"Then don't marry him," came the voice that wasn't Larry's mumbly words, but a deep husky clear voice. I glance at Larry in shock, to see a younger form of a man, before the grief and alcohol consumed his life, before he was mentally impaired from the kick by the horse, it was Larry in his youth, the man he should have been.

Larry didn't need to talk any more, as he sat there and held my hand I realised that this spiritual being has taught me more in the last few weeks about myself then I have figured out in my whole lifetime, I knew what I had to do, after all it's the rest of my life I'm talking about.

"It's okay," he soothed, "everything will work out, you'll see."

Dad gingerly taps on the door.

"It's time poppet," he said poking his head around the door.

I grabbed a tissue and wiped the smeared make-up from underneath my eyes.

"Okay Dad, one minute," I called back.

I felt Larry's hand slip from mine.

"Where are you going?" I asked him.

Larry turned to me with an appreciative smile that required no words but I knew he was thanking me.

"Home," he said as he slowly disappears.

Later

Okay I'm still here and have not been beheaded by Millie, Sid, my parents or members of Rick's family.

It was hard telling Rick that I cannot marry him and it's for the best. Even though Rick pretended to understand and agree, he didn't seem convinced and I'm sure he hates me right now. He said he doesn't but we decided to save face and tell the guests that we cannot get married because of a marriage licence instead.

I mean everyone is here and the mood is good so why kill it.

I got a sorry text from Matt and I told him to come and tell me face to face, to which he said he would only if a lawyer was present.

So I took a photo of all of us having a good time and sent it to him with 'shame you weren't here'.

Then Millie, the bitch, took a shot of one of Neroli's eye pillows wrapped up in a whole packet of cigarette papers and sent it too.

Millie loves to stir.

Rick has asked if I wanted to dance and we did. It was a bit awkward which kind of confirms my feelings for him, Daniel has also asked me to dance and even though it's not awkward, I can't help but feel very nervous.

As I swayed around the dance area making small talk with Daniel, I glance around at the scene.

Millie and Sid are in each others arms with Millie's discreet bump in between them.

Mrs Crankshaw and Maggie are putting their pending drug charges aside to share a joke.

Monty is scouring the marquee floor for food.

All the animals in the petting zoo are being adored by the kids at the reception.

It's such a lovely, lovely day.

"I would like to congratulate you on such a lovely event," said Daniel.

"Thank you," I smiled, "you did pretty good yourself."

"Hmm maybe we need to talk business," said Daniel, "after all I do have some lovely engraved glasses that would've worked well."

I rolled my eyes at him.

Wedding or no wedding, I couldn't be more content than I am now.

I felt a tap on my shoulder.

Mum and Dad appeared behind me with someone that looks like....

Oh no.

"Lisa, who is this foreign woman and why is she insisting you propositioned her husband?"

Facebook Profile.

Lisa Collins.

About me: Well after almost getting married I have decided to be me for a while even though I secretly fancy someone, but I'm not going to rush into that we'll just see what happens aye. So excited about becoming an Aunty to my best friends Millie's baby (which is currently in the process of growing ready for arrival, will let you know how that goes). I run a successful event planning business and a petting zoo, which you can visit for a gold coin donation. I have a wonderful business partner, Daniel. We operate out of our shop called '*Cannon and Collins. Photography, Event Planning and Supplies.*' Check out our page on facebook.

Member of the Country Women's Association (pending investigation of illegal eye pillows).

Spiritual adviser.

18

6 months later

Millie is such a bitch.

She's been in labour now for over 17 hours and won't do any of the exercises or mediation techniques I have taught her and that we practiced in antenatal classes. Okay, yes she is having a baby and I can not imagine how painful it must be, but if she just tries the techniques then it won't be as hard. Besides I'm only trying to help, that's no excuse for her calling me a 'fucken control freaky pain in the arse bitch'.

Sid has just gone to grab a coffee and chill, as he too has been copping a fair amount of abuse.

Daniel and I are getting on great in the business and we work well together, occasionally when the shop doesn't need to be attended, he will take me on his photo shoots as his assistant.

So cool.

I really do fancy him and I'm convinced he feels the same (well I know he does, because I had another reading with the tarot lady and she said I have a secret admirer) but I'm not going to rush into making a move, I really feel we should take time to get to know each other first .

The petting zoo is going well and for a gold coin donation people can book and come and feed and pet the animals. We have a lot of school groups come and now have an alpaca called Larry.

Sid has turned the attic into a bedroom for a B&B, which he will run in between being a stay-at-home dad. It's so cool and even has its own window overlooking the petting zoo yards. Well the old window was already there but we have replaced the old boards with glass and knocked the wall out to make it bigger, the room looks so countrified.

So happy with my life.

Neroli , Tom and Bailey have gone back to her parents in Perth and apart from attending court when she was charged with manufacturing eye pillows filled with illegal substances (for which she only got a small fine, so no biggie) everything is going well and she is now studying natural therapy.

Matt is now with some chick called Melanie and is totally over Neroli, he said she was too ancient for him anyway. But the cool thing is that next school holidays, he is flying over to Perth to see Tom. I'm very proud of Matt as even though Neroli and him are no longer together, he still wants to be part of Tom's life which is so awesome.

The CWA is currently being investigated by the CWA Head Office into the little misunderstanding with the eye pillows, but it's just procedure and I'm sure it's going to be fine. The good news is me, Mrs Crankshaw and Betty have been cleared of any wrongdoing, so it's all good and when the CWA is allowed to run as an organisation again we are never ever making knitted stuff to sell.

Mrs Crankshaw suggested maybe we should just stick to hosting parties for adult products as it seems much safer.

So we have decided to rename our division of the CWA, it is now known as CWA - Chicks with Attitude.

The spotty youths were extremely disappointed after learning that there will be no more manufacturing of eye pillows so they decided to start their own line of 'novelty drafts stoppers'.

Apparently they are doing well.

Rick and I are okay, he left for a while and went on some trip but he's back now and thanked me for stopping him from marring me, saying he didn't feel it would have been right for us as even though I'm a nice girl and all, he didn't feel he loved me enough and didn't know what had come over him. He wants to look up his old childhood sweetheart (the one Jake stole) because he thinks there is still something between them. I said that's fine and we can still be friends, which we are, and I have to say I'm not sad about Rick and I at all. It wasn't meant to be.

Mum and Dad have a different opinion however.

I visit Larry's grave now and then and I swear I still see him playing leapfrog over the headstones occasionally. Bob's death was ruled accidental and Larry's name has been cleared, the cold case is now closed for good and Bob was finally laid to rest. I still feel Larry's presence now and then and have to say, I do miss him. Just the other day I had left a chocolate cake cooling on the bench (yes I have been baking) and when I got back it was half eaten.

Hmmmm.

Millie's screams pull me from my thoughts and the frazzled midwife leaps from her chair.

"Okay, it's time to push," the midwife advises Millie.

Oh my god, where is Sid?

"Where is fucking Sid?!" Millie yells, reading my thoughts.

"Um, I'm just going to get him," I soothed.

"Like fuck you are," she snapped.

Okay, Millie's really starting to be unreasonable.

"Fine, I'll text him," I said pulling out my phone.

Sid must have sensed the text, as he rushed though the door to Millie's side.

Thank god.

I moved to the business end but all of sudden I don't feel so good.

Okay I understand now, maybe Millie's not being unreasonable after all.

I didn't have time to move as suddenly everything goes black and I think I may have hit the floor.

I can't hear anything, it's all peaceful and even though I suspect I have fainted, Larry appears in my line of vision smiling and waving his toothless grin.

I'm so lucky to have met such a gentle ghost, it's still not something I can go round telling people, but all the same, I feel special.

Larry all of a sudden looks like he's about to get into trouble and bolts from my vision just as someone wakes me. I see Sid standing over me with the biggest smile on his face.

"Lisa, it's a girl."

*****